To Gethin

THE
FIRESTONE

FRANCESCA TYER

Dedication

For my family

Acknowledgements

I'd like to thank my family for their continual support and inspiration, in particular my mum for encouraging me to believe in myself and never give up, Rhodri for patiently waiting to read the finished manuscript and for his edits, Christopher for always being there, and my grandma for her editorial advice. I'd also like to thank Richard Hardie for all his help in making this dream possible. Further acknowledgements go to Gina Dickerson for her design and formatting, Maureen Vincent-Northam for her edits, and Authors Reach for welcoming me into their team. Finally, I'd like to thank Janey Bailey for her encouraging feedback and everyone else who has supported me throughout my writing journey.

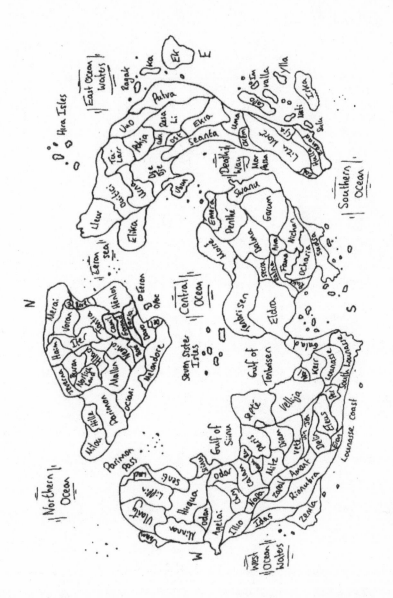

Chapter 1

IT was thirteen minutes past midnight when the airport screens went black.

The voice on the PA system began to falter with the strange guttering sound of a signal cutting out. The lights too started to flicker, splashing the check-in area with a restless effect. One boy looked up from his phone screen and saw the change. He stood apart from the other holiday makers, the hood of his ash grey jumper pulled firmly over his hair. The boy was perfectly ordinary and typically dressed for his age. The only thing that made him different was that today was his fourteenth birthday.

Something buzzed and looking down at his phone the boy was surprised to see the clock on his screen said eight in the morning, yet the sky outside was pitch dark. He looked around the flickering departure hall, pausing to stare with confusion at the airport clocks which read just after midnight. Around him, the hum of voices had grown louder and more agitated as the other passengers became aware of the struggling power systems. Crowds began to gather around the check-in desks, demanding to know what was going on. The boy stood silently amidst the commotion, his phone forgotten as he watched the light above him flicker and go out.

The airport was plunged into complete darkness. It was as if a great shadow had swept in, disturbing the airport with the touch of an unseen hand. Tannoy systems also cut out and absolute silence descended for a split second before it was broken by the sound of hysteria rising in the darkness. An instant later the lights began to flicker on again and the bright orange letters and numbers reappeared on the screens. All around, holiday makers moved from their frozen positions as if released from some spell. Only the boy saw the flicker of a shadow in the corner of the airport fade into nothingness.

'James, are you alright?' James Fynch looked up to see his older cousin Clare glaring at him.

'What was that?' he asked, glancing down at his phone. The time now read quarter past midnight and he frowned again.

'You could stop looking at your phone for one moment!' Clare snapped. 'I have no idea what happened. There must have been a power cut or something. I'm going over there to find out what's going on.' She pointed to the ticket desks where the crowd had gathered. 'Stay here, I'm trusting you not to move.'

James watched as Clare disappeared in amongst the throng. Although she was seven years older than him, he was already several inches taller and objected to her bossiness. He especially disliked the fact that she had been sent to keep an eye on him at the airport. Now alone again, he sighed in relief. Running a hand through his short, dark hair, he glanced around uncomfortably at the mass of suitcases and people. Everything in the airport had returned to normal as though nothing had ever happened. In his mind, James dismissed the fading shadow he had seen as some trick of his imagination, brought on by lack of sleep.

'Attention please, flight BA577 to Valencia has been cancelled until further notice.'

James started, suddenly aware that the system had called out his flight to Spain where he had been allowed to join his parents for his birthday. The rising clamour inside the airport drowned out the loudspeaker and he strained his ears to hear the announcement again. His eyes were drawn to a desk where a harassed looking woman in uniform was talking to a group of passengers and pointing to the screens. He followed her finger and his breath caught in his throat. The word 'cancelled' was now beside several flights, including his own to Valencia.

Glancing furtively around, James stepped away from his suitcase and moved towards the group. As he went forward, a man bumped straight into him and James stopped, scowling in annoyance. The man also came to a halt.

'Ever so sorry,' he said with an apologetic smile. 'I wasn't looking.'

Dressed in a shabby grey suit and carrying a leather briefcase, the man seemed perfectly ordinary. Staring at the man, James shook his head and blinked because in the artificial airport lights, his gingery hair and pale face appeared almost translucent. The man let his words rest for a moment before continuing his hurried walk. James twisted around to take another look, but the stranger had already disappeared.

As James stood watching, his attention was caught by a woman's voice coming from the group ahead of him. Manoeuvring himself through scattered luggage, he began pushing his way to the front, curious to know what was going on. People surrounded him, dressed in flowery prints, and brightly coloured shirts. The scent of sweat mingled with coffee and dusty air conditioning made him feel sick and he wrinkled his nose in disgust.

'Technical errors. Everything is being dealt with as quickly as possible,' the woman was saying. 'I'm afraid that's all the information I can give you for the time being.'

'What do you mean, technical errors?' A man pushed past James and fought his way to the front of the crowd. 'That's absolutely ridiculous. Didn't you see what happened? That wasn't a normal power cut!'

The woman scratched her head. 'We apologise for the problems and delays caused, sir. The airport will of course provide food and hotel services until the issues have been addressed.'

'There are hundreds of us,' another voice stated. 'We'll stay until you give us some proper answers!'

'James, I told you not to move!' Clare's voice cut across the noise. 'It's difficult to keep an eye on you if you wander around.' James thrust his hands into his pockets and said nothing. 'We've been given rooms in a hotel for tonight,' Clare continued. 'It's madness in here, and your flight won't be running for hours. I'll have to ring your parents and tell them you won't be joining them just yet.'

James kept quiet as Clare steered him back towards their bags. The thought of spending his birthday in either the airport or a hotel with his cousin wasn't one which thrilled him. She was the eldest of his six cousins, all of whom he disliked, and he wished she would leave him alone again. With a sigh, he followed Clare out of the airport towards a waiting train.

It was with a sinking feeling that James approached a large grey London hotel fifteen minutes later. Following Clare into the foyer, he was immediately met by a thick, musty smell which seemed to come from the faded red carpet. He looked about with disgust, taking in the peeling wallpaper and damp corners. The plump, blonde woman at the reception desk greeted them with a weak smile.

'Two rooms?' she asked in a forced voice.

'Yes, under Miss Ralston.'

'Of course.' The woman smiled again. 'Rooms seven and eight. Have a pleasant night.'

Taking the grubby keys, Clare turned to James and handed one to him and as she did so, her phone rang. Pulling it hurriedly from her pocket she answered in a tired voice. Glancing up at James, she tapped her watch and mouthed for them to meet at ten the next morning before disappearing into the lounge. A volley of raindrops blew against the revolving doors and James sighed. An escape to Spain would have almost made up for the typical English summer. Although he had been awake for many hours, he didn't feel tired and was instead gripped by the powers of boredom. Taking out his phone he opened a logic puzzle and was soon absorbed by the world behind his screen.

Another shower of raindrops hit the glass and glancing up, he felt an unfamiliar urge to go outside. Slipping his phone away, he checked that the foyer was deserted before stealthily creeping through the doors and out into the early morning gloom. A faint grey mist shrouded everything and made the road ahead almost impossible to see. He had never been out at this hour before, least of all on his own. Absentmindedly, he turned down an alley and found himself in an empty side street, dimly lit by the streetlamps' hazy light. To his left was a tourist shop with closing down signs in the windows and beside it was an empty tattoo parlour. One shop was different from all the rest, situated on the corner and barely visible behind a dying tree. The small black sign looked new and the gold paint said 'Count the Hours'.

Although the shop sign said it was closed, James found himself involuntarily reaching out to try the small brass door handle. To his amazement there was a gentle click and the door swung open, accompanied by the rusty tinkle of a bell. The sound matched the ancient, musty scent of the interior and without a second thought, James stepped curiously into the room before him. As he closed the door, his attention was grabbed by the sound of hundreds of clocks, all packed together on overflowing shelves like nesting birds. Many stood silent among their ticking companions, time frozen between their hands.

A faint glimmer caught James' eye and he reached out, slowly drawing out a small gold clock by its handle. It felt light to the touch; the tiny, intricately worked hands resting still. Strangely, there were no numbers on its surface and the hands pointed to empty spaces.

'Strange one, that one.' A voice as rusty as the doorbell sounded and James jumped. He turned to see an old man peering at him from behind a desk and he wondered if the man had been watching him the whole time.

'Never could get it to tick,' the man continued. He was old, the wrinkles on his face dug deep channels in his skin and his hair was completely white. He wore a pair of round glasses with thick rims that looked unusual on his thin face, but beneath them his eyes shone with the brightness of a much younger man. James stood silently, looking from the man to the clock and back again.

'Came from an odd gent,' the man continued, his eyes fixing on the clock. 'Strange fellow he was, must have had some sort of screw loose. Spoke in a funny way. I've often wondered if I ever really saw him right. One moment he was there, next he was gone and it wasn't until after that I found that clock on my desk. It wasn't ticking, not even then, so I tried to make it work but the hands wouldn't budge.' He sighed regretfully. 'Clocks have their own way you know. Never came again; they never do. They all come in and touch my clocks with their grubby little fingers and whisper in greasy voices.'

James shifted on the spot where he stood. A question was forming in his mind but every time he opened his mouth to speak, the old man started burbling on again. He turned the clock over in his fingers, suddenly realising the man was asking him a question.

'Did you want to buy it?'

James avoided the old man's eyes. 'Erm no thanks,' he muttered. 'I just came in to look.' He was aware of his phone vibrating at intervals in his pocket and replacing the clock on a shelf he turned towards the door.

'That's what they all say,' the man sighed, grumbling. 'What do I bother making them for?'

James came back into the centre of the room, his eyes wide with intrigue. 'You made them?' He tried hard to concentrate as his phone buzzed again.

In the age of machines and technology, he did not think people had skills like that anymore. The man looked through his thick rimmed glasses and held out his hand, pointing to the gold clock. James placed it carefully in his hands and stepped back.

'I made them all, apart from this one,' the man said, looking fondly around the shop. 'I used to have a workshop out the back where I made them, back when this end of the street was still thriving. People used to say wonderful things about them, but not anymore. No one comes to buy them now.'

He stopped speaking and stood staring wistfully into the distance. James moved slowly towards the door but stopped abruptly as his unasked question came back to him. Taking a deep breath, he turned back to the room.

'Is it possible for time to go wrong?'

'That is a strange question from such a young boy,' the old man said, breaking from his reverie. 'Time isn't real, we create it ourselves. Look here at these drawings.' He pulled down a stack of paper from a shelf behind the desk. 'These are diagrams of the clocks I made. Look at the intricacies. It is complex but all man made. If people mess with time then yes, I suppose it can go wrong.' He stopped abruptly and gave a dry smile. 'Well that's enough. If you change your mind about the clock, you know where it is.'

The abruptness of these last words surprised James but he said nothing. He didn't really understand what the old man had been talking about and it certainly didn't explain why his phone had shown the wrong time at the airport. He nodded and turned to go, but halfway to the door the old man's voice stopped him.

'I think you've done something to the clock!'

'Did I break it?' James asked anxiously.

The old man chuckled. 'Quite the contrary, you seem to have made it tick.'

James looked from the old man to the clock in disbelief. It was just coincidence he told himself; it was just an ordinary timepiece. Without a word he went hurriedly out onto the street.

Chapter 2

AN alarm was ringing and James jumped awake. Opening his eyes, he found himself lying on a grimy blue sofa in what appeared to be the hotel lounge. A faint orange light seeping through the curtained window cast a dingy sheen over the room. Rolling over, James pulled his phone from his pocket and switched off the alarm he'd set for mid-morning. An unusual itch on his wrist was irritating him and he rose from the sofa, trying to shake it off. Stumbling towards the door, he caught sight of his tousled form in the lounge mirror and stopped, suddenly remembering it was still his birthday.

Whilst contemplating himself in the mirror, the memory of the gold clock came to him and he smiled. He found himself wondering if he could find his way back to the shop, just to check he hadn't imagined it. It was an absurd idea, but it was one that he couldn't shake off. As he entered the foyer, his eyes fell upon the street outside. It lay completely dark apart from the scattered streetlamps which cast their orange light onto the buildings. James stared. According to his alarm it should be morning, but there was no sign of daylight. He'd only been asleep a few hours and it was impossible that it was night again.

Gripped by curiosity, James hurried out onto the street. For a split-second he thought he saw someone standing in the road ahead, a figure faint against the buildings. He blinked and looked again but it was gone. Glancing around uneasily, he squared his shoulders and set off down the road. Some invisible force guided his feet and before he knew it he was standing in the small street where the clock shop stood. The sign behind the glass still read closed, but he tried the door. It swung open before he could stop it, the rusty bell tinkling inside. He stood in the doorway, unsure of whether to run or stay, but a voice spoke before he could decide.

'I've been expecting you,' the old man said. 'The clock is waiting.' He emerged from behind the desk, grinning at James' confused expression.

'H… how did you know I'd come back?' James stammered, letting the door swing shut.

'Some things are inevitable,' the old man replied.

James frowned. The clock was resting on the desk, glinting in the light of the lamp beside it. He approached it, realising his desire to hold it again.

'How much is it?' he asked, touching the smooth metal with his fingers which still felt numb from sleep.

The old man squinted through his glasses, looking closely at James' tousled hair and wrinkled clothes. 'It belongs to you,' he said simply and quietly. 'I suppose I can't really charge.'

'Belongs to me?' The words came out in a tumble. 'Why? I mean how?'

'Well you made it work, didn't you?'

James looked down at the clock, swallowing several times. 'Not on purpose,' he replied directly. 'I just happened to be in here.' As he turned the clock in his hands, he became aware that beyond the ticking sound, a radio was playing. He pricked up his ears.

'Our headline this morning is of a major power cut that swept across England last night. Reports have come in from several counties, primarily London, Somerset, and Shropshire. Further details will be with you after the weather.'

'Is that about the airport?' James asked. 'Why does it say last night when it happened this morning?' He could feel his heart beating faster as he waited for the old man's reply. Hurrying over to a shelf where the radio stood, the old man switched it off with fumbling fingers.

'Never mind that, it's old news,' he muttered.

'Why's it on the radio now?'

'The power cut was huge,' the old man said suddenly, ignoring James' question. 'The whole country swept into darkness, but no one knew why. No one could figure it out.' He shook his head. 'As I said, old news. It's of no matter, but mark my words, odd things are stirring in the air.'

'Like what?' James asked. He was reminded of the darkness outside and suddenly wondered if the old man was baffled by it too. He had said man-made time could go wrong, but not natural night and day.

'Never you mind,' the man repeated. 'No one understands, least of all me.' He tutted away to himself before continuing. 'Here, take the clock and run home before your parents catch you.'

James had more questions, but he kept his mouth shut. He turned and left the shop quietly, the gold clock clasped in his hand. Looking down at it, he realised that the hands hovered at ten to twelve, the time of his birth. His mouth dropped open and turning back to the shop door, he tried to open it. The handle resisted his touch and he tried again, twisting it more firmly, but the door remained closed.

'It's all wrong,' he called out. 'It should be the morning, not night. You've done something to the clock, not me.'

Silence answered him and swallowing nervously, he rested his eyes back on the clock. It was as if time had skipped straight from morning to night whilst he'd been asleep. He rubbed his eyes, trying to erase the muddled pictures from his mind. It was as the clock hands struck eleven fifty that the lights in the street went out. He went cold, the hairs on his neck standing on end as the sickly orange glow of streetlamps went out. Darkness pressed all around him, so thick that he felt like he couldn't breathe, and a familiar fear seized him.

A suspicion was growing in him, one that perplexed him, and his mind went back to the airport that morning. It was as if a power cut had, for a split second, occurred. The old man's radio had also spoken of a power cut, and now the lights had gone out again. He looked wildly back and forth in the darkness, trying desperately to make sense of it all. A faint rustling nearby made him jump. Broken from his thoughts, he reached for his phone and switched on the torch. The bright light created a circle around him, but it only made the shadows seem more menacing.

Hoping this was just a dream, James forced his legs to move slowly back in the direction of the hotel. His fear was replaced by curiosity, but he found it impossible to order his tangled thoughts. The power cuts, the strange darkness, and the mixed-up times on the clocks circled through his mind. Lost in thought, he suddenly became aware of a light up ahead. Moving closer to it, he saw he was outside a pub where a group of people with torches were gathered.

'What on earth!' exclaimed one large man, balancing a drink

and his phone in one hand.

'I can't see lights anywhere,' a woman in the door stated loudly. 'I've never seen it this dark.'

James moved closer to the doorway, listening with interest.

'It must be the whole area,' another woman joined. 'They had power faults at the airport this morning too, did you hear?'

'Yes, I was there, my flight was cancelled.' The large man shook his bald head impatiently. 'It's ridiculous!'

'They had one like this before,' another man added in a thick Scottish accent. 'It must have been twelve or thirteen years ago now. I—'

He was cut short by the glow of a streetlamp which flickered on again above the group. Others followed until the whole street was illuminated once again and music blared out from the pub. Feeling suddenly exposed, James slipped into a shadowy corner by the door.

'Well I never,' the large man exclaimed, his eyes bulging. 'Turn on the news, Sammy, let's see what they have to say about all this.' He waddled back inside, followed by the rest of the group.

'Unusual for there to be two cuts in a day,' the Scottish man said, shaking his head.

'Shh,' an old lady hissed from her seat. She pointed to the TV. 'We're missing the news.'

Whatever the Scottish man had been going to say was lost. James crept inside the pub, squinting at the TV from the back of the group. A reporter was speaking and James watched the screen intently.

'Breaking news this evening, a power cut has swept across homes in Britain. Many of you will remember the power cut which made the news on the fifteenth of August fourteen years ago. Now, fourteen years to the day and at a similar time, the country has been swept into darkness again. Here with me I have Doctor Ian Roberts on what can be made of the situation so far.'

'I do remember it.' The old lady spoke over the news reader. 'Most odd, I'd never seen anything like it in fifty years, yet now I've seen it twice.' She fell silent, shaking her head to herself.

Standing listening by the door, the old man's words about the radio programme came back to James. He had been listening to old news which must have been from fourteen years ago. It was strange that he had been listening to it on the same day the cut happened again. James shivered. He couldn't help feeling that the old man had known something.

'Tonight has indeed been a strange coincidence,' the man named Dr Ian Roberts was saying. 'Changes in the weather are most probably responsible, caused by minor shifts in the atmosphere.'

James turned away. The clock was ticking gently in his pocket and he took it out, turning it over in his hands. Unbidden, his fingers twisted the little dials until the hands pointed to ten to twelve. When he looked up again, he gaped. The pub door had disappeared and in its place was a hazy white mist. Behind him, the pub looked the same as it had before, with the news on in the corner beside the bar. James reached out to the mist, trying to find the door which had been there before. His hand did not meet with wood, but a thin, cold air and his feet stepped forwards of their own accord.

Chapter 3

THE mist surrounding James was cold and he shivered. When he looked down, his own body had almost disappeared. He looked behind him, hoping to see the pub, but he could only see the swirling mist. It could all be a nightmare, but he didn't remember going to sleep. His whole body felt heavy with tiredness and he pinched himself to check he wasn't dreaming.

Gripped by a sudden hope, James reached into his pocket and drew out his phone. The screen flashed up and he looked for the signal bars, but there was nothing there. All of it was wrong, the flight cancellations, the power cut, the darkness, the clock. Now this too. He didn't understand why it was all happening to him. Looking at the clock in his palm, he wondered if turning the dials would take him back to the pub. He was about to turn the hands when he felt a presence behind him, as if someone was watching. Taking a deep breath, he slowly turned his head. In the mist before him stood an almost indistinguishable figure, faint like a shadow in uncertain sunlight.

'Hello?' James squinted at the figure. He gripped his phone and the clock tightly.

The figure came closer and James shivered. It was wearing a cloak with a wide hood which cast the face into shadow. A few paces before him the figure stopped and a deep but not unpleasant voice spoke.

'So there was something,' it said quietly. 'I couldn't believe it.'

At the sound of a human voice, James' fear abated. 'Where am I?' he asked. 'I don't understand.'

'We are in No Man's Land, the place where the two worlds meet.'

James let out a shaky breath. He couldn't see the man's face, but he fixed his eyes on the shadows beneath the hood. He had no idea what the man was talking about.

'Worlds?' His hands gripped the edge of the bench. 'What worlds?'

'I was not expecting you,' the man said, his voice almost questioning. 'There were movements in the land between but the rumours can't be true.' He shook his head, evidently talking to himself.

'What rumours?' James demanded, crossing his arms over his chest. 'Who are you?'

'Strange, most strange.' The figure ignored James, saying, 'Come and sit.'

Reluctantly, James followed the man. After a short distance a new shape appeared in the mist. It was a low bench made from a discoloured wood which was damp with moisture. The man sat down and patted the space beside him, extending a thin hand towards James.

'My name is Albert.'

James kept his own hands firmly on the bench. He knew it was bad manners, but this was not an ordinary sort of situation. The faint pain in his wrist was still there and he rubbed it irritably. Albert, or so he called himself, retracted his offer of formality.

'Perhaps formalities will wait until later.'

'How do I get home?' James asked, trying to keep his voice steady. 'I don't understand where I am. The time's all wrong, it was like that in the airport too. It shouldn't have been dark outside.' The words spilt out nonsensically before he could stop them.

Albert held up his hand for silence and thought carefully before replying. 'Home is far away, my boy. We are both in a place where we shouldn't be, not the most convenient spot for a meeting.'

'What d'you mean? Where am I, what county?' James could feel his heart thudding forcefully.

Albert laughed to himself again. 'We are in no county. As I said before, this is No Man's Land, the place where the worlds meet. Why and how you are here I just don't know.'

'What? No Man's Land doesn't exist anymore, that was in the war.' James spoke a little too loudly and glanced about him as if expecting someone else to have heard. 'This must still be London.'

'I never expected to see you here,' Albert continued. 'No one has crossed the boundary for hundreds of years, it's almost impossible.' He murmured to himself before turning his attention back to his impatient companion. 'Tell me, what do you know of the things beyond your world?'

James scowled in deep thought. His mind jumped to the idea of heaven and hell but instead he said, 'I've been taught about space, if that's what you mean?'

'That's a start,' replied Albert slowly, 'But what about the things no one ever speaks of without disbelieving?'

'What sort of things?' Despite his initial reservations, James felt curious. The adventurer in him wanted to know more about

Albert and why there were odd things going on.

'Things such as magic,' Albert stated simply.

James inhaled sharply, his fear rising again. 'I don't believe in magic,' he replied abruptly, 'It's just fairy stories for children.'

'Perhaps or perhaps not.' Albert's answers made no sense and James bit his tongue as the other continued. 'To a mere boy like you from a world of swift modernisation, fairy stories as you choose to call it, may seem impossible. Yet for some in this life, magic is most definitely real.'

'What?' James asked. 'Which people? I've only met children who actually believe in it.'

'I mean that there are forces out there which can be labelled as magic.' Seeing the confusion on James' face Albert elaborated. 'When your world was created another was also formed. At the beginning there was not such a divide, but as time went on the two became very separate worlds. Not two separate planets as you might think, but two spaces within the same universe, places across time from each other you might say.'

'That's impossible. Surely science and technology would have detected another world if there was one?'

Albert held up his hand again and his hood fell back a little. James saw his face, exposed to the misty light. He had gingery hair and stubble and a pair of hazel eyes which looked back at James with a curiosity that matched his own. On seeing his face, James started.

'It's you,' he said, 'you're the man from the airport who walked into me.'

Albert inclined his head. 'My world is invisible to yours, as yours is to ours. There are very few who know of ways to cross between. Over the years, as your world forgot how to use magic, the barrier between grew stronger.'

'What's this place for then?' James asked, looking around.

Albert smiled sadly. 'Many hear rumours of another world and try to reach it. They become trapped here.' He paused. 'Not all forces of magic are used for good. Those who know of your world seek to harm it or have power over it for themselves.'

James took a deep breath. 'Where do I come in? Why am I here? Why's the time wrong?'

'Time is something man-made, used in the world to create order. If something shifts in the universe, human time may become misaligned. As to why you are here, I'm not even sure of the answer myself. There was a girl written in the stars. Something has stirred the pattern of the earth; fate has been twisted. I have no idea what to make of it.'

'Can I go home?' James asked. 'I must be in a dream, you're not real, none of this is.'

Once again Albert ignored him. 'In the world I come from, a dark power named The Belladonna has risen. There is a legend named Arvad the Wanderer which speaks of four crystals that have a power beyond human comprehension. The centuries have passed, but no one has ever been able to find them. Now, as the darkness seeks them, the quest must begin again. It has been said that someone would come who could find the crystals and use them for good.' Albert paused and shook his head at James. 'It does not seem possible,' he whispered.

Listening intently, James suddenly realised what Albert was trying to say and gulped. 'Are you… are you saying you think I'm here for that?' He stared at Albert in bewilderment. The idea was mad and impossible.

Before Albert could speak again, a gust of wind blew from the heart of the mist. It swirled about them and for a moment James lost sight of Albert altogether. It felt cold and he gasped for air as everything pressed around him. Out of the silence, there then came a spine-tingling scream.

'What was that?' James called breathlessly.

Something brushed against his hand and he jumped. 'Put this on,' Albert whispered harshly in his ear. 'I fear we have outstayed our welcome. Follow me and don't say a word, we haven't long and I fear it may already be too late.' He moved away into the mist.

Putting on the cloak Albert had handed to him, James ran to catch up, stumbling over the uneven ground. In the cold air, he was grateful for the extra warmth of the cloak. As they went, he noticed the space around them was not completely empty. To their right ran a broken fence, laced with dewy spiders' webs and other benches were scattered here and there. After a short distance, James saw something else appearing out of the white haze ahead. It was a tall mirror, set before a calm blue lake which stretched to the edge of the horizon. As they approached, the atmosphere seemed to change, and an unnatural twilight rested in the air.

Albert stopped abruptly. 'Time grows short,' he said breathlessly. 'Here is a gateway which you must pass through. Whatever you do, don't look at it or touch the reflection.'

In his fear, all James' doubt of Albert's madness disappeared. 'Will I be able to get through?' he asked.

He turned nervously back to Albert, but there was no sign of him anywhere. The stranger had disappeared into the mist and James was completely alone.

'Hey wait!' James yelled. 'What happens if I can't go through?' There was no reply and the only sound was the gentle lapping of water.

The lake spread out cool and dark and James shivered,

wondering what lay beneath its undisturbed depths. The outside edges of the mirror were ornately decorated with unusual symbols and words which he didn't understand. As he drew closer, a cry came from the mist behind him and he whipped around. He thought he saw shadows lurking in the mist and the cry of hollow longing came again. Without another thought, he closed his eyes and stepped forwards into the mirror.

Darkness and silence swallowed him for a moment until he became vaguely aware of the sound of rustling trees. Light hit his eyes and squinting at the scene ahead, he realised he was at the edge of a wood. The leafy trees made it look like somewhere in England which comforted him a little, but their loud whispering made him uneasy. His eyes fell upon a tall grey stone wall visible through the foliage and he gaped at its height. It rose just above the line of trees, casting part of the wood into shadow.

'Arissel.' Albert's voice sounded behind him. 'Named in the old language. That's where we are going.'

James turned to face him. 'I thought I was going back home!' Albert made no reply and James sighed. 'What was that thing that screamed?' he asked, trying a different tactic.

Albert also sighed. 'A lost soul perhaps,' he answered briefly. 'We must hurry. The city is protected, but it's important that when we enter you keep your head down. Don't look at anyone and do not talk to me.'

'Why not?' James looked puzzled. 'Do people know me?'

'No one knows you,' Albert replied, 'But they sense difference and I can't afford for you to be seen.'

'Why different?' James tilted his head questioningly. As far as he was aware, he was perfectly ordinary.

Albert looked at him closely before he spoke. 'They sense the absence of magic,' he said quietly.

Chapter 4

JAMES followed Albert through a small iron gate which led onto an empty street. The whole city was strangely still. No trees rose between the low grey houses and there were no people. Looking around, James shuddered. Every house was the same, with doors painted in dull, uniform shades and windows blackened out.

James hurried to catch up with Albert who had walked on ahead. He kept his head down as instructed, despite the empty streets. The sky had grown lighter and he drew out his phone to check the screen. Nothing had changed and the signal bars remained empty. Looking up, his eyes were drawn to a corner of the street. Someone was standing there, half hidden by the shadows. As if sensing an observer, the figure raised its head. Dark eyes met with piercing blue for a split second before James turned away, but not before he had noticed the thin scar running from the man's cheek to the edge of his lip. James hurried on, forcing himself not to look back.

At the end of the street Albert stopped outside a two-storey building. The black sign above the peeling brown door said 'The Night Inn' in curling gold letters.

'In here,' Albert murmured, holding the door open.

No bell announced them and they silently entered a wide, wood panelled room furnished with tables. The walls were packed with display shelves on which rested various coloured glass bottles. James stared at these with interest but was interrupted by a woman who had appeared at the counter.

'Two rooms?' she asked bluntly and drew a stray brown hair back into her bun.

'Just one for the boy,' Albert replied.

The woman nodded. 'Let me see what I can do.' She turned abruptly and disappeared through a door behind the counter.

Albert looked at James calmly. 'You must stay here. You'll be safe for a while if you keep your head down and tell no one what I have told you. No one can find out, for your own safety, understand?'

James shook his head. 'I don't understand what I'm doing here.' He folded his arms and scowled at Albert.

'I don't understand myself, but something brought you here. It is my task to find out why.' He fell silent as the woman returned.

'Follow me.' She cast James a suspicious look before nodding to Albert.

'The impossible will become possible and the possible impossible,' Albert muttered and went out onto the street.

'Hey wait!' James cried out. 'Wait! You can't just leave me here.' He raised his hands in protest, but Albert was gone.

The woman led him through a glass-windowed door at the back of the room. A flight of stairs rose on the other side and James dragged himself tiredly up them until they reached a small landing surrounded by five doors. The woman directed him to one on the right and James muttered some thanks before entering. The room was small, sparsely furnished with a table, bookshelf, and narrow bed. It was lit by a glowing orb which appeared to be suspended in mid-air. James flung himself onto the bed, yawning widely. His mind was spinning with hundreds of questions as he tried in vain to understand what was happening to him. There couldn't be such a thing as magic, no one believed in that sort of thing, least of all him.

He found his mind turning back to the legend Albert had spoken of. It could do no harm to find a copy and read it, even if it wasn't true. After that, he could find his way back to London and forget any of this had happened. Jumping up from the bed, he went over to the window and looked out, wondering if there was a library anywhere in this strange, dead town. On either side of his window the street stretched out straight and silent, giving nothing away. He sighed and slowly made his way back out onto the landing. Exploring the town was the only way to find a library.

Opening the door at the foot of the stairs, he stopped as he saw someone standing directly in front of him. As the door swung shut the figure turned and he found himself facing a boy of around his own age. He was a little taller than James and his hair was a lighter brown.

'Erm hi,' James said with a grimace and wrapped a hand tightly around his phone.

The boy stared coldly at James who looked down to avoid meeting the hazel eyes. He noticed that the boy was holding a book, half concealed by his cloak. On the front was a picture of a huge beast which looked like something out of classical legend. Seeing James' look, the boy tucked the book out of sight.

'Someone for breakfast,' the boy suddenly shouted, directing his words behind the counter. Turning back to James, he gestured to a small table beside them. 'You can sit here,' he said abruptly and looked away.

James sat down in silence, watching the boy as he took up another book from the table and began to read. A moment later a girl approached the table and placed a bowl of steaming porridge before James. He eyed the food with disgust but his stomach was growling hungrily and picking up a spoon, he took a mouthful. The bland, gloopy texture was nauseating but he clenched his stomach and forced himself to swallow another spoonful. Once he had eaten all he could manage, he pushed aside his bowl and turned his attention to the boy.

'Erm, excuse me?' he asked haltingly. 'Is there a library anywhere near here?'

The boy nodded. 'In the underground city.'

'Underground?' James frowned.

'Underneath all the houses,' the boy replied bluntly. 'Are you new here?'

James paused, 'Yeah.'

'I can take you there if you want,' the boy suggested in slightly warmer tones. 'You'll never find it by yourself.' He sat himself on the other side of the table, looking expectantly at James.

James nodded but said nothing. The boy stood and James followed him out onto the street. He walked a few paces behind his guide, hoping to avoid any questions. The streets they passed through were all identical, straight and narrow with sharp corners. There were no streetlamps and James shivered to think of how dark it must be at night. The whole place was gloomy, the absence of life strangely disturbing. Every street was dead, all fleshless bones in the vast skeleton of the city.

The boy stopped and James came to stand beside him. An iron gate stood before them, barring their way to a street which rose in a steep slope on the other side. The boy raised his arm to the metal in a strange gesture and the gate began to open. James stared as he watched the process, his amazement deepening when he saw what lay on the other side. The street had disappeared and his eyes met instead with the entrance of a tunnel. The boy had already entered and collecting himself, James hurried in after him. He found himself in a wide passageway, lit intermittently by hovering globes of light. It was short and sloped slightly downward towards a large archway and as he stepped through this, James gasped.

'This is the underground city of Arissel,' the boy said.

The cave they were in was so large that no roof or walls could be seen. Above, the airy space was hung with thousands of orbs which glowed like stars in a night sky. Despite its vastness, it was packed with people. Their voices rose loudly into the great space before bouncing back in whispering echoes. Crowds swarmed around market stalls set before small huts which had their doors thrown open. James had been to markets before but he had never seen anything like this. The tables were heaped with books, bottles, food, and many exotic things he had never seen before. He realised with wonder that this was where the life of the city lay.

'I'm William, from the Aeton family by the way.'

James turned to the boy beside him and smothered a laugh. 'I'm James, er James Fynch.' He held in another snort. 'Can I just call you Will?'

The other shrugged. 'Where did you come from?' he asked.

James started, unsure of what to say. 'London,' he gulped, feeling his neck grow warm. 'Where's that?'

James felt the blush grow deeper. He wanted to believe he was still in London, but Will had obviously never heard of it.

'It's difficult to explain,' he said and ruffled his hair

uncomfortably. 'Where's the library?' he then asked, trying to change the topic.

Will broke from his puzzled stare. 'It's in the middle of the city in a courtyard. It's the biggest building down here. Come on, I'll show you.'

Will went on ahead, moving down an earthy street between two rows of low buildings. James hurried to keep pace, but inside he was longing to explore everything around him. Eventually the market streets broke away and he saw the courtyard ahead. It was encircled by low, closed buildings and at its centre stood a large fountain. The stone base was carved with symbols that reminded James of the mirror in No Man's Land. Cast into the air from a single spout, the water cascaded down on all sides, coruscating in the light of the circular orbs. To the right of the fountain rose the library. It had four large stone columns along its front and a set of steps leading up to a heavy wooden door. Above this was a white sign with gold letters which said, 'Elliad's Library'. James sighed with a predetermined boredom.

'I'll come in with you,' Will said, 'I need to find some books too. What're you looking for anyway?' he added.

'It's just a story,' James muttered.

'What's it called? I might be able to help you find it.'

James paused uncertainly. 'Arvad the Wanderer. It's a myth I think but I'm not really sure.'

Will frowned. 'I've never heard of it. Let's go in and have a look.'

James shrugged. He was doubtful as to whether he would be able to find it. Part of him was still waiting to wake up from this nightmare. He followed Will up the steep steps, breathing heavily. Pausing near the top, he turned back to survey the courtyard and surrounding buildings. Through the water of the fountain, he caught sight of a fair-haired boy and girl watching him. As he looked back, they turned away and disappeared into the crowd. James stared after them, his suspicion aroused, but the sound of Will calling for him to follow made him turn away. He hurried up the remaining steps and joined his guide in front of the large wooden door which swung open of its own accord.

The library interior was larger than any James had seen before. Orbs lit up hundreds of shelves that formed a vast maze of corridors. Above this ground level there were three other floors, set around the edge of the room like balconies. Reaching up to these were sets of wooden steps, fixed precariously to the walls. The shelves on the top balcony touched the high ceiling which was crossed with dust darkened beams. The books were all bound in hard covers and were inscribed with either gold or silver lettering. On other shelves, yellow scrolls rested, tightly tied by coloured ribbons.

'It's huge,' James managed to say.

'One of the biggest in the world,' Will replied proudly. 'It's got everything in here, every book I've ever looked for anyway. I'll take you to the myths section so you can look for that story. I'm sure it'll be there somewhere.'

At the end of the first aisle, a dead end met them. James was about to turn back when the shelf began to move, swinging slowly to the side to reveal a new aisle before them. His mouth dropped open in amazement but he tried to hide his expression from Will. The same thing happened several times before they came to a small set of steps which led down into another room. Will stopped at the bottom.

'The first section has myths in,' he announced, gesturing to the shelves before them. 'You might find something here. I'm going to go and find some other books but I'll come back and find you.'

The smell of old books rested in James' nostrils as he began moving along the shelves. He brushed the book spines lightly, collecting dust on his fingers. The boredom he had anticipated fell away as he read the titles of ancient volumes. There was one called 'The Legends of Ancient Sorcery' and another named 'Myths of the Seven Sisters'. He knew Arvad's tale was just a myth, but he felt curious about it and picked out each volume with fresh eagerness. At the end of the seventh row of shelves he stopped with a sigh. Row after row had produced nothing on Arvad. Albert must have been lying, or else completely mad. He sat on the floor, putting his head in his hands. He had heard of escaped lunatics before and it wouldn't surprise him if Albert was one.

Looking up disconsolately, James' eyes rested on two majestic volumes standing side by side. As he reached forward to pull one out, a thin green book dropped to the floor and from its covers fluttered a single sheet of paper. Kneeling where the book lay splayed, he picked it up and looked with curiosity at the map drawn on the front page. It depicted four masses of land, each divided into regional sections. Puzzled, he began to flick through the pages, trying to find where the loose one had fallen from. At the back of the book he paused and caught his breath. Beneath his fingers was the title he had been looking for, 'Arvad the Wanderer'. It was a single page, the writing tightly scribbled and blotched in places. In one swift movement, he tore the page out and shoved it in his pocket, glancing guiltily around him.

Suddenly, he became aware of voices close by. Straining his ears to locate the sound, he realised it was coming from behind a door to his left. Standing, he crept closer and leaned in to listen.

'I don't understand any more than you do. It's impossible.' James frowned. He was sure that the voice belonged to Albert. 'Seven hundred years since it last happened,' the voice continued, 'and no other recordings ever in history. Seven, the number which all magic is based upon and to which Arvad himself is linked. It can't just be coincidence.'

'He shouldn't be here, we must return him to his world,' another male voice responded.

James' breath caught in his throat and he stared hard at the door. They were talking about him and why he was here in this so-called other world. Stepping forward again, he pressed his ear to the door.

'Do you have reason to believe fate has changed, that it is a boy instead?' The same voice spoke again.

'Why is he here otherwise? How did he get here if it were not intended?'

There was a pause. 'I believe in him as little as you do, it merely seems like a strange coincidence,' Albert muttered quietly.

On the other side of the door, James didn't dare breath. His hand slipped into his pocket where the cold metal of the gold clock brushed against his fingers.

'It's not possible. If we sent him, he would surely fail,' the second voice insisted. 'He must go back before he learns too much. People will grow suspicious.' The other voice dropped to a harsh whisper. 'The boy stumbled here by chance, he doesn't belong.'

'What're you doing?' Will's voice sounded behind James and he jumped guiltily away from the door.

'I thought I heard something,' James replied quickly.

Will squinted suspiciously but moved on. 'Did you find the myth?' he asked.

'No, there was nothing here.' James wasn't sure why he hid the truth from Will. The boy knew nothing about the story anyway.

'What did you want it for?' Will asked, moving back towards the main room. James followed behind, quickly forming an answer.

'Just curious,' he mumbled. 'Someone told me about it and I thought it might be interesting.'

The two boys fell silent and Will led James back through the library. They made their way down to the courtyard which was still crowded with people. Passing close to the fountain, James felt a coolness in the air and reaching out, he tried to catch the droplets in his fingers. Suddenly, a hand struck his arm down.

'Don't touch it,' Will hissed beside him. 'Don't you know about the fountain?'

James looked at his companion in bewilderment. 'It's just water, isn't it?'

'The water has the power to purge all memories,' a voice said. 'It is a cruel world where people grow afraid. There are whispers in the crowds and you must fend for yourself against the darkness.'

Chapter 5

'DID you hear that?' James asked, looking around for the source of the voice.

Will frowned. 'Hear what?'

'The voice, just now.'

'There are voices everywhere, what are you talking about?'

'Right next to us, how did you miss it?' James persisted. He looked about again, convinced that the voice had sounded right next to him.

'I didn't hear anything. I don't know what you're talking about.' Will shrugged. 'It was probably someone walking past.'

James folded his arms and began to walk again, back towards the tunnel mouth. He felt tired, barely able to lift his feet from the earthy ground. Will soon overtook him, silently leading the way back towards the inn. Rounding a corner, James passed close to two men arguing at the end of a narrow alleyway. Their voices were clearly audible, and he couldn't help overhearing.

'What did you find?' The first man spoke in a harsh whisper.

'Nuffing,' the other replied in similar tones.

'What do you mean nothing?' the first snarled.

'Like I said, nuffing. Nuffing for you, ol' Scarface.'

'Don't call me that! I won't take nothing back to her.' The

first man suddenly grabbed the other by the collar and spat into his face. 'Find out about the rumours or you'll pay.'

'I will, but if I find out, you'll be ve one to pay. Ve reward is part of ve deal.'

There was a small burst of light and a yelp. James stared as the light hovered for just a second before it evaporated. He must be mistaken, magic didn't exist, it was impossible. Shaking his head in confusion, he walked on, following Will out of the underground city. Retracing their steps, the boys made their way back to the inn. It was empty inside when they entered, and James sat down at one of the tables whilst Will disappeared behind the counter. Glancing around to check the coast was clear, James took the torn sheet of paper from his pocket and, placing it on the table, began to read.

'This is the tale of Arvad the Wanderer as I was told it, many years ago. Arvad, meaning wanderer, had ambitions beyond ordinary men. Legend has it that he lived in a small village with his six elder brothers. They were not wealthy, but nor were they poor, and they had enough to live by. Each of the seven sons had a small sum of money bestowed on them by their aged father to provide them with all they needed for the years to come. Their mother was no longer alive and the house was falling to ruin, yet their father divided all he had between his sons. This tale is not about all seven brothers however, but of the youngest alone.

One morning Arvad set out from home at sunrise. At the time he was living, a darkness had fallen on the world and cast it into shadow. It had spread from the Western lands into the North and the whole world was soon under its spell. Arvad had heard of a powerful magic that could defeat the dark and this is what he set out one morning to find. He searched for many days and many nights, travelling the world from dawn until dusk, but he found nothing. Although he had magic within him, he was searching for something greater which came from the world itself.'

James stopped reading, unable to decipher the next set of lines. Turning the page over, he continued to read as the writing became clearer again.

'Arvad went across the sea to the Southern continent and searched there for many months. It became an obsession to find the power that could be used to destroy the dark, yet he also learned that such power could bring eternal life. He searched the four continents for many years, gathering as many clues as he could. Soon he was no longer a young man but middle aged and growing weary of his search.'

James paused again where the words blurred together and sighed with frustration. The story didn't seem to be telling him anything useful at all. He lowered his eyes to the last paragraph.

'One night, Arvad built a fire, weary with his troubles. As he observed the flames he felt a change stir within him. He looked up to the sky where the air was bright and clear and then to the stream running beside him. Earth, fire, air, and water surrounded him and he felt their power. A great strength grew within him and kneeling there on the bare earth he closed his eyes, letting the tide of magic fill him.

Arvad summoned the earth, air, water and fire to listen to him and from each he begged a favour. He asked for a power from each element that when combined would grant him eternal life. In return, he gave them each a gift. Then the earth, the air, the water and the fire each bestowed on him a crystal. These had the power to destroy both evil and good and bring eternal life. Yet Arvad knew that it was not his fate to be the one to use these crystals. He asked the elements to take them once more and hide them within themselves until the day came when someone should find them.'

The rest of the story was absent and leaning his head on his arms, James closed his eyes. The story was a myth, a fairy tale that someone had decided might be true. There wasn't such a thing as eternal life, or magic. Albert's idea that someone had to find these crystals was a trick which he had somehow become involved in. It was possible that Albert was indeed mad, but that did not explain the strange clock shop, nor the power cut or the place within the mist. James tried to focus his mind on the facts but found himself gradually drifting towards sleep.

He was suddenly wrenched from his thoughts by a blinding pain which shot through his arm and neck. Sitting upright with a sharp yell, he pulled up the sleeve of his cloak. It felt as if a fire was burning him and he gripped his arm in agony. A dim glow shone around him and looking down, he saw a globe of transparent light resting in his palm. He held it out before him, staring at it with a mixture of fear and awe. The globe was weightless and cast a pale glow about the room. As the light grew, the pain faded, leaving only a faint tingling behind. Looking closely at his wrist, he gaped with fresh amazement. A mark was emblazoned on his skin, a plain circle with an inner ring of seven intricate stars. He touched his wrist gently but could feel nothing. The mark seemed to grow within the skin itself.

'Are you alright? I heard a noise.'

James looked up to see Will had entered the room and he covered his wrist hurriedly. 'Yeah fine, I dropped something that's all,' he lied.

Will approached the table and sat. Reaching out he picked up the piece of paper which James had forgotten to replace in his pocket. It was in his hands before James could grab it.

'Arvad the Wanderer,' Will read. 'So you did find it in the library.'

James held his breath, wishing he could sink through the floor. Will's eyes were already scanning down the page.

'It was just that page,' James replied quietly. 'It was the only thing I could see.'

There was a silence before Will looked up again. His face bore a puzzled expression and he carefully laid the sheet back on the table.

'What's it for?' he asked. 'Why are you reading just a page if you can't find out the ending?'

James swallowed. He wished he could tell Will everything, but Albert's warning rang in his ears. The light in his hand and the strange mark on his wrist made Albert seem less mad after all.

'You wouldn't believe me if I told you,' he said, folding his arms.

'Try me,' Will insisted.

James paused uncertainly. It could do no harm to tell Will just a little of what he knew. Taking a deep breath, he met Will's gaze squarely.

'The myth is meant to be true,' he began. 'The four crystals were hidden ages ago and no one has been able to find them. The tale says someone is supposed to discover the crystals and use them to destroy the dark.' James stopped, awkwardly running a hand through his hair. It all sounded stupid when said aloud.

'Who told you to read it, and why?' Will said after a pause. 'Were they trying to scare you about dark magic?'

James looked down at the table. 'I was told that the darkness is growing but the crystals can destroy it. I wanted to find out the truth.'

He saw a strange look pass over Will's face, one of confusion mingled with astonishment.

'The person, the one supposed to find the crystals, you think it's you?' Will's eyes grew wide. 'It's just a story you know, none of it's true. Someone must have been playing a game with you.' He gave a short laugh.

'I don't know if it's me,' James sighed. 'I don't understand, but I think that I should maybe find out.'

'Wherever you've come from, it must be strange,' Will said and stood up.

James noticed that he had something tucked under his cloak and squinted at it. It was a book, the same one as before. He wanted to ask Will about it, but the boy had already walked away. In the doorway behind the bar, he turned again to James.

'There is dark magic, but the dark can't be completely destroyed by anything,' he said and left without another word.

James remained at the table for just a minute longer before escaping to his room. He flung himself on the bed and lay completely still, thinking hard. His head was torn between logical reasoning and the prospect of adventure which Albert's words had hinted at. Will's disbelief had annoyed him and this, alongside the conversation he had overheard in the library, strengthened his desire to find out the truth. Something in him wanted to prove that Arvad's story was real and that he, James Fynch, was part of the quest. Reaching into his pocket, he slowly drew out the small gold clock which he hadn't touched since No Man's Land. Holding it up to the dim light, he squinted at the thin gold hands. To his surprise, they had moved, and he instantly understood that the clock was keeping time with his world.

Outside his window, the sky had turned to twilight. Lying on his back, James raised his hand, trying to recreate the light in his palm. His attempts grew weaker until he eventually drifted into a restless sleep, entering like a shadow into a dream. A figure was before him, a black shape that was blurred at the edges. It was standing in a pale mist, a ghostly dream figure, but he wasn't afraid. Somewhere in his mind a voice was whispering with gentle urgency, trying to catch the dreamer's attention. Whether it was male or female was uncertain and he listened intently. He reached out towards the figure, but his hand only met with air.

'Go,' the voice whispered, 'go now before it's too late. The moon is full tonight. Soon it will begin to wane and with it goes the light.'

James awoke to the sound of screaming.

Chapter 6

THE thud of many feet sounded on the street outside, accompanied by panicked shouts. Opening his eyes, James stared into the darkness of his room, listening fearfully to the chaos below. Heart beating heavily, he rose from his bed and crept over to the window. The moon was hidden behind a cloud and he could only just make out figures in the darkness below. Shadowy people were running from the surrounding buildings and down the street in small, tight groups. Their shouting was loud and frightened, but their words were indistinguishable.

The voice from James' dream telling him to go quickly was still fresh in his mind. Although everyone outside was running, he didn't know where they were heading or why. He wondered if the dream figure had wanted him to follow the crowd or go another way. Tearing himself away from the window, he hurried over to the door, pausing only to grab his phone and Arvad's tale from beside his bed. He shoved them deep in his trouser pocket alongside the tiny gold clock. Having collected his few possessions, he flung open the bedroom door and hurried downstairs. On entering the main inn room, he stopped abruptly as his eyes rested on Will and a woman standing by the back door.

'We have to go,' the woman whispered harshly. 'What are you waiting for?'

'I've got to get something,' Will mumbled under his breath. 'I left something behind.'

The woman sighed. 'If you mean the boy, leave him. There's something strange about him, I don't like it.' She shook her head firmly and hurried out of the door, beckoning for Will to follow.

James gulped, trying to keep his breath steady. Albert had warned him that people thought he was different, but he hadn't believed it. Part of him had wanted to believe that he was still in London where he was an ordinary boy amongst the crowds.

'I was coming to get you!' Will called across the room and James jumped, realising he had been seen.

'What's happening out there?' James asked and moved closer to the door. He noticed the woman had disappeared.

'We need to get somewhere safe,' Will urged. 'There's been at attack at the north end of the city. They're coming this way. Hurry up!'

'Who're coming, who're they?' James waited for an answer which he already knew.

'The dark, the dark have come.' Will looked at James with fear in his eyes. 'Maybe you were right.' His eyes searched James' face for a moment before shifting to the door. 'Follow me,' he hissed, his voice urgent again. 'We'll have to go through the back streets.'

Outside, people were still running. From above it had seemed like a scene in a play, but now James was struck by the closeness of it. The screaming and the fear were so real that it took his breath away. As he and Will passed through the door, there was the sound of shattering glass behind them. Both boys ducked instinctively, sheltering their heads from flying shards. Several pieces struck James' cheek and he felt a small trickle of blood burst from his skin.

'Run,' Will whispered hoarsely. 'Run and don't stop.' He grabbed James' arm and pulled him violently out onto the street.

They began to run, down the first street and into the next. Although it was quiet behind the houses, James could see lights blazing against the sky at the other end of the city. As he stared up at the flashing brightness, the moon suddenly peeped out from behind a thick purple cloud and he gaped. Against the white shining sphere rested a dark shape that only myth and films allowed him to recognise. It was a dragon and on its back, sat a shadowy rider. He felt his whole body go numb and he suddenly realised what the dream figure had meant. When darkness covered the moon, the light went out.

'James, come on,' Will shouted. 'We'll have to go a different way to everyone else. This side is already blocked.'

Breaking from his trance, James hurried to follow Will who had begun to run again. He was so focused on keeping his legs moving that he didn't see the dark shape lying in his path and was brought abruptly to his knees. Although it was dark, he could just make out a lump splayed on the ground beside him. Crawling cautiously closer, he reached out and prodded it suspiciously. Above him, the moon appeared again, and he recoiled at the sight before him. A dead man lay there, his eyes open and glazed.

'James, come on, we'll get killed.' Will stopped a short way ahead and tired to catch his breath.

Fighting down a sick feeling, James pointed to the body with a shaking hand. 'Is he dead?' he asked.

Will was silent for a moment. 'We're nearly at the gates,' he replied at last and turned away.

James couldn't get the dead man's face out of his head. He'd never seen death before but now he could feel its presence everywhere, haunting his every move. Will's voice forced him to push these thoughts to the back of his mind, but he could feel them festering there.

A flash suddenly lit the sky and the boys looked up. Directly above them hovered the dark silhouette of the dragon, framed by the moon. James felt the air in his chest constrict. Will began to slowly creep alongside the buildings and James followed, hidden by the shadows. As they turned into another street, James glanced back and saw three dark figures emerge on the path behind him. Before he could turn away, a bolt of light shot down the street and burst against a building close by. He remained still but from the corner of his eye saw Will stumble as a shard struck him.

'Keep going,' Will gulped. 'We can't stop, not now.'

The city gates stood open, swinging on broken hinges. Only one figure stood blocking their passage out of the city and James stopped, waiting for direction from Will.

'There's a small building further along the wall,' Will whispered with a grimace. 'There's a hidden door inside which leads out of the city. My dad showed me once, said it was used for smuggling. We'll have to run into the next street and hope the guard won't see us. I'll go first, you follow if it's clear. OK?'

James nodded, heart thudding. He watched nervously as Will moved his injured leg and limped out into the open space between the streets. The guard remained still, oblivious to the movement behind him. James held his breath until Will had turned the corner and was safely hidden in shadow again. The guard still hadn't moved and James paused only briefly before stepping forward himself. After a few careful movements, he broke into a run, dashing across the street to join Will. The sudden action caused the guard to turn and the peace was instantly destroyed by a blast of light. It was sharp and white and shot towards the boys in an unwavering stream. James looked at Will in panic and they both ducked.

The light followed closely behind them as they began to run again, keeping the city wall close on their left. After only a few metres, Will held up his hand for James to stop. In front of them stood a low, dilapidated building, its door slightly ajar. Pushing it open, Will stepped inside and James cautiously followed. It was dark, but Will produced a small light in his hand which lit up the cold, empty space around them.

'Where's the door?' James asked.

'Along the back here I think, hang on.'

Will ran his hand along the wall and stopped in the centre. There was a small flash of light and James watched in amazement as the wall melted away to reveal a narrow doorway. Will didn't notice the look, his attention focused on wrenching the stiff door open. It burst inward in a cloud of dust and, looking through it, James saw the vague outline of trees. Drawn towards freedom, he stepped through the door into the wood beyond. He longed to stop but Will paced on, determined to leave the city behind. They only came to a halt once the walls had disappeared behind a thick cover of fir trees. Will knelt and took out his wounded leg.

'There's a splinter of wood in it, can you get it?' he asked James.

James paused, repulsed by the thought, but Will's pained face encouraged him to kneel also. Putting his fingers on either side of the splintered piece, he squeezed until there was enough wood to pull. Will uttered a sharp groan as the piece came out. He quickly covered the wound with his cloak and leant back against a tree, looking at James.

'Who are you exactly?' he asked. 'You're not from here, you're different. Tell me the truth.'

James was silent for a moment before he spoke. 'I'll tell you, but you won't believe me,' he answered quietly. 'I'm not even sure that I believe it myself. I come from another world, a place completely different to here. It has cars and electricity and fast food, things which don't seem to exist here.' He stopped, guessing Will wouldn't be able to follow. 'There's another world, one without magic,' he began again.

Will stared at him in disbelief. 'Another world, without magic?' He shook his head. 'Does that mean you can't do magic? How are you supposed to fight the dark if you can't do magic?'

'I don't know,' James replied simply. 'I met someone from this world who told me about Arvad. He told me about a quest to find the crystals, but I'm not sure that I really believe him.'

'I didn't believe the dark would come, but they have,' Will stated. 'What if it is true? What if you are meant to find the crystals?

'That's what I've got to find out, whether it's true or not. I have to try, but I don't know where to start.'

James looked way into the trees. It was cold and he shivered, pulling his thin robe tightly around himself. Moonlight wavered through the trees which danced in a sharp wind. The light created a silver pattern on the ground that looked like swirling water. The shadows that were untouched by this light made him shudder and he closed his eyes.

'Arthur?'

A thin voice came through the darkness and both boys

jumped at the sound. Into the circle of wavering light came a girl of about their own age. She had long blonde hair reaching to her waist and her skin was so pale that James couldn't help staring. He thought he recognised her and after staring a moment longer, he realised she was the girl he had seen standing by the fountain in the underground city.

'Have you seen my brother?' she asked, looking from one to the other. Her face was tear stained and her nails had been bitten down to the skin. Will and James both shook their heads and she frowned.

'Who are you?' James asked bluntly.

'I'm Aralia,' she said and pulled up her left sleeve. James stared in amazement. On her wrist was a circular mark like his own, only hers was filled with a half moon. 'Who are you?' she then demanded.

Before they had time to answer, they were interrupted by a boy who came rushing through the trees. His hair was as fair as Aralia's and on seeing him she darted forward.

'Arthur! What happened to you?'

'I lost you,' he replied briefly before glancing suspiciously at James and Will. 'Who are they?' he asked Aralia.

'What're you doing here?' Will asked tersely, ignoring Arthur's query.

'The entrance to the underground city was blocked and we had to come out this way,' the boy answered in an equally abrupt tone. 'We managed to get past the guard but got separated.' He turned to sister with a frown.

'D'you know what was happening back there?' James asked in partially feigned ignorance. 'Why was there an attack?'

Arthur shrugged. 'All I know is that they were the Shadows.'

'Warriors of the South,' Aralia added, seeing James' puzzled face. 'They fight for a force known as the Belladonna, or so we were told. They've never been here before. I don't know why they're here now.' Her voice trembled as she spoke.

James turned away and lowered himself to sit by a thick tree trunk. Will joined him and the boys watched the siblings sit down a short distance away, huddling close together in the cold. Will's face bore a strange expression and James watched him from the corner of his eye.

'There's a place my dad told me about,' Will said into the silence. 'It's a village further north, in the next region. A man lives there who knows about crystals. Maybe that's where you should start.'

'Can you tell me how to get there?' James asked.

'No,' Will replied shortly. 'I can't understand where you've come from, or that there's a place without magic, but I'm coming with you. I'll show you the way.' James was surprised by the response and nodded to Will in thanks. There was a pause before Will spoke again. 'The dark came for a reason, didn't they?' His voice shook slightly and he kept his eyes fixed on the ground. 'They've never been here before, there must be some reason.'

'I don't know,' James replied truthfully, 'I don't exactly understand either. I was told of The Belladonna, but I didn't believe it. I don't know what to believe.'

Will stared directly at him, his eyes wide and fearful. 'The dark must know you're here' he whispered. 'They must be looking for you.'

James fell silent, gazing blankly into the silvery night. Will too went quiet and after a while, James heard his breath grow softer as he drifted into sleep. In the half-darkness, he stretched out his hand and imagined a light there, growing in the depths of his mind. Slowly, a shape began to emerge, taking the form of a bird. As he watched, the fiery creature rose from his fingers, up towards the night sky where it faded and was gone.

Chapter 7

BOTH boys awoke early. The sun had barely risen, and only a faint glow glimmered through the trees. It was different from the moonlight but just as beautiful. A chill, like those of early autumn, hung in the air and James shivered, wrapping his cloak about him. His stomach rumbled and delving into his pocket, he pulled out a few stale pieces of chocolate. He threw one at Will who sat up with a groan. Aralia and Arthur lay a short distance away, still sleeping. They looked so alike that James thought they must be twins.

'We'll have to go before they wake up,' James whispered to Will. 'No one else can know what I told you.'

'We can't just leave them here,' Will responded. 'They're on our side.'

James sighed. 'I saw them in the underground city, but that doesn't mean we can trust them. I don't even know the truth myself. I can't tell them what I don't know for sure.' He pushed himself up from the ground and stood looking down at Will. 'D'you still want to join me?'

'You don't know the way without me,' Will answered simply. He too stood and glanced uncomfortably at the siblings. 'There are lots of stories about them anyway,' he continued. 'My mum says they were thrown out by their family. The rumour is that they're only half human you know, but I don't know whether that's true.'

'What? That's not possible.' James looked over to the siblings in disbelief.

Will shrugged and turned away. 'I guess we'll never know,' he replied absently.

Will brushed over the ground they had slept on, covering any traces they had left. He began to move towards a small path, just visible through the trees, and James hurried to follow. Their route took them directly past the sleeping siblings and as they went by, Arthur mumbled something in his sleep. James and Will froze, but Arthur merely turned over and slept on. A thin stream joined the edge of the path and they paused briefly to drink from it, the cool freshness quenching their parched mouths. James dipped his face into the swirling whirlpool, washing off the grime and blood which had stuck to his skin. Beside him, Will rinsed his wounded leg which had begun to heal.

Once refreshed, the boys began to walk again. The stream continued to run alongside the path until the thickening brambles eventually blocked it out. In several places the boys were forced to slash their way through with sticks as the route became lost amongst the ivy choked trees. The stream occasionally reappeared again until it eventually dropped away into a small waterfall.

'Just keep going, at some point the wood must stop,' Will called to James. 'I remember standing with the woods behind me, I'm sure we must be going the right way.'

'I thought you knew where you were going?' James questioned sharply.

'I've never been to the village,' Will returned, 'but it's near the border and I know how to get there.'

'How did your dad know about the crystal man?' James jumped over a thick brambled patch as he spoke.

Will slowed his pace but didn't turn around. 'I don't know, I never asked,' he replied quietly.

'What does he do?'

There was a pause before Will answered in a low voice. 'He was a historian and a researcher. He travelled a lot, trying to find new information. A few years ago he was working on something secret and wouldn't tell anyone what it was. He went away to do research one day and never came back. That's when we moved to the inn. We don't even know what happened to him.'

James didn't know what to say and so kept quiet as they continued along the overgrown path. He slowed his pace, allowing a small distance to grow between himself and Will. Ahead, the trees began to thin and he could vaguely see the outline of hills on the other side. The sight of them filled him with hope and he slashed the brambles aside with increased energy. In front of him, Will pushed on in silence, never once turning to look at James. It wasn't long before they left the last few scraggly trees behind and emerged into the open. Wild hillside sloped before them, thick with long grasses, weeds, and bracken. Small copses of trees were also scattered across the hills, well distanced from one another. James noticed that the leaves were beginning to turn yellow, even though it was still August as he believed.

Will came to a halt and pointed to the slope on their right. 'That's the border of the Gamad region,' he said. 'We climb up there.'

Neither complained of their hunger or tiredness as they began to ascend the slope. The grass was over half their height, and this made the climb more difficult. Although they were shielded from the wind, an afternoon chill had replaced the morning sunshine. Half way up they paused to look back over the view. Behind them were the fields they had crossed, framed by the dark mass of brambled wood. The city was nowhere in sight and the only sign of habitation was a small group of houses clustered together in the distance. James caught sight of movement in one of the fields and turned to see what it was. He could just make out a group of animals huddled together but didn't know what they were.

'What are they?' he asked Will, pointing to the fields. They looked like cows, only they were smaller and had pure white skin.

'They're Purina,' Will answered. 'People keep them for their healing powers. Their eyes produce a silver liquid used in some medicines. They can only survive in the north because their skin burns in the heat, but the liquid is traded all over the world.'

'Is it valuable?'

'To the regions who can't get hold of it easily, yes, but it's fairly common in the north.'

A new flash of movement caught James' eye near the trees below and he turned his attention to it. He looked again, scanning the edge of the wood until his eyes finally rested on a black cloaked figure. It hovered there for a split second before disappearing back amongst the trees. He suddenly felt Will's hand on his back, pushing him to the ground.

'Someone's watching us,' Will breathed.

'I know, I saw,' James returned. He raised his head a little and ducked again. 'It's appeared again,' he announced in a nervous voice. 'We'll have to crawl. The grass is long enough to hide us until we get to the top. Can you crawl alright?'

Will nodded and stretched his palms out over the rough ground. Side by side, he and James began to move up the slope, trying not to disturb the grass around them. James cast frequent glances behind him, half-expecting to see the black cloaked figure scaling the slope in close pursuit. At each slight rustle of grass he froze, but the hillside lay empty, only disturbed by himself and Will. It felt like they crawled for hours, their faces scratched by the grass and their knees sore and bruised. The top seemed to stay in one place, never coming closer. James had to stop several times to catch his breath, but Will ploughed on undeterred.

Will reached the top first and James joined him shortly after, panting heavily. Both boys stood and looked nervously down on the shrunken view below. To their relief, the black cloaked figure was nowhere to be seen and they turned away to scan the rest of their surroundings. They were standing on a narrow plateau which rolled gently down into a small valley. To their left rose another hill but a small opening revealed the silver ribbon of a river on the lower ground behind it. Right where they were standing was a small rise on which rested a group of stones set in a circle. Some words were etched on one of the these and James read them aloud.

'Here is marked the border of the Gamad and Camil regions.' He turned to Will. 'Are we in Camil?'

Will nodded. 'We have to go into Gamad, down there.' He pointed to the stony valley below. 'Hopefully we'll get there before it gets dark, it doesn't look far. I think the village is close to the border, but I don't know any more than that.'

The bracken and loose stones made it difficult to stay balanced, but they reached the bottom safely. They found themselves standing in a field at the heart of the valley, surrounded by rolling slopes. A short distance to the left, James spotted a group of houses which had been hidden from above.

'Over there,' he said breathlessly to Will. 'It must be the village.'

Both boys were weak with hunger, but they began to stumble in the direction of the houses. As they approached, they saw that the village was surrounded by a broken wire fence. The houses were built from rough cut stone and stood jumbled together, each overcrowding the next. Some rooves had caved in and many of the doors stood swinging on rusty hinges. The gardens too were untended, overgrown with weeds and scattered with rusting tools. A rusty metal gate appeared to be the only way into the village and the boys ventured tiredly through.

'It looks abandoned,' Will said in a hushed voice. 'It's all in ruins.' He kicked at a broken spade handle and sighed.

James nodded, his heart sinking. 'I thought your dad came and spoke to the man here? Did he say anything about the village itself?'

'No, I don't think so, but I can't remember all the details. I didn't think I'd ever need to come here to speak to the man. Maybe it's not the right village at all.'

James wandered to the doorway of the closest house. A rusty spade stood by the door, surrounded by broken flowerpots. Inside, the broken windows cast an eerie light over a small front room. He slipped into the house and looked around the space which had been taken over by cobwebs and dust. The fireplace was cold and empty, charred by the soot of many fires. Something was written on the mantelpiece, a small engraving barely larger than his hand. He went closer, brushing away a layer of grime. The words were written in a strange language and he read them aloud in a faltering voice.

'*Oreauq mativ manretea ni sirbenet. Oge mus sugav.*' It was like no other language he had ever read before and he turned his eyes away, disinterested.

Emerging from the house, his eyes fell on a dilapidated church which stood opposite. Its walls were smothered with dying ivy and the doors swung from rusty metal hinges. The remnants of a graveyard rested in front of it, the headstones barely visible under the long, wild grass. Will was walking amongst these fallen memorials and James went to sit on the crumbling wall surrounding them. His legs ached and he could barely hold his head up.

'Anything interesting?' Will asked, coming to sit beside him.

'Nothing, the house was empty,' James replied with a yawn. 'There's nothing here at all. It was a stupid idea coming here when I don't even know what I'm looking for.'

Will rubbed his tired eyes. 'The man might know something about the story, or about the crystals at least. I'm sure my dad said the village was by the border, it must be this one.' His face looked slightly grey in the evening light which cast shadows all around them. 'We might have to sleep in one of the houses for the night,' he added.

'It's all empty,' James muttered. 'There must be another village somewhere. This one looks like it's been abandoned for years.' His voice was heavy with disappointment.

Behind them, another voice then sounded. It spoke quietly, as if fearing to disturb the long, still shadows. 'Not completely abandoned,' it said. 'How may I help you?'

Chapter 8

AN old man stood behind them, his back bent with age and his kind face deeply wrinkled. He wore a battered, old brown cloak with its hood drawn half way over his head. In his hand he held a small bunch of wild flowers with star like blue heads that were ringed with a frill of yellow. He was standing by the church gate, leaning lightly against the tumbling wall which was itself only held up by strands of tough ivy. A pair of blue-grey eyes watched the boys from under hooded eyelids. James jumped down from the wall and stepped forward to meet the old man.

'We're looking for someone,' he said and met the man's gaze unflinchingly.

The old man didn't blink. 'Who is that you look for?'

'A man who knows about crystals. He lives somewhere in this region, near the border. We thought this must be the village, but it's empty.'

The man smiled, cracked toothed and wrinkled. 'Follow me,' he chuckled. 'I know where you might find him.'

Will and James looked at each other nodding and the old man smiled again, turning towards the slope in front of them. They followed him, past many run-down houses which looked melancholy in the fading light of the day. It was strangely beautiful but carried with it a great sadness that rested over the village like a cloud. The air was oddly heavy, seeming to quiver about them and James shivered with it.

It wasn't a large village and they soon left it, starting up a path ahead of them in the wake of the old man. He didn't stop until he reached a small cottage, hidden in a little nest of slopes. This too must have once been beautiful but was now old and crumbling. One small patch of flowers grew by the wall but the rest of the garden was bleak. To the back of the cottage a group of fir trees spread to the top of the slope, casting a large shadow over it. The building itself was made from grey stone and had two small windows facing in the direction of the abandoned village. It was not very large but looked comfortable enough and going up to the door, the old man opened it before standing aside to let the boys in.

At the end of a tiny passage was a door which they were ushered through. Everything was dark until the man created a light in his hands and sent it upwards where it cast a soft glow above them. The room they had entered was small and lined with shelves of books. They stretched all the way around, from floor to ceiling, making the room feel almost claustrophobic. In the centre was a table, set with four chairs and scattered with bottles, paper and a cup with a broken handle. The smell of the space drifted between dampness and a dry must which caught in their nostrils and made James sneeze. There were no windows, but they could see well enough. The old man gestured for them to sit, sweeping the things from the table into his arms. James and Will sat awkwardly, looking at each other in unspoken anticipation.

The old man disappeared briefly and returned carrying two steaming bowls of stew and several mugs. He set them down before the boys who hungrily breathed in the warm, unfamiliar scent which hit them. James wasn't entirely convinced by the greyish mass, but his stomach was grumbling and casting all doubt aside, he began to eat. All manners disappeared as the boys wolfed the food down with noisy gulps.

'You look hungry, eat it all up,' the old man said, 'then you can tell me what you came for.'

'You're the man aren't you?' Will asked through a mouthful of stew.

The man laughed. 'An excellent deduction. Of course I am, who else could he be? My name is Kleon.' He chuckled to himself again. 'I'm most curious as to why you came to find me.'

'You met my dad, Nicolas Aeton,' Will said before James could answer. 'I remember him telling me about you.'

Kleon nodded slowly and squinted at Will as if trying to discern a resemblance. 'I did indeed meet Nicolas many years ago. He was a fine historian. What does his son want from me now?'

James decided it was his turn to speak. 'Have you ever heard of Arvad the Wanderer?' he asked, diving straight in with hopeful energy.

Kleon shifted his gaze to James, but his expression revealed nothing. 'I might have I suppose. Say I have.'

James' heart immediately sank and he ran his fingers through his hair self-consciously. 'It's an old myth,' he continued, 'I don't know all of it but it talks about four stones, or crystals.' Kleon's eyes lit with a little interest but betrayed nothing more. James saw the look and went on, a little encouraged. 'Each crystal is for one of the elements, earth, air, fire and water. We don't know anything else about them.'

'What would two young boys want to know this for? Kleon

set down his mug without removing his gaze from James' face.

James squirmed under the weight of the question. 'J... just a project,' he stammered, 'for school. We thought you might be able to help us as there aren't any books about it.' Suddenly remembering the page in his pocket, he drew it out and handed it to the old man uncertainly. 'I couldn't find the other pages,' he said quietly.

Kleon took it up and began to read. It didn't take him long and he laid it back on the table, his eyes narrowing. 'I have read parts of it before,' he stated thoughtfully. 'Few people know of the tale as it was kept secret for many years. Many of those who read it believed they were destined to find the crystals and achieve eternal life.'

'Do you think the story is true?' James asked, swallowing the last mouthful of stew.

'It has elements of truth,' Kleon replied. 'Crystals do indeed hold great power and can, under the influence of magic, be an incomprehensible force.'

Will cast James a look before speaking. 'Can you tell us about the crystals?'

'I see the firestone is the only one spoken of in detail, but I might be able to help you.' Kleon stood and began running his fingers along one of the bookshelves. 'I don't know what the crystals are, but I have some ideas,' he said over his shoulder.

His fingers eventually rested on a large green volume and he pulled it out. He returned to the table, spreading the book before him and began to flick through the rough pages. The boys watched him anxiously until at last he stopped at a page in the centre, passing his fingers over the lines.

'Yes,' he whispered to himself, 'yes.' Neither James or Will wanted to interrupt him and waited until he was ready to speak again.

'I've lived on my own in this place for many years,' he said quietly. 'I've tried to uncover many secrets of the world, some I've achieved, others I have not. I have studied many crystals and their healing powers. As the firestone is not the specific name of any crystal, its type is difficult to discern.'

Kleon pushed the book over to them and pointed to the open page. At the top was a simple ink drawing of a jagged crystal. Kleon touched the image and suddenly it glowed on the paper, leaping to life off the page.

'This is a type of jasper, known as heliotrope,' he said, pointing again to the glowing image. 'It is a bloodstone, known for its strength and represents fire to the belief of many. This may be the crystal referred to as the firestone.'

Will leaned forward and reached out to touch the page but Kleon pushed his hand back.

'Don't touch it,' he hissed. Will looked acutely embarrassed and withdrew his hand quickly.

'Have you seen one before?' James asked, ignoring Will.

'I have seen a few in my time, it is often used in jewellery and for protection. It is expensive, as with many stones.'

'Why are crystals used in the tale? Why not something else?'

Kleon adjusted his cloak and smiled at James. 'Crystals are an ancient power, used for healing. They are close to nature but can also be used by man. They carry both the power of the natural world and that of the human, which makes them one of the greatest powers on earth.'

James nodded slowly. 'What makes it a fire stone?' he asked. 'How's it made I mean? Does it come from fire?'

Kleon shook his head. 'No, it does not. People just attribute the crystal properties to the elements, but beyond that there is no real connection.' He turned his eyes to the book again and continued to flick through the pages.

His response had not been the one James had hoped for and again he felt at a loss for speech. Kleon flicked to another page and began muttering to himself again. A new image appeared on the paper, a red crystal, polished and shining in the light above them.

'The ruby,' Kleon explained. 'It says here that it is a cleanser of blood and diseases and is the stone of energy. Large pieces of this crystal are valuable and extremely rare.' He stopped and peered at the boys, taking in their dishevelled appearances with curiosity. Gently, he closed the book and returned it to the shelf.

'Where do people find rare crystals?' Will asked curiously. 'Is there a place where they come from?'

Their host sighed. 'I am sorry I can't be of more help, but I know where you might go. There are caves only a day or so's walk from here across the hills. The dwarf like race there study these stones more than I and may help you.'

'Dwarves?' James gulped and quickly looked away to avoid the old man's penetrating stare.

'They can be uneasy around people so be careful,' Kleon said. 'They are strange creatures who mine deep into the ground to uncover the wealth of the earth, study it and protect what they find. I warn you not to be too inquisitive. It is late now,' he continued. 'I will offer you a bed for the night. It can be dangerous to wander about in the dark, I often find, especially for a couple of calves like you.'

James nodded gratefully, and the old man got up, gesturing for them to follow. They crossed the hallway into the room opposite where they found a mattress resting by the discoloured beige wall. A few pictures adorned the room and there was a small window bordered by disintegrating curtains. On the floor were more books, stacked into dusty piles and these filled much of the space. Kleon went out and returned with a few blankets which he cast onto the floor.

'Sleep,' he said abruptly and left again, closing the door behind him.

Left alone, the boys looked about curiously. Sleep was not the first thought in their minds as both were longing to discuss what had just passed. Will flopped down onto the mattress and sat with his arms drawn over his knees and his face between them. Despite his aching legs, James chose to pace about the small room, his shoulders slumped, and his hands thrust into his pockets. Turning his back to Will, he took out his phone and pressed the on button. To his surprise a light shone from the screen, despite the days without charge. He turned it over in his hands, feeling comforted by the cold, familiar rectangle. The signal bars were still empty and the time blank. Strangely however, the rest of the screen fizzled like a television losing signal.

'D'you think the firestone is one of them, a ruby or a jad… whatever it was?' Will asked from the bed.

James hurriedly tucked his phone away. 'Jasper? I don't know, we need the rest of the story.' His tiredness returned to him as he sat on the pile of blankets and his head drooped.

'Do you think the myth is true?' Will questioned through a wide yawn.

James pulled a blanket around himself and chucked one towards Will. 'I'm beginning to believe it,' he said quietly. 'I think we have to find out more about the crystals, that way we'll find the truth. If they exist, then surely the myth is based on something.'

He lay down facing away from Will and closed his eyes. Will sighed and extinguished the light which Kleon had left with them and they both gradually drifted into sleep. James found himself once more as if he were awake, in a place surrounded by mist, and a shadow which he felt he knew passed before his eyes.

'Look behind you and in front. Beware of those who seek to stop you on your path towards the truth.'

The voice was closer than before, whispering all around him. Still, when he opened his mouth no sound came out and he looked around desperately. The warning seemed to again suggest that this task must be destined for him, even if he didn't want to believe it. The misty figure came into view but it was stepping away from him, back through the haze. Its face, whether a man's or a woman's, was hidden under a dark hood. The mist swirled as the body moved, reminding James of the white clouds in No Man's Land. He reached out to the figure, trying to stop the dream from fading. Looking down, he saw his own body had disappeared and by the time he raised his head again, the figure had gone.

Chapter 9

JAMES awoke with a start. It was still the early hours of the morning and light was just sifting in through the tattered curtains. He rolled over stiffly, cold from his uncomfortable sleep on the floor. Groggy eyed, he sat up and glanced over to the bed where Will still lay snoring peacefully. A spider resting in a web on the window above Will was just beginning its breakfast and James turned away, his stomach turning.

Rising from his makeshift bed, he tripped on a book and kicked it away irritably. The hard cover jabbed his bare foot painfully and he gritted his teeth. Looking around, he saw the book had come to rest beside a stack of large, dusty volumes. Its cover had fallen open to reveal the pencilled image of a crystal. With sudden curiosity James leant forward and grabbed the book before sitting down on the grubby floor. The room wasn't bright enough for him to see properly so he shifted to sit under the window where a line of pale light spilled beneath the curtains.

The book was like the volume Kleon had shown them the night before, only it was smaller and the words were packed closely together. The page James had opened bore the title 'Moonstone' and a small paragraph of writing which rested below a simple sketch. Flicking through the pages, he searched for the letter 'J' until he found a section about the jasper crystal. The image was again just a basic outline and the whole page was scrawled in tight, handwritten script. The text only offered some basic details which Kleon had already relayed. Wondering if the images in this book could also come to life, James held his hand over the page and closed his eyes. He imagined colours seeping into the sketch and a light glowed blue in his hand, but when he looked down again there was nothing.

James sighed and turned the pages again, hunting for the ruby. It was there too, laid out just as the other crystals were. He was close to shutting the book when he saw a faint mark at the top of the page, a circle filled with a perfect seven-pointed star. Gently holding his hand over the page once more, he watched as the light glowed in his hand. Something started to happen on the page, the writing beginning to ripple across the yellowed paper. He stared as the wavering text settled into new lines, etched between the original rows of words.

'Personn posseth a magyk far les than the cristal,' he read slowly. *'Thy commeth fro the erth itself and in hevens far.'* He was struggling to read this strange language which was only partly English. It reminded him of Middle English texts he had glanced at a few times at school but had never bothered to read. He concentrated again.

'Sem seed the ayr, water and fyr hath also plaid a part. Fyr it of the erth and of ayr but yet desireth more. Tis sed no fyr burhn al tyme but shuld it hav the chance wuld cunsume tyme. Fyr posseth the hart of cristal, which can only groweth if bestowed a gift, that of tyme. The natur of such is for personn grew himself, for non yet has this gift.' James paused and raised his strained eyes. The writing was slightly faded in places and he could hardly understand it.

'*Oother cristal there be fro erth, the ayr and water. This too must tak a gift, also of which personn has ne fund. Shud this cristal be in hand, which must need a power non can know, he will live eternal. So it is seed as I have herd, the myth sprung from ancient land as told by sage who reches for high heven. Thys writ, should I hide it in erth for rite man to find and red. Then shal this myth of legend become now true.*'

James came to the end of the text and gaped at it. Going over to the bed, he shook Will who was still peacefully sleeping. Will rolled over to face the wall with a groan which was muffled by the woollen blanket wrapped around him. James continued to shake his friend with unwelcome enthusiasm.

'Will, Will, wake up.'

'What, what is it?' Will sat up with an irritable expression and looked at James through half closed eyes.

Ignoring Will's sleepiness, James shoved the book into his hands, pointing to the page he had just been reading.

'The firestone is a ruby, I'm sure of it.' He tapped the page excitedly. 'Read this, I found it on the floor. What d'you think it means?'

Will rubbed the sleep from his eyes and looked down at the book, noting the strange writing with evident disgust.

'Really? You want me to read this?'

'Yeah, I think it might help us. 'Read it, just read it.'

Sighing, Will began to read. James paced up and down the small room, winding his way through the piles of books. His impatience grew greater every minute until Will relieved him by finally looking up.

'You said you think the firestone is a ruby, where does it say that?' He frowned at James.

James went and sat on the bed, taking the book from Will. He held his hand over the page. A light glowed and the words began to shift again, back to their original form. The page was as James had first found it, with the image of the ruby resting at the top. He handed it back to Will, watching his face closely.

'The writing about Arvad's myth is disguised inside the page about the ruby. Surely whoever wrote it there meant it to be a clue?'

Will kept his eyes fixed on the book. 'You can do magic,' he said quietly.

James felt a heat growing on the back of his neck. Not knowing how to answer, he passed quickly over the comment. 'It must be the ruby,' he continued. 'I don't think it could just be coincidence. Kleon talked about the dwarves. They'll be able to tell us more about the ruby.'

'We should ask Kleon where he got this,' Will said and, reaching over, closed the book with a thud.

'What does this mark mean?' James asked, pointing to the circle at the top of the page.

Will squinted at the circle, tracing its circumference with his eyes. 'It's a family symbol, like the ones on our wrists. Usually it means the author of the book. Kleon might know.'

Both rose from the bed and went out into the hallway. No sound came from anywhere in the cottage and they crept carefully into the room they had sat in the night before. To their surprise Kleon was already there, his back facing the door. They could just make out a book resting between his hands, the pages lit by a tiny ball of light which rested on the table. As if sensing their presence, Kleon turned to greet them and gestured to the table which was already set for breakfast.

'I trust you slept well?' he asked as the boys sat and began to eat hungrily.

After swallowing a few mouthfuls, James took the book out

and laid it on the table. Kleon looked at it for a moment before turning a questioning gaze onto James.

'Where did you get that?' he asked in his cracked voice.

'I found it on the floor in our room,' James replied carefully. 'We were wondering where you got it from?'

Kleon reached out his wrinkled hand. It was so old that the skin seemed to have sunk away and left only his bones, yet he held the book in a strong and steady grip.

'Yes,' he murmured. 'I remember now. A crystal book if I'm right?' He began flicking through the pages, coming to rest on the one about the ruby.

'The ruby,' he murmured and held his hand over the page. There was a glow of orange light but nothing happened. James looked at Will in surprise but neither of them said anything. Kleon shut the book with a gentle thud and placed it back on the table.

'I found it in the village many years ago in one of the houses. I was the only one who remained.' He did not elaborate on this point. 'It was the only thing left in the house, half buried under the floor. I couldn't tell you which house it was now, but I still wonder who hid it there and why, for I have many books of a similar nature. I wonder what was so special about this one. Anyway,' he moved out of his reverie, 'keep it if it will be of use to you.' He pushed the book back towards James who took it and thanked him.

Kleon left the room, taking the breakfast things out on a tray. James waited until he had disappeared before turning to Will with a puzzled frown. Evidently whoever had hidden the book in the village knew about the secret page. He could think of no other reason why someone would need to hide it. The other question resting in his mind was why Kleon hadn't been able to reveal the hidden words. He didn't feel he could ask it however, as he didn't want Kleon to know the secret. When the old man returned, he brought with him two packages of food which he handed to Will and James. They thanked him and he led them to the door, opening it onto a grey day. Outside, a wind had risen and the village below lay shrouded in mist.

'Follow the path up through the trees behind my house,' Kleon advised. 'It will take you a few days to reach the caves, but the path will lead you there. It's an old track which has linked the caves to the village for centuries.'

After thanking him one last time, the boys exited the house. Kleon watched them go, returning their waves as they disappeared up behind the trees. Not far along the path, both boys heard the sharp snap of a twig somewhere behind them. They whipped around, scanning their surroundings with suspicion. The warning in James' dream suddenly sprang back to him, the figure telling him to look behind. He pulled his hood up further over his face, afraid that the snap was some misplaced footstep, someone who hadn't wanted to be heard.

'Did you hear that?' Will asked nervously.

James nodded and took a few steps backwards. 'I can't see anyone or anything, but it sounded quite close.' He peered back down the path, between the trees, but there didn't seem to be anything there.

'D'you think it's possible that whoever we saw from the top of the hill could have followed us?' Will whispered. 'Someone who wants to keep an eye on what you're doing.'

'They want to stop me finding out the truth,' James replied quietly. 'I... I had a dream last night where a voice told me that I had to watch out for people trying to do that.'

'You had a dream telling you that? That's mad, I thought you said no one else knew about this quest.'

James shrugged. 'I know, but someone clearly does, and they're trying to help me. Come on, let's hurry.' He began to walk up the path again, his mind set on reaching the caves as quickly as possible.

They walked all day, only stopping to eat some food and drink from a stream. As it grew dark, they found a place to rest under the shelter of a few brown-leaved trees. They took turns to stay awake, fearful that they were still being followed. James slept fitfully, dreaming of his parents, the power cut, and everything that had happened since then. When Will woke him, the sky was just growing light. He took his turn on watch, shivering in the cold which grew sharper as morning came on. When the sky was no longer getting brighter, he shook Will awake. They ate a small portion of the bread Kleon had given them before rising and starting to move again. They walked for several hours, passing over slopes and through thin copses until they broke out onto a small plane. The view was the same on all sides, hills, valleys and trees, with small villages dotted in between.

'We must be nearly there,' Will said, shaking out his damp cloak. A light suddenly filled his face and delving into his pocket he drew out a tightly folded square of paper. 'A map, I forgot it was in here,' he said cheerfully.

James took the paper and spread it out between his hands. To his amazement, he saw not seven continents, but four, placed at separate quarters of the globe. Each continent was divided into small segments, titled with words James didn't recognise. At his touch, one segment of land on the north continent turned dark, as if stained with a blot of ink. Will grinned at him and pointed to the dark patch.

'That's Gamad, the region we're in. The map fills in whichever region the holder is in so you always know where you are. My dad gave it to me for a birthday once. I didn't realise it was in my pocket!'

James grinned back at Will. He chose not to speak of his world and how different this map was to any he'd seen before. Will would only ask questions, or worse, wouldn't believe him. Looking out at the plane, James suddenly felt a tingling in his wrist. For a split second, he thought he saw a path winding through the trees ahead and out onto another plane.

'What is it?' Will asked, noticing James' blank face.

James shook his head. 'It's nothing. I thought I saw something but I'm just tired. Come on, I'm sure we're nearly there.'

A pale sun was trying to break through clouds, glinting down through the treetops as they passed under the trees. By the time the boys broke out onto the barren plane, the air was already warmer. The terrain around them was rough, scattered with rocks and sharp tufts of grass. A few scrubby trees stood leaning towards the wind, their leaves already shed. In the north, the sky was iron grey, hanging like a dead weight over the land.

'This must be it,' James said, looking around without much enthusiasm. The brief image he had seen in his mind matched the scene which lay before him.

Will shivered. 'I can't see anyone about, it looks empty.'

Like the ruined village, the landscape around them was deserted. James spread out the map again and squinted closely at it, as if trying to find some clue.

'There must be a cave entrance somewhere then,' he said. 'We're just not looking closely enough.' Occupied with scanning the rocks around him, he didn't see Will's face turn pale.

'They are here.' Will's voice came out in a harsh whisper. 'Look.'

James turned. Coming towards them was a troop of tall figures. He had expected the dwarves to be small like the ones he'd seen in films, but this perception was entirely wrong. The group coming towards them was not as he expected at all and he suddenly felt the strong desire to run.

Chapter 10

THE group of dwarves had encircled them before they had time to hide. They were strange looking persons, much taller than the boys, and broad shouldered. The older dwarves had beards that almost reached past their knees whereas the younger dwarves' chins were still mostly bare. Each carried a long wooden staff engraved with three diamond marks. James and Will looked at their captors warily, their eyes never leaving the circle that imprisoned them.

'What's your business on Ona territory?' one wiry haired dwarf asked, baring his gold-plated teeth in a snarl. Will recoiled, turning his head away to avoid the shower of spittle.

'Ona territory?' James asked with a frown.

'We, the Ona people,' the gold toothed interrogator snapped in his husky voice. 'Don't you know that we don't welcome strangers here?'

'We thought you were dwarves.' Will spoke out before he could stop himself.

The faces of those surrounding them darkened. Will turned red and James turned to glare at him. Another Ona then stepped forward into the circle, coming to a halt next to Will who lowered his eyes to avoid the angry stare. The Ona opened his mouth to speak, revealing a row of uneven yellow teeth.

'Never call an Ona a dwarf,' he hissed. 'Never! Dwarf is the name of our half-brothers on the Western Continent and does not belong to us.' Reaching forward, he snatched the map which Will now held.

The gold toothed Ona held up a hand for silence and gestured for his companion to return to the circle.

'Take them inside,' he commanded. 'Take them to the chief and tell him they were trespassing on our land.' He raised his staff and brought it down hard on the earth with a hollow thud.

Before James and Will could protest, two Ona came and grabbed them firmly by the arms. One was old, the other young, but both had fierce green eyes and dark, curly hair. Wordlessly, they began propelling the boys forward over the barren plane, neither loosening their grip. After a short distance, an outcrop of craggy grey rocks came into sight, the top sheltered by a cluster of leafless trees. As they approached, the boys noticed a small opening in the left of the rock face which was only visible from these close quarters. Through this gap they were unceremoniously shoved, one after the other, and the rest of the Ona clan followed.

Beyond the entrance was a dimly lit passage which sloped narrowly downwards. It reminded James of the underground city in Arissel, but he knew it would not be the same. Several Ona dropped away from the group but four stayed with James and Will, forcing them down the passage. They walked for a short distance until, on rounding a corner, they found themselves in a brightly lit cave. Three figures stood before them, each wearing a thick, woollen robe embroidered with three diamonds. James felt his heart flip as he noticed sharp daggers thrust into a thick belt around each Ona's waist. The three looked at the boys with a cruel kind of interest, their faces grimly set.

'Two more imposters,' Gold Tooth growled and spat on the floor at the boys' feet. James made a face and stepped backwards, only to find the old, green eyed Ona blocking his way.

The robed figure standing on the left licked his lips with a wide, purplish tongue. 'Your names?' he asked. His voice was rough and deep, causing his words to come out as a growl. 'Who dares come to the place of the Ona race? Either you are ignorant or foolish.'

In response to the question, Will pulled up his sleeve to reveal his symbol, a semi-circle shot through with a diagonal line. Slowly and uncertainly, James followed suit. He saw a curious flicker pass through the Ona's eyes and hurriedly covered his wrist, wondering if his symbol was somehow different.

'Your business?' the same Ona asked, his lip curling.

James took a deep breath, buying himself time to focus his thoughts. 'We were told you could tell us about a crystal,' he muttered uncertainly.

There was movement from the middle Ona who stepped forward and fixed James with a piercing blue stare. His eyes were rimmed by small black lashes which made their colour even sharper. Unlike his two companions, he wore a large gold badge on his chest, set with a small, black crystal.

'Who told you this?' His eyes bored into James who found himself unable to look away.

'A man named Kleon,' James replied. 'He thought you'd be able to help us.'

'And what do you want to know?' the Ona sneered.

James gave a small shrug. 'Anything you can tell us about rubies.'

A deep, unpleasant laugh met his words and the Ona turned to Gold Tooth. 'You know where to take them to answer their questions.'

Gold Tooth grinned widely. 'Follow me,' he said sharply and prodded Will and James in their backs.

Silently, the boys entered the passage once more. They had no idea where they were going and James held his breath quietly as the passage grew darker around them.

'Aren't you worried?' Will whispered to him in a thin voice.

James swallowed. 'No, are you?' His words came out brusquely.

'No,' came a determinedly steady reply.

'Stop whispering,' the Ona ahead of them snarled and they fell silent again.

There were several doors set along the tunnel at uneven intervals. Most were shut fast but some leaned ajar and James peered through, catching glimpses of caves filled with shelves and boxes. As the passage grew darker, he had to reach out and touch the walls to feel his way along it. The rock was damp and earthy beneath his fingers and the air too was thick with moisture. In the darkness, James felt his eyelids start to droop and he had to keep jerking his head upwards again, focusing on keeping his feet moving. Every time his eyes closed, he was back at home in his own bed, solving logic puzzles on his laptop. He could even hear his parents' voices yelling up the stairs. He wondered if they had come back from their holiday now and if they missed him at all. To him, their distance felt perfectly ordinary.

The air grew gradually warm again and James realised the tunnel must have been sloping gently downwards without him noticing. A new passageway had opened to the left, barred by a single grey metal gate and lit by a glowing orb. He squinted as the sudden light burned his eyes, but he still tried to see through the door at the other end. Another light inside glinted on piles of strange black stones resting on shelves. Beside these were groups of pale pink and white crystals which he didn't recognise either. As he glanced for those few moments, he felt his phone buzz in his pocket. Hurriedly, he reached inside his cloak, shielding the screen light in its folds. Someone was calling him but there was no number and the signal bars were empty. A cold fear gripped him and he quickly ended the call.

'Stop!' The command from ahead brought James from his wild thoughts. 'Go through the gates,' the Ona snapped and gestured to another gate to their right which was hidden in shadow.

Without thinking, James passed through, followed by Will. It was already too late when they heard a click and whirled around to find the gates had been closed behind them. Will leapt forward, coming into sharp contact with solid metal bars. On the other side, they could see the form of the gold toothed Ona retreating down the orbed passageway which provided the only light.

'Hey,' James yelled, 'let us out!' He reached out and shook the bars with frustration.

'We're trapped, it was all a trick,' Will said beside him. 'They were never going to help us; we were idiots to come here.'

James shook the bars again before sliding his tired body onto the hard, stone ground. 'What're we going to do?' he asked tiredly.

Will came and sat down on the floor next to him and let out a long groan. 'We shouldn't have trusted them! Why would they tell us about the ruby? They had no reason to help us. We've got to get out of here before they decide to kill us.'

James nodded numbly and removed his cloak, wrapping it up into a pillow to put behind his head. The silence rang in his ears, lurking in every shadow. He was tired but his eyes flickered open and shut again as he lay on the cold earthy floor. The memory of the body lying in his path in Arissel wouldn't leave him and he swallowed, his stomach churning. He had never been afraid of death before, but Will's words made him think about it in the darkness. The only death he knew was that of his sister, but that had happened several years before he was born. Now the prospect haunted him and he didn't know what to think or feel. He hadn't wanted to believe that this quest was dangerous, but he was beginning to realise the truth.

'You seek ruby?' A soft feminine voice, laced with a foreign accent, broke the silence of the prison cell and both Will and James leapt up.

'Who's there?' Will whispered, nervously scanning the semi-darkness.

On the other side of the bars stood a woman. She wore a thin green cloak over which her reddish hair was splayed in long, loose strands. Although tall, she had a delicate frame and her thin, ringed finger gripped the bars of the cell.

'What d'you know about rubies?' James demanded, keeping well back despite the bars dividing himself and the stranger.

A gentle laugh fell from the woman's lips. 'I am from Ona race, what do I not know about crystal. They are force more powerful than man, force that is both good and evil. I can help you.'

'An Ona!' James exclaimed. 'Why would you help us?'

'Not all seek to harm you. I study crystal to find them but also help other understand their meaning. I hear you speaking of ruby.'

Although wary of the Ona, James was aware that she was their best hope. He looked questioningly at Will who responded with a shrug.

'We're looking for a fire ruby,' James said.

'A fire ruby?' The woman's voice sounded puzzled. 'All rubies have link to energy and fire element, but I have not heard of this fire ruby.'

James frowned and rubbed his tired eyes. 'Are any rubies sourced from fire?' he asked.

'I haven't heard of this. Perhaps non-natural formation using powerful magic might include fire. People try different method to find and make ruby because they are rare.'

'Are there different types of ruby?' Will questioned, taking a step closer to the bars.

As he spoke, there came the distant sound of footsteps. The Ona turned and looked down the passageway with a quick, wild flick of her head.

'I must go,' she whispered, 'but I promise to be back before much time passes. Here, I have brought food. Rest and do not be afraid, they won't come back yet.'

These last words rang ominously in James' ears and he shuddered to think what might happen when their captors did come back. He took the food thankfully and returned to his place on the floor as their helper slipped out of sight. Will sat down in the opposite corner of the cell and began absent-mindedly drawing lines on the earthy floor. They shared out the bread and meat Elra had brought but both were too tired to talk. Silence pressed between them until they eventually drifted into restless sleep.

James awoke from his fitful doze to the sound of a continuous buzzing. He had no idea how long he'd been asleep and looked around with confusion before realising the sound was coming from the floor beside him. His phone lay next to his cloak on the earthy ground and he picked it up with fresh fear. The numberless caller was ringing him again, even though the signal bars remained empty. In a sudden spurt of irrationality, he pressed the green button on the screen and held the phone up to his ear.

'Hello?' His voice sounded empty and shook slightly. There was silence at the other end as no one answered.

'Who's there?' he tried again, his voice stronger this time. Nothing happened and he quickly ended the call. Something was wrong, no one from his world could possibly reach him and no one in this world used technology.

'Hello?' The voice made James jump and he clutched his phone tightly. The voice hadn't come from the speaker however, but from somewhere outside the cell.

'Who's there?' he repeated in a hushed voice. 'Where are you?'

He scanned the darkness nervously, hoping the voice belonged to the female Ona. A light flickered on and he looked toward it. A figure stood in the adjoining cell, swinging the soft beam over James and the still sleeping Will.

'It's you!' The person belonging to the voice held the light up higher and James caught sight of a pale white face looking back at him.

'Aralia?' He recognised the face of the girl they had met back in the wood outside Arissel. 'What're you doing here?'

Another figure stepped from behind Aralia and James saw it was her brother Arthur. The two boys looked at each other with an unspoken defiance, James' brown eyes meeting Arthur's greenish grey.

'How long have you been in here?' James asked abruptly. 'How did you get here from the wood?'

Arthur moved past his sister to stand by the bars. His white blond hair shone brightly in the light which she now held still on her narrow palm. James was once again struck by how similar they looked and he couldn't help staring. Arthur gazed back at him with wary eyes.

'We've been here for hours,' Arthur replied shortly. 'I don't know how much time has passed.'

James suddenly wondered how much they had heard. A few hours ago, the Ona woman had been speaking to them about the firestone and the ruby. He rubbed his eyes and looked back at the two white faces before him. Aralia watched the ground for a few moments before raising her head to meet James' gaze. In the half-light, her white skin made her look not quite human.

'The fire ruby,' she whispered. 'Are you really looking for it?'

Chapter 11

THERE was a long silence whilst James tried to clear his thoughts. The corners of the cell lay in shadow, but he remained in the circle of light. Arthur and Aralia had heard it all and James knew it would be dangerous to let them go with this information. It would be better to keep them on his side. They were now wrapped up in the secret of the firestone and must become a part of his journey to discover the firestone and the truth.

'Yes, I'm looking for a firestone.'

His answer was simple but bore all the weight of a secret which shouldn't be told. He turned his head away but from the corner of his eye could see the siblings looking at him blankly.

'What is it?' Aralia asked tentatively after a moment of silence. 'What is the firestone and why're you looking for it?' She began biting the nails of her free hand whilst she waited for an answer.

'Why d'you want to know?' James asked defiantly. He kept his face turned away, focusing his eyes on the shadows.

On the ground in front of him, Will stirred and suddenly sat up. He looked at James through groggy eyes before turning his gaze to where Arthur and Aralia stood.

'What're they doing here?' he mumbled, looking from them

to James and back again.

Before James could gather the words to reply, Arthur began to speak. 'We followed you, that's why we're here and that's why we want to know why you're looking for this firestone.' He stopped abruptly and both Will and James stared at him disbelievingly.

'You what?' Will spat. He glared at Arthur before turning to James with a sudden look of understanding. 'It was them following us, they were the people at the bottom of the hill.'

James nodded but didn't speak. It was all beginning to make sense and he felt relieved that someone more dangerous hadn't been following them. The atmosphere in the cells was tense and the four watched each other suspiciously. Reaching into his pocket, he drew out the book Kleon had given them and the sheets of paper bearing Arvad's tale which he'd tucked inside. He held both up for Arthur and Aralia to see but kept far enough back so they couldn't read the words.

'The firestone is one of four crystals which can destroy the dark.' From the corner of his eye he saw Will's expression change but refused to meet the confused stare.

'The dark?' Arthur asked, his tone curious.

James nodded. 'People using dark magic. It's growing stronger all the time and apparently these crystals can defeat it.'

'Dark magic has always been around,' Arthur returned. 'Why's it suddenly worse?'

'I don't know, I don't understand any of it,' James answered truthfully. 'I'm trying to find out the truth. All I know is that the crystals need to be found before the people using dark magic get to them.' He sighed and sat down on the floor again, letting his head fall into his hands.

'Why you?' Aralia spoke gently. 'Why're you trying to find

this firestone?'

Raising his head again, James looked directly into her eyes. 'I don't know,' he repeated. 'The quest might not be mine, but if it is, I'm going to find out.'

He decided not to mention his world or the conversation with Albert and what he'd overheard in the library. The bare bones of truth would be enough to stop Arthur and Aralia asking questions, or so he hoped. Still holding the book, he leant forward and pushed it through the bars.

Arthur took it and held the light up to it, gesturing for his sister to come and join him. Silence fell over the cells and James felt a new fatigue wash over him. He closed his eyes, listening to the shuffling sound of Will taking a seat near him. Uncertainty lurked about them in the shadows, made darker by the light which pushed them away. The bars surrounding them, sealed by a strange, unbreakable magic, crushed any hope of escape. James felt himself slowly drifting further and further away from the earthy walls, into a world of tired thought and shadows.

'Are you awake?' A soft feminine voice roused James from his momentary sleep. 'It's Elra if you remember,' the voice continued, 'but I don't think I told my name.'

Opening his eyes, James saw the friendly face of the female Ona hovering by the bars. The light in the other cell had been quickly extinguished and Arthur and Aralia were hidden by the darkness.

'I'm awake,' James whispered back.

'Me too,' Will's voice mumbled beside him.

'I have a key,' Elra whispered. 'It is a key that lets you out. I came before but you sleep long. I play dangerous game and in return for your freedom, I ask for something.'

Both boys stood hurriedly and gathered up their cloaks. James felt suspicion rising in him again but still reached into his pockets in search of something that might act as payment. Amidst the wrappers and other jumbled things, his fingers brushed against three coins. He drew them out and tentatively held them out to Elra who took them with interest.

'What are they?' she asked, turning them over in her palm.

James was grateful for the semi-darkness which hid the coin surfaces. 'Some silver and gold pieces, I found them.'

He nervously watched her turning over the pound coin and two fifty pence pieces. She smiled faintly and tucked them into her pocket.

'I never come across these before,' she said simply.

There was the sharp click of a key in the lock and a squeak as the gate swung open. Elra stood beside it, beckoning for the boys to step out. As they went through the gate, James stopped and looked over to the adjoining cell where Arthur and Aralia still hid in the darkness. He turned to Elra.

'Can you help them too?' He pointed towards the cell. They had the crystal book and the page of Arvad's tale and he couldn't go on without them.

'I've only one key,' Elra replied. 'If they are friends of yours and wish to be free, they must crawl under bars and into this cell. There's no time to waste.'

Will was already calling softly to Arthur and Aralia. They immediately followed his instructions, their movement indicated by the sound of scuffling. Arthur appeared first, squeezing himself under the low spikes which ran along the under edge of the bars. These caught on his cloak but he continued to push himself through, leaving pieces of fabric behind. He was nearly through when his shoe became jammed between two spikes and he looked helplessly up at Will and

James.

'Hurry,' Elra whispered. 'Help him! We have time not to waste.'

Together, James and Will grabbed Arthur's arms and tugged. On the other side of the bars, Aralia frantically tried to free the shoe and push Arthur forward. After a few rough pulls, his foot came free with a pop and he let out a gasp of pain. James tried to help him up but Arthur brushed him away and turned back to help Aralia through. As she was smaller than her brother she slipped through easily and stood quickly, brushing off her clothes. Elra gestured for the four to step from the cell before locking the gate behind them.

'Hurry, hurry,' she whispered again. 'Follow me and don't make sounds.'

'Where're we going?' James asked, but Elra hurried away down the passage, her hood pulled up high over her head.

The four followed her silently, not daring to utter a sound. Arthur was limping slightly, but his stern expression kept James from offering him help again. The passage floor began to incline slightly as they walked and the air grew gradually lighter. They soon spotted faint daylight ahead and Elra stopped, turning to them with an expressionless face.

'End of passage is opening onto moor which stretches under these hills. It is dangerous way, made to trap any who escape. There are no houses for long way, and many mist rises.'

Reaching into the pocket of her cloak, Elra drew out a small cloth bag. She held it out to James who took it, feeling its weight in his palm. Curiously, he reached inside and pulled out three small polished red-brown stones which glittered faintly in the pale light.

'The ruby,' Elra whispered, 'in polished form. More common

than many but still rare and expensive to buy.'

James felt the smooth stone beneath his fingers before handing it to Will who had his palm outstretched. He held up the second and third stone to Elra.

'Are these rubies too?' he asked.

She nodded and pointed to the smaller of the two. 'This is blood ruby, like many, was found in Garia. Some can be treated with heat to improve their colour, but it can be dangerous. Maybe this is what you look for. Only those with skill find such precious jewel. Each region lay claim to wealth found and it is complex. Many laws make it difficult to find valuable things, but to purchase them costs too much money.' She reached out and picked the larger crystal from James' hand. 'This is star ruby; it is maybe rarest and has asterism inside it.'

James hardly heard these latter words as he focused his attention on the blood ruby in his hand. Blood made him think of energy and energy of fire. He was sure they must be looking for a blood ruby and therefore they would have to go to Garia to find out more about their source. As he looked at the ruby, there came a sound from somewhere in the passage behind them. Elra whipped the bag from him and returned the crystals to it with urgency.

'It would cost much to be found with these,' she said in a harsh whisper.

Footsteps sounded and they all turned to each other with desperation in their eyes. The sound was coming closer and was suddenly accompanied by a shout.

'Stop, traitor!' The voice was deep and masculine.

'Go,' Elra urged, 'go quickly. Leave me, I'll be safe. Please, hurry before they find you.'

In panic, the four of them thanked her and hurried towards

the opening. Just as they were about to step out, there came a sharp cry. They all stopped in their tracks, convinced that the voice belonged to Elra. There were other voices too, talking in rough tones and they strained their ears to listen.

'Please, they escaped.' Elra's pleading voice reached them. 'They'll be lost on the moor.'

'There's a price on their heads, did you know that?' The same male voice snapped out the words with vigour.

Another voice took over from the first, smooth and vicious. 'I want the boy; I will pay a fine price. My name is Kedran. I could kill you for letting them go, just as I killed that old fool Kleon who told me I could find them here.'

There was a gasp from Elra, followed by one from James. He caught Will's eye and saw a desperation there which matched his own.

'You killed Kleon, he was good man,' Elra cried. 'There are not many good men in this world. Kill me if you wish but I never will help you.'

Kedran laughed. 'You seem almost too pretty to die, but even innocence must end.' He laughed again. 'You helped these children escape and now you'll pay.'

There was a scream of agony followed by a soft thud. James turned to the other three, his eyes wide with fear. Some strange part of him wanted to stay, but the more rational part told him to run. Breaking from his stiff position he hurried out into the light, followed by the others. He was struck by the brightness of the daylight, even though the sky was closed and grey. As his eyes adjusted, he realised they were standing on the outer edges of a moor which stretched outwards for miles. Hazy mountains rose to the right, marking where the ironed-out landscape ended. There were only a few trees in sight and no houses at all.

They were in the middle of nowhere, under a dull canopy of sky which met the land at the edge of the horizon.

Chapter 12

THE landscape had a hardness about it and the sky glared coldly back at them. It was as if some unseen hand had wiped all life away. James looked at the moor through half shut eyes, feeling the cool wind blowing against his face. He stepped numbly away from the protective overhanging of rock by the cave entrance and rested his feet in the marshy grass.

'We have to cross this?' Aralia asked, breaking the sickened silence. 'It's so empty.' Her voice trembled slightly, as though she was forcing the words out.

James made no reply. Instead, he began to walk, hardly caring where he went. A raindrop fell onto his cheek and he looked at the darkening clouds with a shiver. The view ahead had grown hazy with sheets of rain and swirling mist which had easy passage across the flat moorland. There was no shelter and the only choice was to meet the rain head on. Hearing the footsteps of the others behind him, he turned. They looked at him expectantly, as if hoping he had a plan or knew a route across the moor. He ignored them and walked on, trying to arrange his swirling thoughts.

Elra's scream still rang in his ears and he felt sick at the remembrance of it. He had never heard anything like it before, not even when a girl at his school had cracked her head. Forcing his thoughts away from this image, he turned to dwell on the rubies Elra had shown them. The blood ruby, like many of its kind, had come from Garia. James knew he had to go there and find out anything he could about the blood rubies.

'Elra spoke of a place called Garia,' he suddenly said aloud. 'Where is it exactly?' He kept walking at a quick, determined pace and the others hurried to keep up.

'The next region,' Arthur's low voice answered. 'Garia borders Gamad, the region we're in now. Why do you want to know?' He drew level with James and cast him a curious glance.

James let out a sigh, relieved that Arthur hadn't questioned his lack of geographic knowledge. 'The blood rubies,' he replied through a short breath, 'found in Garia.' Slowing his pace, he drew cool air into his lungs to calm his racing pulse.

'The blood ruby?' Will questioned. 'We're looking for a fire ruby, aren't we?' He brushed several raindrops from his eyes.

A light mist had crept up around them, completely obscuring the surrounding moor. It was thin and damp and clung uncomfortably to their clothes and skin.

'Elra said rubies can be treated with heat, meaning fire of some sort,' James answered steadily. 'Fire is an energy and so is blood. Will, d'you remember Kleon reading from the book which said the ruby is linked to energy and…'

'Cleanses the blood,' Will finished for him.

Although Will's face lit up with understanding, the mention of Kleon made him turn pale. There was an unspoken question resting on both boys' lips, but neither wanted to ask it. James hurriedly continued to speak.

'The ruby cleanses blood which is symbolised in the blood ruby and is treated by heat and fire which links back to blood energy.' He looked at the others. 'It's one big circle, it all links together.'

Arthur nodded. 'Arvad must have used unnatural magic to make the ruby so powerful. He must have put the ruby in the fire and used its heat energy to create the power of the firestone.'

Their conversation was cut short as they were hit by a deluge of rain. It lashed down in stinging swathes and was so heavy that it created a mist of its own. James grabbed Will's wrist and shouted to the others.

'Hold on to each other. Don't stop, keep moving.'

'There must be trees somewhere,' Will yelled back. 'I'm soaking already.'

The water streamed down their faces and seeped into their clothes. Beneath them, the ground grew steadily softer and James was afraid they might sink. Holding each other's wrists, they tried to walk quickly but the driving rain made progress difficult. James tried to look ahead through his dripping eyelashes but still couldn't see any sign of shelter. Suddenly, Aralia uttered a yell.

'What is it?' James shouted through the noise of the rain thudding in his ears.

'Nothing,' she replied sheepishly. 'I thought something touched me but it was my cloak.'

James rolled his eyes but he could see Will grinning widely and smiled also. In the growing gloom, Arthur created a light which bounced off the rain and back onto their tired faces. They walked dejectedly on for a while, but it grew dark much quicker than any of them had expected. As the rain began to lessen, they decided to stop and rest for a short while. A few low stones were scattered around on the grass and the four companions perched themselves on these, shivering miserably.

Reaching into his pocket, James instinctively felt for his phone. His fingers curled around wrappers and bits of screwed up paper, but the cool, familiar rectangle wasn't there. Desperately, he searched his other pocket and those in his cloak too but found nothing. His phone must have fallen out whilst they walked, he thought hopelessly, and began to scour the surrounding area with his eyes. The only other thought that crossed his mind was that someone could have stolen it from him, but that was unlikely.

'Will!' he hissed to his friend who was hunched over beside him. 'I've lost something.'

'What is it?' Will asked.

James paused, unsure of how to describe his phone. 'It's something from my world, I can't really explain,' he said bluntly. 'It looked like a black rectangle. I need it back, I have to find it.'

Beside him, Will went pale and looked down at the ground, opening his mouth to speak and then shutting it again.

'How important was it?' he eventually asked, still fixing his eyes on the ground.

'It had information about me on it and if someone finds it…,' James stopped and rubbed his forehead hard. 'Maybe someone stole it,' he added despairingly.

He watched as a faint blush spread into Will's cheeks. 'I know that no one stole it,' Will muttered uncomfortably. 'Something was making a noise in the caves and I woke up. There was a bright light coming from something next to you, so I picked it up. It was just before Elra came to let us out.' Raising his eyes, he looked at James with a puzzled expression. 'What was it?'

James looked at Will in disbelief. He clenched his hands in his pockets and tried to keep his face calm. Arthur and Aralia were watching him and fearing they had overheard, he got up and moved away. He stood with his back to Will and putting his face between his hands, closed his eyes. It was too late to go back; his phone was lost for good. The Ona would find it and take it; they would find out everything about him. They would see it and know he was different; know he was from another world. He heard Will get up behind him and walk a short distance away, where he began talking to Arthur and Aralia. After a while he sat again and listened until his friends' voices died away.

The four rested for a few hours but their wet clothes made them fidgety and uncomfortable. They rose miserably from the slippery rocks they were perched on, shaking the water out of their cloaks. The rain had grown heavy again and, after eating a little of the food James and Will still had, they began to walk. The flatness of the moor offered no landmark and they walked without direction. Feeling a light tap on his arm, James turned to see Aralia had come up beside him.

'You're not from here, are you?' she said softly. 'You're somehow different.'

James cast her a sharp glance, surprised by her question. He felt his neck grow warm and nervously ran a hand through his damp hair, causing it to stand on end. Aralia watched him expectantly, but he didn't dare turn to face her. Instead of speaking, he merely nodded.

'What's it like, where you come from?' Aralia put a hand to her mouth and began to chew on a nail.

Taking a deep breath, James turned to look at her. 'It's a world where magic doesn't exist,' he said quietly.

She stared at him but said nothing. He looked back at her, watching confusion and disbelief pass across her face. Her lips opened as if she were about to ask a question, but she wordlessly sealed them again. James turned away uncomfortably, not knowing what to say.

'What do your parents do?' she asked eventually.

James sighed, feeling somehow impelled to tell her the truth. 'My dad runs a newspaper and my mum works for him,' he said quietly. His parents had worked at the newspaper ever since he could remember. He turned to Aralia. 'What about yours?'

She dropped her eyelashes and hid her face in the shadow of her hood. 'My mother was a dryad,' she began.

'A what?'

'Not fully human,' Aralia replied, but offered no definition. 'My father was human and such relationships are against the law. My mother was sent away after I was born and my father disappeared.'

She stopped speaking suddenly and James felt a little embarrassed. Silence fell between them and they walked on without looking at one another.

'Where did you get the book, the one with the ruby in it?'

Aralia's question was simple. It served as a token of her acceptance of his secret, even if she didn't quite believe him. James gave a small shrug.

'Someone called Kleon gave it to us when we found it in his house. Why d'you want to know?'

He stepped over a rough stone in his path and looked at her expectantly. From the corner of his eye, he saw Will and Arthur drawing level and falling into line beside Aralia.

'I've been thinking about the book you showed us, the crystal one.' Aralia cast James an uncertain glance before continuing. 'The author said the book was buried for the right person to find, and I think Arvad found it. That's why he decided to go looking for the power that could end the dark and bring eternal life. He didn't create the power, it was a myth already.'

James nodded slowly, turning his mind back to the strange, half-English words. They hadn't made much sense to him, but Aralia's explanation seemed logical.

'How did you understand all that?' Will joined the conversation, glancing at Aralia with admiration.

'I've read that language before,' she replied with a faint blush.

'It makes sense, what you're saying,' James acknowledged. 'Arvad read the book and found the power it talked about. He got the crystals but died before he could use their power. How does this help us though?'

Aralia smiled faintly. 'The tale and the crystal book talk about the gifts Arvad gave to the elements. He gave the gifts to claim power and then got the elements to hide it again in the form of the crystals. The firestone can only be freed if given the same gift. The book says that no fire is eternal, but it desires to be. Maybe whatever Arvad gave the fire made it eternal because that is what it desired.' She stopped speaking and James grinned at her.

'That's what the bit about fire desiring to consume time meant,' James said, turning to Will. 'It meant the fire wanted to be eternal and in return for the gift, Arvad got the firestone.'

Aralia nodded. 'The firestone has to be hidden inside the eternal fire. We need to find out what the gift was to help us find the fire and the firestone.'

A shout suddenly sounded behind them and they all turned, scanning the empty moorland. It came again and again, growing higher and more desperate. Then, from the haze of rain there slowly emerged a shape, a dark, indistinct form that was evidently not human. It was about the same height as a man, but it had a long tail which viciously licked the air. The eyes were a deep red, ringed with a pale greenish yellow and around its head was a set of scales. It seemed to be whispering something, but the crooning lisp was too quiet to understand.

'It's an Akas,' Will said, his voice filled with fear.

'What the hell is that?' James asked, for a moment forgetting his annoyance about his phone.

'They're called Akas,' Will returned. 'I've read about them. They live on moorland like this and try to catch anyone who walks across.'

'What do they do with trapped people?'

'Guide them to marshland and drown them, or make sure they never find their way off the moor.'

As Will spoke, the creature drew closer. The other three backed away but James stood staring at it, completely mesmerised. He found himself wanting to hear what it was whispering, and he listened intently, trying to understand the words.

'Come with me,' it whispered. 'I can help you. You don't need to stay; I can give you shelter. I know what you're looking for.'

'You do?' James heard himself say.

'I know everything. I know your darkest secrets, your dearest wishes. Come with me, I can give you answers and show you the way.'

James nodded to the Akas. Somewhere, he could hear someone calling to him, Will or Arthur perhaps. A flash of light burst into the rain and he turned to see Arthur standing only a few feet away from the being. His arms were outstretched, and light burst from his hands, hurtling towards the creature where it burst against its flesh.

'Don't listen to them, the half humans and the boy. You're not like them, you're different. Come with me, I can help you.'

James kept staring at it, hardy blinking. He could feel his feet step forwards towards the whisper, drawing him in. Then he heard another voice inside his head, whispering with an urgency he couldn't ignore. 'Run, run,' it urged. Another shape was rising in the rain behind the first and he suddenly broke from his trance. Turning to the others, he echoed the words he had just heard.

'Run, run!'

Chapter 13

THE shape hovered on the moor, the snake tailed, red-eyed creature from some nightmare. It stood still at first, but as the four friends began to run it moved slowly after them, trailing in their wake. Aralia was struggling to keep up and Arthur grabbed her arm, pulling her along with him. James was gasping for breath, but he kept going, trying to keep pace with the other boys. A shout from Will made him stop in his tracks. He saw that Will too had stopped and stood pointing to a shadowy mass which lay ahead.

'Look,' Will said breathlessly.

A dark rise of trees stretched before them, spreading far out into the distance. The trees were tall, thick firs which grew closely together, shutting out the light. Beneath them, the rough ground was strewn with needles and the tingling scent reached James' nostrils on the restless air. There appeared to be no obvious way in through the thick branches which cast dark and quiet shadows over one another.

'It's an Anagroma,' Will whispered, his face incredulous. 'I've heard about them but never seen one.'

'A what?' Aralia asked.

'Anagroma, it's like a reverse mirage.' Will shook his head to himself. 'You know how we couldn't see any trees on the moor? Well this was here the whole time, but it's disguised by natural magic so people believe the moor is empty. It's all a trick. A mirage makes you see things that aren't there and is natural, but this uses magic to disguise things which are there.'

'What's natural magic?' James looked at the trees ahead with a puzzled frown.

Aralia answered him in her soft voice, but kept her eyes fixed ahead. 'Magic formed by nature rather than humans,' she said. 'It's the most powerful kind of magic, even stronger than elemental magic which is where humans command nature.' She stopped talking and stepped after Will who had gone on ahead.

The ground became hard and brambled as they gradually drew level with the first line of trees. James parted the branches and peered through them at the darkness beyond. The light coming from behind them only revealed closely packed trunks which cut off any accessible pathway.

'Do we go in?' Aralia asked breathlessly, her voice loud in the close silence. 'Is it safe?' She began to bite her nails distractedly as her eyes roamed over the trees.

'We don't have much choice,' James replied, his own heart sinking at the thought.

Kneeling, he separated the bottom branches and peered through. The trunks were still packed closely together, but the branches were old and less dense.

'It's tight, but if we crawl we might be able to get through.' He spoke with determination and received nods from the other three.

On hands and knees, they pulled the lower branches apart and with Arthur first, entered the forest one by one. The needled branches tore at their wet skin, and the brambles, which fought for space among the trees, stabbed with malicious relentlessness. They were still soaked to the bone, but the sense of panic had abated a little as the branches hid them from the Akas and other dangers of the moor. In the gloom which enveloped them, they were forced to crawl blindly as no one wanted to risk creating a light. There were no creatures here, no sound of birds singing or of twigs cracking under the weight of some animal. The whole forest was dead, filled with an undisturbed peace.

The four crawled at a slow pace, fighting against the undergrowth. Their hands and faces were raw and bleeding, but no one uttered a complaint. From the back of the line, James could just make out the shapes of the others in front of him. The branches pushed aside by Will, who was in front, kept springing back and slapping him in the face. He accepted each slash patiently, unwilling to raise his voice in the silence. They crawled in the gloom for a long while before the line abruptly stopped. Craning his neck to see ahead, James saw that a path had opened amongst the trees. Dimly illuminated by the only light that managed to push through the trees, the lower branches had formed an archway over the path.

'It's all so dead,' Arthur whispered, voicing all their thoughts.

Rising from their knees, the four companions stood and gazed around them. The pathway seemed to be the only logical way to go but they approached it nervously, their feet crackling loudly on the needled earth. Feeling something wet on his leg, James paused to pull aside his cloak. A thick trickle of blood seeped out of a cut, visible through a tear in his trousers. He was about to cover it again, when Aralia stopped him.

'Let me,' she said.

She tore off a piece of her own cloak and directed a reluctant James to stand still while she bound the cut. James rolled his eyes at Will but the other was engaged in pushing aside a large clump of weeds beside the path.

'I thought it was,' Will whispered and turned to the others. 'Look, it's a gravestone.'

Aralia uttered a small squeak of horror and shrank back. Rising from his seat, James moved curiously over to Will and knelt by his side, pushing the weeds back further to reveal the crumbled surface of a stone. It was leaning at an awkward angle, beaten down by the years. Its edges were almost completely worn away and the writing on the surface was rough and indistinct.

'There's no name,' James said. 'I wonder whose it is?'

'There's a symbol on it though.' Will ran his hand over the cold stone surface. 'A name of some sort, but the words aren't there anymore.'

'D'you think it's the only one here?' Aralia asked, looking around nervously.

James too turned to look at their surroundings, his eyes slowly adjusting to the dim light. A short distance along the path another rectangular shape could be seen, another stone. Arthur hurried straight towards it, but James remained by the first grave for a moment longer. Something about the symbol looked familiar to him and he ran his fingers over it, trying to remember. It was a circle filled with a star, but it was so faint that he wasn't quite sure how many points rested inside. He counted six or seven but couldn't be sure. Still trying to recall why it was familiar, he got up and went over to join the others.

'Does it have a name on it?' he asked, bending down to look at the other gravestone.

'It says Celaeno, but I can't read the family name,' Arthur replied. 'I guess it's nothing important.'

They saw no other graves as they went along and guessed those had been the only two. As they walked, the sky above them began to grow dark and the forest became more eerie. None of them had any idea how far the forest stretched on for, but it seemed never-ending. When it became too dark to see, they decided to stop and rest in a small clearing just off the path. James offered to stay awake on watch first as he wanted time to think. He sat with his back against one of the trees, watching while the other three wrapped themselves in their cloaks and slipped into a shivering sleep. James also shivered, despite the trees sheltering him from the wind. He pushed himself against the tree behind him as if hoping its trunk could offer some warmth.

He sat trembling in the darkness, his mind alert to the unknown dangers that might be lurking in the shadows all around him. Something about the graves disturbed him, but he didn't know what. He was sure the symbol was familiar, the circle and the star with six or seven points. Unable to remember, he sighed with frustration and closed his eyes. The breathing of the others became regular and as he listened to it, he felt himself drifting off with them. He tried to wake himself up again, but his eyes kept closing and he passed in and out of consciousness.

A twig snapped somewhere nearby and James sat up, suddenly and completely awake. He leapt to his feet and stood with his hand on the tree trunk behind him, scanning the darkness. To his left, he then noticed a small light glowing between the thick branches, flickering in and out of sight. Wrapping his cloak tightly about him, he moved cautiously towards the wavering light which took him onto the path. For some reason he didn't feel afraid and crept on, breathing so quietly that it hurt his throat. Ahead, the light continued to flicker through the branches and he was forced to step into the undergrowth.

'Hello?' he called softly but there was no reply. 'Who's there?' he tried again.

Pulling aside a few more branches, he suddenly found himself looking into a small clearing. A young woman was standing there, her back turned to him and her silvery hair fell down the length of her body in waves. She was dressed in a long, silver gown which also fell to the ground in soft panels and in her hand was the light which James had followed. It lit up her figure and cast the surrounding trees into deep shadow. Her other hand rested on a dark spinning wheel which looked as if it hadn't been used for years. The woman herself was faint in the darkness, looking as if she were not really there. In the wavering light she seemed restless and James watched her with wide eyes. He was about to turn away when a voice spoke.

'Why don't you come out? I can see you.' It was a soft voice, one that belonged to the wavering light and shadow.

A little startled, James stepped out of his hiding place but remained close to the cover of trees.

'A boy,' the woman whispered, her back still turned. 'What brings you here?'

James stared speechlessly at her faint form, wondering how she could see. He was unwilling to tell this stranger the reason why he was here.

'You can speak to me you know,' she said softly. 'I don't bite.'

Taking a deep breath, James offered a simple answer. 'I'm going to Garia.'

'Through the Lover's Wood? You must have been lost on the moor. No one comes here if they can help it.'

'Why not?' James asked, stepping a little closer.

'It is a burial place, one where many lovers are buried. You saw the graves.' She uttered a deep sigh and James shuddered, wondering how she knew. Moving her hand a little on the spinning wheel, she spoke again. 'The wheel,' she said calmly. 'The wheel spins out the fates of all who enter the wood.'

Her answer made James shrink back into the darkness. He was grateful that she was facing away from him and couldn't see his expression.

'Whose graves are they?' he asked in a faint voice.

The woman didn't answer immediately and in the short silence, James could feel the dead emptiness of the forest pressing around him. Despite the figure's presence and that of his friends close by, he felt completely alone. This world remained unfamiliar to him, a place where strange creatures and humans lived alongside magic. It was a concept he still struggled to believe and understand even though he stood here now searching for a way to reach the firestone before the darkness.

'This forest has many graves,' the woman said. 'It all began when two lovers died here many years ago.'

James shivered and briefly closed his eyes. 'We'll leave in the morning and find our way to Garia. Where does the path lead to?'

'The path?' She laughed, a faint but pitying laugh. 'The path leads to nowhere. You may go around on it forever and never get out of this place.'

'Who are you?' James found himself asking before he could stop himself.

'My name is, or was, Celaeno. I am one of the seven sisters, the only one who still walks this earth.' She turned her head a little to the side, but her face remained hidden. 'I can't look at you,' she said gently. 'To do that would frighten you.'

A realisation dawned on James and he felt his heart flip. Celaeno was the name they had looked at on the second grave. The figure looked faint because she wasn't really there, she was a ghost.

James swallowed down the wave of fear that suddenly washed over him. He fixed his eyes on the spinning wheel and kept them there while he spoke.

'The other grave, who was buried there?'

Her head snapped up but she remained silent and the emptiness once more pressed around them.

'His name was Arvad,' she eventually said. 'He was a brave man, but a foolish one who lived a dangerous life.'

James' mouth dropped open but he quickly shut it again, unsure of whether Celaeno could see him. She seemed able to sense everything going on around her without having to look. He couldn't believe that Arvad's grave was here, right in a forest which they had stumbled across by chance.

'You knew him then?' James stuttered out the question. It didn't seem possible that Celaeno had been alive seven hundred years ago.

'I suppose I did.' Her answer was short, but it gave James a flicker of hope.

'Did he ever talk about crystals when you met him?' His voice rose excitedly, and he tried to check it but instead found himself stepping forward again until he was standing directly within the circle of light.

'Arvad never spoke of crystals, he lived a life of crime and died in prison long after me.' Celaeno's voice drifted away and James detected a note of sadness in it, despite her feigned carelessness.

'In prison?' James' eyes grew wide. 'Where? Why's he buried in the forest?'

'The prison is in Garia, not far from here, but no more questions,' she urged. 'The Hidden City, home of the Necromancers and Alchemists is the place for such things. Go, your friends are looking for you. The longer you stay the longer it will take you to leave. I never did.'

Her last words brought a chill to James' heart. He turned and began to push his way back through the trees, pausing for just a moment between the branches. Celaeno's voice came again, a little louder this time, and James sensed she had turned around to face him.

'Don't forget you have magic. In this place you will need it.' She fell silent and James was left to walk away alone.

Chapter 14

AS James approached the clearing again, he saw Arthur, Aralia, and Will standing together talking. The sound of his footsteps made them turn and he noticed the concern on their faces.

'Where've you been?' Will asked, folding his arms. 'We've been looking for you.'

Walking past them, James went to stand at the edge of the clearing beside the path. He wondered if everything Celaeno had told him about Arvad was written in the missing pages of the tale. The single page torn from the library book didn't offer many details about Arvad's travels.

'James?' Will's voice sounded behind him.

James turned to find his friends looking at him expectantly. He grimaced at them, wondering how to tell them about Celaeno and what she had said.

'He, Arvad I mean, died in prison,' he began haltingly. 'A prison somewhere close to here.'

'In prison?' Will asked in surprise. 'How d'you know that?'

'I fell asleep when I was meant to be on watch,' James admitted. 'I heard a twig snap so I woke up and there was a light the other side of the path. I followed it and found someone, a girl who knew about Arvad. Her name was Celaeno.' He was self-consciously aware that he was missing out details, but felt it was better not to elaborate. 'The first grave we saw, it was his.'

'Celaeno, the name on the grave?' Arthur asked, his eyes widening. 'Are you sure you weren't dreaming?'

James ignored the question as he could see the same doubtful looks pass across Will's and Aralia's faces.

'We need to go to the prison,' he said with finality. 'If Arvad died there, then there must be records about him and maybe clues about where he sent the firestone.'

'Arvad didn't hide the firestone,' Aralia responded with a frown. 'The story says he asked the elements to hide them and gave them a gift in exchange. Even he can't have known where it was hidden.'

'We're back to needing the missing pages,' Will said gloomily. 'Maybe the prison is the best place to go, there might be clues there.'

'We have to find out,' James replied, and the others nodded.

In agreement about the next stage of the journey and excited by the new clues, they stepped out onto the path again. The arch of trees continued to curve over above them, decorating the path with dappled shadows. Looking around, James saw that there were more crumbling graves scattered amongst the trees. He couldn't shake off Celaeno's words of warning that the longer they stayed, the harder it would be to leave. Turning his attention back to the path with a shiver, he saw that Will had stopped and was pointing to one of the graves.

'Look,' he said in a small voice. The stone looked just like all the others they had passed, but James followed Will's finger and saw it pointed to the name 'Celaeno'.

'We've come in a circle,' Aralia stated. 'We didn't turn off the path at all, it's not possible. There must be more than one

Celaeno.'

'No,' James replied quietly. 'This path is magic, there's no way out. The girl I spoke to, she said the longer we stayed the harder it'd be to leave. She was talking about the path.'

'You're right,' Will said in amazement. 'It's not just magic, it's another Anagroma. The magic makes us think we're going somewhere, but we're not.'

Aralia sank to the ground and Will joined her while Arthur and James remained standing on the path. A way out seemed impossible and James didn't understand enough about magic to use it as Celaeno had suggested. He closed his eyes and tried to think in the same way as he did when playing logic games on his phone, but it was much harder trying to picture everything in his mind. He found himself wishing that he still had his phone, even though it was useless without a signal.

'What's that?'

James opened his eyes to see Aralia pointing through the trees with a trembling hand. Standing in amongst the branches was a group of grey figures whose cloaked bodies looked strangely translucent. A faint light emanated from each of them, casting an eerie glow through the trees. They stood like sentries, barring all possible routes apart from the enchanted path ahead.

'They're ghosts,' Arthur breathed. 'All of them are ghosts.'

Aralia went pale and moved to stand behind her brother. 'What do we do?' she asked quietly. 'They're not moving, they're just watching us. What do they want?'

James closed his eyes, trying to block out the eerie light all around them. Somewhere in his head he could hear a voice, the familiar tones of the dream figure. It was indistinct but he forced his mind to focus on it, shutting himself off to the outside world.

'Look past the mirage, you have magic, use it.'

The soft voice repeated the words until James had heard all of them. Keeping his eyes shut, he imagined the path ahead and let a light grow around it in his mind. Suddenly, he saw an image etched on his eyelids, a scene with grey sky and a small village which rested just north of the forest. The path led straight out of the forest and came to an end just outside the village fence. This vision reminded James of the one he'd seen and dismissed on the way to the Ona caves. Now, he knew that the path in his mind was the only way to get out of this haunted place. He quickly opened his eyes, expecting the picture to stay with him but as he saw the forest again, it disappeared. All he could see were dark trees filled with thin, grey ghosts.

'Will,' he whispered. 'You said an Anagroma is like a mirage. If the path is one too, then there must be a way out but we just can't see it. Mirages are illusions which trick the eyes. If we shut our eyes, we won't be able to see the mirage and then we can't be tricked by it.'

A look of understanding dawned on each of their faces and James himself was amazed that he'd come to this conclusion.

'Let's try,' Aralia said urgently, casting a nervous glance at the figures around them.

Quickly and quietly they formed a line, each holding on to the person in front. James was at the head with a frightened Aralia clinging onto the back of his cloak. Closing his eyes, he took a slow step forward, followed by another. The atmosphere began to change around them, growing darker and closer. James could feel pine needles and rough brambles scratching at his skin, but he didn't dare open his eyes. He waited to feel open air on his face and to see light through his eyelids, but everything remained dark. After a few moments he heard Aralia gasp and the line jolted to a halt.

'What is it?' he heard Arthur ask. 'Rai?'

'They're following us, the ghosts are following us.'

James strained to keep his eyes closed but could feel his eyelids trembling. Opening one eye slightly, he let a sliver of light in. In the narrow image revealed to him, he saw the ghostly figures gliding through the trees all around them. They were reaching out their hands as if trying to touch the four friends as they went past. James shut his eye again quickly.

'Close your eyes,' he whispered fiercely. 'It's all a trick, they can't hurt you. Don't look at them.' Taking another step forward, he felt Aralia's hand slip from his cloak. 'Don't let go,' he hissed. 'We'll lose each other if you let go.' He felt her hand again and walked on, picking up the pace.

'Light,' Will suddenly said. 'James, Arthur, Aralia, open your eyes.'

Opening his eyes, James looked around but could only see the same, gloomy darkness penetrated only by the faint glow of the ghosts.

'What light?' he asked irritably.

'Mirages are made by light, so they aren't there when the sun disappears. An Anagroma is the opposite. We need light to see past the illusion.' He grinned widely and holding out his hand, formed a light in his palm.

Arthur and Aralia did the same and slowly, James followed suit. He watched in fascination as the glowing ball formed in his hand and he held it out in front of him. All four of them let their light shine out onto the path, creating dancing shadows around them. For a moment nothing happened but then the ghosts around began to fade and their pale glow disappeared with them. A new light was visible up ahead. An opening had formed between the trees and daylight shone through. Laughing in relief, James hurried forward and the others followed behind, none of them stopping until they burst out into the open.

The sky was dark grey and the air felt cold, made worse by the damp still permeating their clothes. Their cloaks were dirty with mud and their faces too felt grubby and unwashed. The dim gloom of the forest spread out behind them and no one wanted to look back. Standing at the edge of the forest, a new sight of low hills met them. The grass was green again, but the trees had been browned by autumn. Over the next hill they could see a village nestled against a slope, and more houses were spread out on the lower ground. It was comforting to see habitation again and the four started towards the village.

As they approached, they realised that the houses overlooked a large lake. The water stretched out for a good way, coming to rest at the edge of the vast forest. The trees cast a shadow over half the water, contrasting with the other side which lay bright and glassy. Despite this light, the water looked almost black and lay unusually still. A fence ran around the edge of the first house and they stopped beside it, peering into the village. A woman stood a few metres away, sweeping something up from outside a front door. Beside her sat a child from whose hand fluttered a string of yellow butterflies which quickly evaporated. A cobbled lane ran alongside the first row of houses and a small inn stood at the end of it. Unlike the abandoned village James and Will had seen on their first day, the gardens here were well tended and the houses were intact.

As they stood looking, a man's rough voice sounded behind them and they turned tiredly. He stood leaning on a wooden post and chewing on a piece of grass. He was dressed in an old brown cloak which was covered in moth holes and gave him the appearance of a weathered farmer. From underneath this cloak there peeped a stained and patched shirt which was tucked into a pair of worn trousers. Beside the man stood a dark-haired girl of around eight or nine. She watched them through large blue eyes that were neither friendly, nor hostile. The man spoke again but his words were in a language none of them understood. Seeing their blank faces, he began to speak English in a strange, guttural accent.

'What are four children doing here, four stranger?' The man stared at them coldly. 'Stranger never come here, through forest.' James saw his hand twitch by his side as if on the verge of using magic.

'We're looking for Garia,' Aralia said. 'Are we near it?'

A flicker of curiosity passed through his eyes but was quickly dampened. Bending down, he said something to the girl and tried to push her towards the houses, but she stayed firm. The man rose with a sigh and spoke again in English.

'Why do you want Garia?'

'The prison,' Arthur said hurriedly. 'Is it near here?'

The girl's eyes grew wide and she looked up at her father, tugging at his sleeve. He didn't respond and so she grew very still, just watching. Just then a woman called from one of the houses and the man, apparently her husband, yelled back in his own tongue.

'That is border,' the man suddenly said in English and pointed with a solid, well weathered hand towards the lake. 'Black lake there, this is border to Garia where prison built. It is not far, but dangerous. No people go there unless criminals.' His voice dropped to a harsh whisper. 'Magic not allowed there, no one choose to go there.'

Breaking from his silence, James spoke quietly. 'How far to

the prison?' he asked.

He could see Will gaping at him as if he were mad and the man too was watching him searchingly.

'Come into village and eat with us,' the man said, ignoring the question. 'My wife asks you to join us. There I may tell you more.' Taking the grass from his mouth he said something to the girl who ran off ahead of them. 'Come,' the man beckoned. 'Welcome to my village.'

Chapter 15

THE man led them towards a small grey house which had a neat garden path running up to the open door. On the other side lay a dark, cramped kitchen, its brown walls hung with herbs and dried flowers. A table in one corner was set ready for breakfast and the man gestured for them to sit at it.

'Please sit,' he urged them and placed himself at the head of the table. 'My wife Maja has made food. My name is Rolf.'

Almost as soon as they were seated, Maja brought over plates of food which she laid before each of them. Smiling, she wordlessly mouthed and gestured for them to eat. James eyed a strange looking pile of meat before him with apprehension, wrinkling his nose at the strong smell. It looked dry and leathery but he took a piece and began to eat hungrily. It tasted as it looked, but it filled the hollow place in his stomach. Silence reigned while they ate, accompanied only by the occasional clink of a cup or plate. The young girl kept quiet during the meal, but she continually watched the four strangers with her wide, blue eyes. When they had all finished, Maja cleared the table whilst Rolf brought over a pencil and some paper.

'Let me draw map for you,' he suggested in his thick accent. 'Here is forest, with village and lake.' He drew out the scene with an accomplished hand and pointed to each landmark. 'This line is way to prison, round the lake. I go once, not again. You see strange things.'

'What kind of things?' Will asked abruptly.

Rolf looked at Will with a haunted expression in his eyes. 'I cannot say. Things so terrible that they may not be spoken, not even to Maja. Garia is evil place and I know not why you want to go there, but not my business.' He stopped short and handed the map over to Arthur.

'Thanks,' Arthur said quietly.

'You know it dangerous, fill with bad people,' Rolf warned. 'Be careful.' Rising from his chair, he went over to the front door.

Restless in his own seat, James also stood and Will, Arthur and Aralia joined him. One by one they thanked Maja who smiled at them and took four packages from the shelf beside her. She handed one to each of them with a nod and mimed chewing. There was no way to thank her enough and she ushered them modestly out of her kitchen before returning to her work. Rolf led them back through the garden and up the cobbled lane towards the open slope beyond. Many of the cottage doors now stood open and the villagers stared unashamedly at the strangers walking past. James bowed his head, uncomfortable with the unwanted attention. Once outside the village again, he turned to Rolf with a grateful smile.

'Thanks for the food and the map.'

Rolf also brushed aside the thanks. 'Be careful,' he warned again and waved as they began to move away. 'It was good to see stranger here,' was his final call.

Turning back to wave one final goodbye, they saw Rolf had replaced the grass in his mouth and stood watching them go with a searching expression.

Just over the edge of the slope, they were suddenly hailed by a young female voice. Stopping short in their tracks, they saw Rolf's daughter standing half hidden by the trunk of a large tree. She was silent for a moment until at last she plucked up the courage to speak.

'I take to border,' she said slowly. Her accent was thicker than her father's and much less polished.

Arthur shook his head at her in a superior manner. 'It's dangerous,' he pointed out gruffly. 'Shouldn't you be at home?'

She tossed her head and looked defiantly at him. 'I go, you come.'

Before they could stop her, she had skipped off down the slope towards the edge of the black lake and all they could do was follow. They hurried after her, watching her dance away from the village, her hair blowing in the breeze. The lake was glassy and the closer they got the blacker it looked, its unfathomable depths plunging down into nothingness. A few lily pads floated gently on its surface, clearly undeterred, their pale white flowers absent now in the autumnal cold. The long grass surrounding the lake trailed into the water, creating ripples at the edges. It could have been idyllic, but the cool darkness of the lake changed the whole atmosphere.

Ahead of them, the girl wound her way around the lake, stopping every now and then to see if they were following. They wound on behind her, treading the damp grass with lighter hearts than earlier that day. James walked beside Will as a gesture of his forgiveness for the phone incident. Leaning over the water, he saw his face peering back at him, vaguely reflected in the smooth, black mirror. It was dirty and scratched from the brambles and needles in the Lover's Wood. Will also leant over and seeing his own grubby reflection, scooped up some water and splashed it over his face. James knelt beside him and followed suit. The water was sharp, but it felt refreshing to rub away the grease and grime.

As James touched the water, he noticed a change occurring within its depths. A familiar figure appeared on the surface standing within a white, swirling mist. Closing his eyes, he cleared his mind, but on opening them again found the image had gone. His friends were watching him with odd expressions.

'You look like you've seen a ghost,' Will commented with a grin. 'Everything alright?'

James took his hand from the water and dried it slowly on the hem of his cloak. He glanced around him, checking that the girl was well out of ear shot before he spoke.

'I keep seeing and hearing someone in my head, someone who tells me about danger ahead and helps me,' he began. 'I can't see who it is because there's a mist and every time I try and speak they disappear.'

All three of them stared at him in disbelief, but it was Aralia who spoke.

'It's impossible.'

'What is?' James asked, puzzled by their reaction.

'There's a form of magic which allows people to speak through their minds, a kind of telepathy or mind magic. It has to be practised for years before it's mastered and so only the high circles of priests, enchanters, and necromancers really understand it.' Aralia shook her head. 'There are other people who know how to do it of course, but never someone our age.'

'You think...,' James cut himself short and stared back at her, slowly understanding what she was saying. 'I can't even keep a light lit in my hand for long,' he stated with bewilderment.

'If you can't speak to the figure, then it's not two sided, but it's still amazing that you can hear the voice,' Arthur joined.

'Are you coming?' The voice of the young girl startled them. She paused only briefly before skipping away again and the four hurried to follow.

The lake swept around in a graceful curve and the girl soon broke away from it, never seeming to grow tired of running. As the village and lake fell out of sight behind more hills, she eventually stopped and waited for them to catch up. With a small hand she pointed between the slopes which were dim and bleak in the grey light. They followed her finger and saw smoke rising into the sky and the buildings of a town which stood out like a dark blot on the landscape.

'Prison that way,' the girl whispered, her eyes wide. 'I step no more.' She drew a note from her pocket and handed it to Aralia. 'Please, for my father. He in prison, may you take?'

'I thought your father was Rolf,' Aralia said with a frown.

The girl shook her head. 'Rolf is brother, father's brother.'

'Your uncle,' Aralia helped her. 'Of… of course we'll take the letter.'

'Tell him it from Alva.' She squeezed Aralia's hand and smiled gently.

James looked at her, right into her blue eyes which were so startling in the frame of her dark hair. He saw something hidden in their depths which was lost as she turned away from him. Aralia bent down and pulled something from her pocket. It was a small chain with a simple green glass bead on the end. She pressed it into Alva's hand.

'Thanks for guiding us,' she said softly. The girl smiled again and then ran away back towards the lake.

The four began to walk again, over the grass and away

towards the town. The atmosphere around them had changed once more, perhaps due to the sudden absence of magic. As they drew closer to the town, the buildings became clearer but the dark smoke rising from them choked the air. Any signs of nature had been built over and the ground surrounding the town was dry and cracked as if struck by drought. A few remaining strands of dying grass stood weakly fighting against harsh weeds. The bareness of the land and the odd warmth in the air made the whole place seem strangely desert-like and the four friends gazed at it in awe.

A short distance away from the town another vast building rose, built from a smooth, sandy coloured stone. It was like an amphitheatre, circular, with arched openings all around it and several storeys high. The town itself was unusual, the buildings darkly coloured in contrast to the amphitheatre and were all oblong structures linked to tall towers. A string of people were slowly making their way from the town to the amphitheatre, all cloaked and hooded and many dragged their feet behind them. The black smoke hung in a haze everywhere, stinging eyes and noses. Unable to see what lay the other side of the buildings, the four began to walk down the slope that led towards the amphitheatre.

'What's it for?' James whispered, more to himself than the others.

Directly ahead of them a small archway lay empty and they slipped through in single file. On the other side was a long, curving stone corridor and Will, who was at the front, beckoned the others to follow. Several open arches ran along the right side and then to their left a stairway appeared, winding upwards. Cautiously they began to climb, passing by several other passages until they reached an abrupt end. In front of them was a locked door and a single archway which opened onto a small stone balcony. Passing out onto this, the four found themselves looking out onto the town and the green slopes beyond.

Leaning over the edge, James looked down and was surprised to see people on the ground directly below him. Hidden behind the curve of the building were rows and rows of men and women, all working at the earth with bare hands. James was close enough to see that there was a mixture of old and young and even a few small children. Many laboured with trembling arms but no one ever stopped to rest or even look up. There was a hush, a deep silence that no one broke and they kept on working relentlessly at the dry ground.

'Where are we?' James asked in a whisper. He stepped back from the edge and rubbed his eyes as if hoping the scene would disappear.

Arthur let out a short breath. 'Slaves,' he whispered, 'All of them.'

'What?' James asked in horror. He hadn't realised slaves still existed, even in this other world.

'Rolf said there were things here that he didn't want to talk about,' Arthur replied. 'I don't know what they're here for, but I don't really want to find out.'

'Maybe this is the prison,' Aralia added unexpectedly. She turned to the boys for confirmation of her idea. 'Maybe the prisoners are used as slaves.'

Will nodded vigorously in agreement. 'A prison, just not the type we expected.'

James was only half-listening to the conversation as he had caught sight of a boy of around his own age amongst the rows of slaves. He was dressed in a brown faded cloak and his hood had fallen back on to his shoulders to reveal longish dark hair.

Bent to the ground, his hands and arms moved slowly as if he were tired. As James stared, the boy lifted his head as if he sensed someone was watching him. His eyes, completely expressionless in their pain, looked back at James. The dark, youthful face was the only one that saw the observers above. He only stopped for a moment before some weight seemed to fall on him and he returned to his work.

'Let's go.' James tried to swallow the emotion in his voice and moved back from the arch, trying to forget the boy's face.

The sound of running feet suddenly roused them. They looked around wildly for somewhere to hide but there was only a small space on either side of the archway. Quickly, they darted over to these, Aralia and Arthur on one side, Will and James on the other, all crushed uncomfortably close to one another.

'Stop breathing down my neck,' James hissed at Will. On the other side Aralia giggled and he scowled at her.

'Can you see anything?' Arthur was trying to lean over his sister's shoulder but she pushed his head back.

'Not yet,' James whispered back and drew his head back in from the archway.

As the footsteps grew louder, they all fell silent. Voices now reached their ears too, words spoken in the same harsh language that Rolf and Alva had used. The sounds came closer and closer until the footsteps stopped right outside the balcony where the four stood frozen. As he was closest to the edge, James held his breath and peered cautiously around the corner. A row of brown cloaked figures stood lining the stairs, their backs bent, and their faces hidden. At the front were two people dressed in black, their faces covered by deep hoods. One of these figures turned and James whipped his head backwards, cracking it against Will's. There was a grunt of pain from both, followed by fearful silence.

James could feel his heart pounding. He had drawn his head back quickly, but not before he had seen the man's face under the black hood. It was one he had seen before, the rough, unshaven face marked by a thin scar running from cheek to lip. The face belonged to the man he'd seen on the empty streets of Arissel, whose hard eyes had stared at James as if they knew exactly who he was. He shuddered and, pressing himself closer to the wall, placed a trembling finger on his lips.

A cough and the sound of someone sniffing the air came from beside the balcony opening and James tensed. He was afraid that the scar-faced man had seen him and would discover them hiding on the balcony. The sniff was however followed by the faint click of a door opening and the sound of footsteps growing gradually fainter. As the door slammed shut, James let out a long, shuddering sigh of relief. Stepping from his hiding place on unsteady legs, he looked at his friends before peering cautiously through the archway.

'There's a door out here,' he whispered. 'That's where they disappeared.' He left the balcony and walking across to the door, gave it a sharp push. It creaked uneasily under the pressure but after another shove it slowly opened.

'What're you doing?' Will hissed. 'We don't want to follow them. Shut the door.' He leant against the archway.

James paused by the door. 'There was a man there, someone I saw in Arissel. I don't know who he is, but I don't trust him.'

'In Arissel? Are you sure he's the same person?' Aralia asked.

James nodded. 'I'm sure. He has a long scar running down his face which makes him easy to recognise.'

Still holding the door open, he stepped through it and beckoned for the others to follow. Arthur and Aralia hurried to do so and Will followed on behind. A long, curved passageway greeted them, both sides punctured with arches which were open to the air. Glancing through one of them, James found himself looking down into an empty arena, surrounded by rows of unoccupied seats.

'What's it for?' he asked in a hushed voice. 'Look.'

'The prisoners I'd guess,' Arthur replied after a quick glance. He didn't elaborate and the others were left to imagine its purpose.

A sound came from below and two figures appeared in the ring facing each other. Moving to the arches on the other side of the passage, James observed a new trail of prisoners was making its way over, forming the same straggled line. He shivered and closed his eyes, not wanting to see their misery. Suddenly, a scream came from behind him and before he even turned, he knew whose voice it was.

Chapter 16

'RAI?' Arthur was quietly calling for his sister, desperation rising in his voice each time he said her name. 'Rai?'

Will too picked up the call, moving further down the passage. Aralia's name merely came back as an echo, a ghostly word reverberating against the walls.

'What happened?' James hurried over to the inner side of the passage again. Aralia's scream was still ringing in his ears and he shook his head, trying to forget it.

'I don't know, she just disappeared,' Will replied. 'I didn't see anything, I only heard her screaming.' He went over to the outer arches and scanned the land between the amphitheatre and town. 'Who could've taken her?'

'Rai,' Arthur called again. 'Rai?'

James went to stand by Will. 'The dark,' he said quietly, 'they're everywhere. Someone must know we're here and they've taken her as a bribe. Whoever it is knows we'll go after her and they'll expect us to pay.'

Arthur began to walk down the passage at a quick, nervous pace. Seeing him move, Will and James hurried after and placed themselves on either side of him.

'I can't just stand around talking.' Arthur looked at each of them desperately. 'I've got to find her before they hurt her. I've got to take the risk. This is all your fault,' he added under his breath. Although he didn't direct the words at anyone specific, James felt their sting and gritted his teeth.

Resisting the urge to bite back, James followed Arthur and Will as they moved on ahead. At the end of the passage they reached a flight of steps which wound steeply downwards into the heart of the amphitheatre. The boys began to descend quickly, knowing that Aralia now had to be their focus. The steps wound back down to ground level and they came out into a short, passage which had no arched openings. Although it was dark, none of them dared create a light as they remembered Rolf's warning about the law against magic. Up ahead, the path branched out in two directions, one lit by daylight and the other dark. Stepping past Arthur, James headed towards the first and gestured for the other two to follow.

'This one must go outside again,' he said hopefully.

The boys hurried down the passage and soon stood outside on the barren landscape again. Looking up, James realised they were standing within view of the rows of slaves they had seen from above. None of them looked at the boys and they simply continued to work with bent backs and downcast eyes. Each line of slaves worked at a long trench, digging deeper and deeper until they were forced to jump inside the groove to continue their shovelling. They dug with their nails, scooping the earth into piles with bloodied hands.

The sweaty, grimy smell of unwashed bodies reached James's nostrils and he pinched his nose shut. Arthur however stood undeterred, scanning the lines of slaves with his sharp eyes. James wandered into the first row before stopping. Cautiously, he reached out and tapped a nearby slave on their shoulder.

There was a long pause before the head came up and James saw a familiar face looking back at him. It was the same dark-skinned boy who had raised his head and seen him on the balcony, the pleading eyes now sparkling suspiciously. The boy said nothing and James addressed him loudly and slowly.

'Have you seen a girl here? A blonde girl in a black cloak.' The boy frowned as if he hadn't quite understood and then shook his head.

'She looks a bit like me,' Arthur said, stepping forward. He waited while the boy stared at him intensely before shaking his head again.

James let out a sigh. 'Is this the prison?' he asked, trying a different line of questioning. He wondered whether the other slaves were listening, even if they never looked up.

Looking at James again with the same expressionless stare, the boy opened his lips and tried to speak. After several attempts he shut his mouth again and shook his head desperately.

'I don't know if he understands anything,' Will muttered under his breath.

A haunted expression came into the boy's eyes and he opened his mouth again. A couple of words came out, spoken in a slow and stuttering voice.

'Lu… Lucifer's place.'

'Lucifer?' James recognised the name from his world but couldn't remember why he knew it.

'Devil,' the boy said and hung his head again. 'Slaves of Lucifer, bound to earth.' His sentences were short and stunted and it was difficult to understand what he was saying.

James stared at the boy's chaffed and bleeding hands with revulsion. Many of the nails had been ripped off and the skin underneath was raw and peeling. Glancing down at his own unhardened hands, he felt a deep sense of guilt and placed them in his pockets.

'What're you digging for?' Will voiced what they were all thinking. 'Are you planting something?'

The boy crushed a piece of earth in his hand and let it fall before he answered. 'Place, magic is forgotten. I, we, must search for.' He paused and pointed with a shaking arm to the slopes where the boys and Aralia had come from. 'Them. Earth, dug by us, thousands of years. Now here.' He pointed back to the trenches.

James gulped and a strange expression came into his eyes. 'Is that the prison?' he asked again, this time pointing at the amphitheatre.

The boy cast his eyes at the building and his glance was unsettled. He shook his head. 'Prison by black lake.'

'The black lake? The one over there?' Will pointed to the way they had come.

The boy jerked his hand the other way, shaking his head. 'No, lake over there, twins.'

'What's your name?' Will asked before he could stop himself.

A lost look came over the boy's countenance and he avoided eye contact. 'I have no name, none of us do. Not many can speak, lose voices after years of silence. I'm one of only ones left.'

James looked at the other slaves and understood at last. 'What happens over there?' he inquired, nodding to the amphitheatre.

Their nameless companion shuddered. 'Some freedom there, if they fight. I don't want to see.' Suddenly he fell completely silent and his head dropped again. It was the same weight that James had seen push it down when he had watched from above.

There was nothing else to say but as James moved away someone grabbed his arm. He looked down, expecting to see the boy's raw fingers but instead found his cloak clutched by a wrinkled hand. It shook slightly despite the firm grip and James slowly turned to see who held him. An old man stood in front of him, a pleading expression held in his weak grey eyes. As James looked back, he became aware that the man's other arm was missing and he worked with one hand only. The voice came out quietly, sounding as if it had not been used for many years. James could hardly hear; the crusty words were mere whispers in the open air.

'Stranger come.' The man's accent was strangely husky, the r's heavily rolled and the t's almost lost. As he spoke, his eyes lit with a mad fire and he gripped James' arm even harder.

'Many year…, questions,' he continued before stopping to catch his breath in a long wheeze. 'Questions,' he repeated. 'Dangerous.'

He fell silent for a moment and let go of James' arm. Holding his own arm out before him, he violently shook back his worn sleeve. The movement revealed an empty circle on his wrist and he began to trace its circumference with his eyes. His lips moved and a singular, hollow word leapt out.

'Forever.'

James, Will, and Arthur looked at each other. They all thought the same thing, that this man must be mad from his years of silence. As they started to step carefully away, a rumble of thunder sounded overhead. The air suddenly seemed much thicker and warmer, pressing closely around them. James looked up at the sky and as he did so, felt a tug on his sleeve again. Looking down, he saw the man glaring at him fiercely.

'Alati, Alati,' the man whispered. He began repeating the word over and over in a deranged whisper until his arm dropped and, bending over, he began to work again.

James moved away and hurried to catch up with Will and Arthur. Together they began to walk towards the town, eyeing the dark buildings with distaste. The first street they came across was roughly paved and hazy with dark smoke. This had stained the surrounding buildings, turning the large grey bricks to a sooty black. Behind them the amphitheatre had disappeared, lost behind the dark windowless structures which loomed over them. Directly ahead was a long low building which stood with its door wide open. Gripped by fresh curiosity, James made his way towards it and peered around the door. A strong smell hit him, different from the smoke, but just as unpleasant. It burnt his nose with a hot and pungent scent which made his eyes sting. Inside he could see a small room crowded with shelves of paper and after a quick glance around to check the coast was clear, he slipped inside.

Tentatively approaching the first shelf, he lifted the sheet of paper closest to him and briefly scanned it. On it was a list of names with symbols inked beside each of them. He replaced the sheet with disinterest and chose another, only to find a similar list.

'Names, just names,' Will stated, coming to stand by James.

'They must be the names of all the slaves.' James put down his sheet with disgust and shuddered as he watched Arthur pick up a pile of faded yellow paper.

'The Lost Years,' Arthur mumbled, reading the title aloud. 'Most of it's in different languages. Rai could translate but I don't understand any of it.' He sighed and returned the papers to their shelf with a thud. As he did so, a small note fell out from between the sheets. It was tightly folded and picking it up, he began to undo it layer by layer.

'There's nothing in here, come on,' James said and headed to the door.

Absent-mindedly, Arthur shoved the piece of paper into his pocket and followed James back out onto the street. It wasn't far to the end of the street and on reaching it, James took a right turn. Here again low buildings stretched out on either side, but here the doors were closed. The street was empty apart from a stray cat which watched the three boys with a pair of weak yellow eyes. A stack of wooden boxes rested beside one of the buildings and Will went over to them. Although they were bolted shut with thick metal locks, he tried to prise open the lids of the two largest ones.

'Locked fast,' he reported back to James and Arthur.

The sound of a door opening made all three of them jump and they dashed to hide behind the building. A split second later a red-haired woman emerged from a side door and bent down to pick up the boxes. She paused momentarily to glance suspiciously around her before re-entering the building. The door didn't quite shut behind her and James looked at his friends questioningly. Arthur and Will nodded to him and after a count of three they all moved together, driven towards the door by an unspoken agreement.

Chapter 17

INSIDE the building was a long room fitted with low, oblong, tables that were lit by floating orbs. There was no sign of the woman and the boys allowed themselves to wander about freely. An array of intricate wire and metal mechanisms rested on the tables and among these were many pieces of paper with complex designs drawn on them. Some designs matched pieces already made but others were new and untried. Beside one image was a black stone and James picked this up. It felt heavy in his palm and he closed his fingers around it.

Something rattled somewhere outside and he started before turning to Will and Arthur in panic. One by one they crept towards the door where they stopped and peered cautiously out. The sky had grown even darker as the heavy clouds clustered together, threatening imminent rain. Directly before them in the street stood two black cloaked figures. The face of one was completely covered but James realised with horror that under the other cloak was Scarface. He was holding the other figure by the arms with one thick hand whilst his other fumbled to unlock the door of the building opposite.

The boys remained hidden within the building entrance as they stood watching the proceedings. Having successfully opened the door, the man turned to look at his prisoner with hard eyes that glinted cruelly in their hooded sockets. His mouth twisted into a cruel smile and he spoke in a rough voice.

'Where is he?'

'Where's who?'

James instantly recognised the voice of Aralia and held his breath. Beside him, Arthur started forward but Will put out an arm to restrain him.

'There's no point in us getting caught too,' he hissed.

Back on the street, the man gripped the door so hard that his knuckles turned white. 'The boy,' his snapped. 'Where is the boy?'

Aralia's reply came out calmly and steadily. 'What boy?'

James let out a sigh of relief. At that moment, a new figure emerged on the street. It was the same red-haired woman whom the boys had seen enter the building just before them. She had come out from a side door and walked heavily across the street, her thick frame thwarting any natural grace. Seeing her face fully for the first time, James noticed that half of it was inked over with a black tattoo. The image was of an unusual flower wound around with leaves and stood out against the woman's reddish hair. On reaching the spot where Aralia and Scarface stood, she smiled harshly, revealing buck front teeth.

'The boxes are safe now,' she said in a low voice and James strained to hear. 'Someone was dumb enough to leave 'em outside. I don't know where the other brat got to, it's 'er job not mine.' She put her hands on her hips and hissed loudly. 'Where is 'e then?'

'His whereabouts are unknown, but he'll come. They'll want to save her.' Scarface pinched Aralia on the arm and she cried out.

Arthur instinctively stepped forward again, but Will kept a hand firmly on his arm. The smoke all around them seeped into their noses and mouths, making it hard to concentrate. James felt slightly sick and his mind started to spin dizzily. With a great effort, he focused his attention on what was being said.

'What d'you want with me?' Aralia was struggling against the man's strong grip. At each wrench, his hand only clamped down harder and she bit her lip to stop herself from crying out again.

'This is a slave town and a factory town,' the woman said coldly. 'Here the slaves are born, they work, they die, and are cremated in the towers. You, dearie, will follow the same fate if you don't start talking.'

With a firm hand she pushed Aralia towards the open door. Aralia tried to struggle again but the man gave her a shove, so hard that it brought tears to her eyes. She glanced back as best she could and seeing her looking, Arthur raised a hand in the hope that she would notice him. Her eyes roamed past him once before she was propelled through the door and was lost from sight. It was flung open again a few minutes later and the man and woman exited, locking the door behind them. After waiting for them to disappear, James, Arthur, and Will stepped simultaneously from their hiding place and hurried across the street. Arthur knocked sharply on the door and pressed his ear against it.

'Rai, it's us, are you alright?' There was a long silence in which no one answered. 'Rai?' he called again.

'He took the key and there're no windows,' James whispered to. 'There's no way in, not unless we use magic.'

'It's forbidden here remember,' Will joined in, shaking the door handle. 'One of the seven regions where magic is illegal, and we need it.'

A rumble of thunder followed by a flash of lightning made them jump. The air was hot and stuffy and James fanned himself with the edge of his cloak, trying to clear his mind. Beyond the thunder, another sound slowly reached their ears, a faint banging which came from inside the building. He pressed his ear to the wall, trying to work out what it could be. At close quarters it sounded like the clank of machinery, but he couldn't be sure.

'What is it?' Arthur asked, also placing his ear against the wall.

James shrugged. 'I don't know, it's hard to tell.'

The sound was ominous, almost like the beating of drums. As they stood listening it grew gradually louder, joining the rumbles of thunder intermittently splitting the air. It sounded close and James called for the others to follow him and hide between the buildings. Finding themselves observers again, they watched the street until a short line of brown cloaked figures came into sight. The faint drumming came from their feet which were fitted with metal heeled shoes, and these clanged against the paving stones.

'The slaves,' Will whispered.

Leading the group was a woman James didn't recognise and she brought her charges to a halt in the middle of the street. Each slave proceeded to remove their cloak and place it at their feet before standing straight and silent in their threadbare tunics. The woman passed down the line, stopping at each slave to inspect their wrists. She kept glancing towards the building Aralia was in and her right hand toyed with a key. Suddenly, Arthur uttered an exclamation and James turned to him sharply.

'The slaves, we have to pretend to be slaves!'

'What?' James stared at him. 'Pretend to be slaves?'

'Yes,' Arthur whispered back hurriedly. 'Here's the plan. The woman is checking the symbols of the slaves before they go into the building. When she's finished, we join the back of the group as they go past and follow them in.'

Will shook his head and planted his feet firmly on the street. 'Arthur, you're mad! It's too dangerous. We don't know what's inside the building.'

'We don't know until we look,' Arthur retorted. 'Anyway, d'you have a better idea?'

Will and James both fell silent, unwilling to argue. The excursion into the amphitheatre and Aralia's kidnap had already delayed their journey longer than James liked to think. Any plan that would get them out of the town quickly was a welcome one. The sight of the scar-faced man filled him with foreboding and he wanted to leave before anyone discovered his whereabouts.

'Now!' Arthur whispered beside him.

James snapped back to the present and watched as Arthur slipped from their hiding place. He had cast aside his black cloak and jumper and stood in trousers and a vest in the street. Just in front of him, the line of slaves was slowly winding its way towards the building. Hurriedly, James stripped off his own cloak and hoodie. Tucking them under his arm, he slid to stand beside Arthur, and Will reluctantly followed. Ahead of them, the woman had unlocked a door set a little way along from the one Aralia was locked behind. The group processed through and the boys followed, keeping their heads bent low as the slaves did.

The room inside was dimly lit and filled with three rows of desks behind which sat several men and women. On each desk was a pile of paper, several pens, and a box of what looked like ink stamps. At the back of the room was a thick metal door but aside from that the place was windowless and bare. James, Arthur, and Will watched as the first few slaves were each directed towards a desk. Once there, they were forced to speak their name which was written down on a sheet of paper and then stamped. Following this, each held out their wrist and in a flash of light a black circle appeared on their skin, covering over their original symbols. James cast Will a horrified glace, suddenly realising the meaning of the black mark. 'Forever,' the old slave had whispered. The slaves were trapped in a circle with no end, bound into service forever.

There was no way to escape. They were stuck in the line of slaves, moving gradually closer towards a horrific fate. It was the first time James had felt truly terrified of what might happen. He hadn't quite believed he could lose everything he knew, could be hurt. Every previous incident had threatened danger but there had always been some way of escape. Here there was nothing, no door to run through, no friend to help them. In front of him, the queue moved forward and he was only one person from the front. He turned to the others in panic, only to find they had disappeared. Scanning the room desperately, he saw Will being shoved towards a desk at the back, closely followed by Arthur. Left alone, all he could do was walk forward to the desk in front of him which now stood empty. A large, brown-haired woman sat in front of him, her pig eyes framed with huge glasses.

'Ize?' she demanded. James looked at her blankly. 'Nam, nom?' she tried again.

James understood. 'Kleon of the Elra family,' he lied quickly, using the first two names that came into his head.

The woman wrote this down and picking up a large stamp, thrust it down on the paper. The print came out reading Dorea da, but he didn't know what it meant.

'Turra,' the woman then said brusquely and tapped her wrist

for ease of translation.

James cast one last, hopeful glance around the room. Nothing had changed. There was still no way of escape and even the main door was blocked. Slowly, he pulled back his sleeve and stretched out his arm over the desk. As the woman raised her hand, a load crash sounded across the room. She dropped her arm and stood, trying to see what was going on. James too craned his neck to see over the groups of slaves. A slave lay on the ground in the corner, a trickle of blood running down his face. Above him stood Arthur, his fists rolled into tight balls. James stared at the scene in shock, not knowing what to think or do.

He caught sight of Will beckoning to him through the chaos and began to push his way through the slaves who had begun to chant in some foreign language. Will was lost from sight until reaching the back of the room, James saw him standing beside the metal door. Will put a finger to his lips and gently pushed it open. A grey room greeted them, furnished with a single desk and chair. On the chair sat a figure and at the sound of someone entering, they turned. James and Will both found themselves staring into the terrified face of Aralia.

'How did you get in?' she asked in a small, tremulous voice. 'Where's Arthur?'

'I hoped you'd be in here!' Will exclaimed. 'No time to explain how we got in. Come on, get up. You'll have to run with your hands tied like that, d'you think you can?'

Aralia nodded, her expression slightly bewildered. 'The man, he was in the caves, he…'

'Come on,' Will commanded, cutting her off abruptly. 'Follow me, there isn't much time.'

Bursting from the back room, Will ran across the desk-filled space, heading for the main doorway. A fight had broken out between the slaves and they stood lurching at each other with fists and feet. Seeing Arthur caught in their midst, Will shouted to him before continuing out onto the street. Outside, the rain was battering the pavement and flashes of lightning appeared in the distant sky. It had grown darker again, the sky was made even blacker by the cloudy smoke which continually poured out of the towers. Although the air was cooler, the burning smoke still seeped through and the knowledge of what it was made James feel sick.

'Go, run!'

Arthur's voice sounded behind them and at his command, they began to run. After a few paces, James stopped still in the middle of the cobbled path. He was sure he could feel someone's eyes on him and he shivered involuntarily. Slowly, he twisted his head and looked back down the way they had come. Standing beside the building they had left was Scarface and his female companion. Both were watching him, their bodies motionless and their faces holding no expression.

'Pst,' James hissed at the others who had moved on ahead. 'We're being watched.'

They turned and stared down the street to where James directed his eyes.

'Why aren't they moving?' Aralia asked quietly. 'They're so still.'

As the last word left her lips, there was a sudden flash of purple light which joined a sharp white blaze of lightning. Light shot down the street at high speed, narrowly missing the spot where the four friends stood. Aralia let out a sharp squeal but remained fixed in a position of terror. Another flash ricocheted off the grey stone walls near them, creating a zigzag of purple over the paving stones. Behind the brightness, James saw the shadows of the man and woman standing with their hands outstretched.

'Run!' he yelled. 'They're trying to kill us.'

They began to run again, dodging the bolts of light which shot towards them. The man and woman followed in pursuit, never ceasing their flow of magic.

'What do we do?' Will shouted. 'They're not stopping.'

'Here, this way,' Arthur yelled back. He turned off the street into a narrower one without slowing his pace.

Gasping for breath, James ran at the back of the group where the bursts of magic bounced dangerously close to his ankles. As he passed into the next street, he noticed a doorway slightly ajar to their right and tried to shout out to alert the others. Finding he had no breath left to call, he pushed himself to catch up with Aralia and tapped her on the arm.

'There,' he managed to pant and pointed towards it.

The message was passed on and without further conversation they ran to the door and slipped through, slamming it behind them. A deathly silence descended, punctuated only by the sound of heavy breathing. The space they were in felt small and they were forced to huddle together. No one dared speak for fear of their enemies hearing them. A single flash of light shook the door and they all started. The wood trembled on its weak hinges, the vibrating sound echoing around the interior. A momentary calm was then broken by voices, sounding so close that they could hear every word.

'They can't go far, Kedran. No one can run for long in Garia.'

It was the woman speaking.

A hand fell against the door and it opened slightly. James clamped a hand over his mouth to dampen his breath that was still coming out in short gasps. The door opened a crack further, letting in small flecks of lightning which still tore at the sky.

'Let's not waste time here.' The man's voice sounded and the hand slipped from the door, leaving it to swing open in the breeze.

Inside the room the four watched in terror as the street and their enemies became visible. Neither of them turned however and they disappeared around a bend. Everything outside went still and after waiting a moment longer, James let out a shuddering sigh.

'Kedran,' he whispered.

'I tried to tell you before,' Aralia said. 'Scarface and Kedran are the same person. He was in the caves and he's now here too. He's been following us the whole way. He must be working for the dark, for The Belladonna.'

Wordlessly, James stepped out into the rain. 'If we're being followed, then there's no time to waste,' he said. 'This is a race and races don't go on forever. One of us will win, and I can't let it be The Belladonna. I have to make sure the light succeeds.' He took a long stride forwards, restless in his need to make up for lost time.

This time no one ran but they kept up a steady pace through the remaining streets. They could still hear the chanting behind them but ignored it as they hurried towards the edge of the town. It wasn't long before they reached it and found themselves looking out onto a cluster of barren slopes. Turning to glance back, James saw the town lying silent and brooding behind him, the darkness hiding its terrible secrets. Despite heavy legs they all walked quickly, desperate to get away from the town. James knew it wouldn't be long before they were followed again and he wanted to be as far away as possible.

The darkest hours had already passed by the time they reached the tip of the tallest slope and found themselves looking down at the black lake. Although much larger than its twin, it spread out with the same glassy darkness below them. The night was dark, but the glow of a half-moon revealed a scattering of trees surrounding the lake and more hills behind. In the lake's centre was a small island, empty apart from weeds and a singular tree. The most striking feature however was the dark, concrete building which rose from the steep right-hand bank.

'There it is,' James whispered. 'We made it. Down there is the prison we've been looking for.'

Chapter 18

FROM the top of the slope, James could see the reflection of the prison wavering on the water like a dark wound. He watched it with fascination, wondering what lay hidden beneath the glassy surface. To the left of the prison, a small light came into sight, winding its way towards the trees. Upon reaching them, it paused for a moment before bobbing back towards the building and out of sight.

'Guards,' Will said as they all watched the light disappear. 'They'll be everywhere. We need to figure out a plan because we can't just break in there, especially without magic.'

'Maybe we could create a distraction,' James suggested. 'Two of us could divert the guards and the other two could sneak inside.'

Arthur shook his head. 'No, the guards won't be tricked that easily. They're trained to deal with dangerous criminals, we've got no hope.'

Silence fell and they watched as another light, gleaming faintly against the lightening sky, began moving around the edge of the lake. As he looked, James made his peace with the idea that there was no way into the prison without taking a great risk. His heart sank at the thought and closing his eyes, he tried to think through his tiredness.

'The letter.' Aralia spoke quietly and fumbling in her pocket, drew out a folded piece of paper.

'What letter?' James squinted at the paper as Aralia held it up.

'The letter Alva gave us for her uncle, remember?'

Arthur took the letter from between his sister's fingers and frowned. 'What about it?' he asked.

Aralia sighed and with a swift flick of her hand, took back the letter. 'We have a letter for a prisoner,' she said excitedly. 'If we take it to the guards and say what it's for, we'll have a way in. Even if it doesn't work, we should try, for Alva's sake.'

'She's right,' James said quietly, fixing his eyes on the shadowy prison below. 'It seems like a good idea and it's the only one we have.'

By the time they reached the bottom of the slope the sky was light. The lake didn't look as menacing as it had in the dark, but it still bore a strange, brooding quality. Directly ahead of them, the vast bulk of the prison rose upwards on the lake bank, the walls set with many barred windows. Two heavy metal doors rested at the front of the building and two guards stood in front of them. Both were dressed in grey-green cloaks embroidered with a badge of four overlapping bars. Catching sight of the approaching strangers, both guards stiffened and stood to attention.

'Turette!' One called out and held out his arm in a gesture that suggested they should stop.

Obligingly, the four came to a halt and waited as the guard hurried down the slope towards them. On reaching them, he began tapping his wrist and mimed pulling up his sleeve.

'Vismé, vismé,' he said, repeating the gesture.

They all pulled up their left sleeve and waited as he inspected each one. His eyes lingered a moment longer on James', but he turned away without comment. Taking the letter out of her pocket, Aralia held it out to the guard who took it and scanned the name on the front. He frowned before proceeding to unfold the layers and run his eyes over the words. When he looked up again his eyes were completely expressionless. Aralia pointed to the letter and then towards the prison.

'A letter, for a prisoner in there,' she said, watching the guard's countenance grow vague. 'Capsive,' she tried again and pointed to the prison. 'In there. Can we take it in?'

The guard turned away and walked back towards the door, the letter still in his hand. He held it out to his companion and the two began talking in rapid voices. Eventually, the first guard beckoned to the four and glancing at each other with anticipation, they followed his summons. As they came level with the door, the guard flung his arm up and the metal structures swung slowly open.

'Olegg!' the guard barked at them and passed through the open doorway. Uncertain of his meaning, the four followed him nervously inside anyway.

A long, grey painted corridor met them, empty apart from a smaller set of metal doors at the opposite end. The guard led them through these and into another corridor which looked much the same apart from having several more doors. Opening one to the left, the guard gestured for them to pass through in front of him. Inside was a tiny, windowless room furnished with a few hard chairs and a desk at which a grey-robed woman sat. The guard passed over to the desk, placed the letter on it and left without a word.

The four were left standing uncomfortably while the woman slowly placed a pair of glasses on her nose and began to read through the letter. She read slowly, her eyes dragging over the words one by one. When at last she finished, she stood and jerked her head for them to follow. Outside in the corridor again, they tailed the woman right down to the end where she opened another door. They were immediately met with a long, concrete-floored passage lined with barred cells. Glancing inside the first cell, James swallowed uncomfortably as his eyes came to rest on an inmate. A brown-cloaked man was sitting on a stool behind the bars, head in hands. Beside him was a bucket, a threadbare mattress, and a jug of water. James hurried past to the next cell in which a woman lay sleeping, curled up on the mattress. There were eight more cells on either side, but James bent his head to avoid seeing inside the rest.

Up ahead, their guide had stopped beside the last cell and was barking something at the occupant. Moving closer, James watched as a middle-aged man rose from his stool and approached the bars. The guard handed him the letter, which he took and unfolded hurriedly.

'My Alva, my Alva,' he muttered to himself in a thick accent which sounded just like his daughter's. As he read his face grew lighter, but it fell again as he folded up the paper and tucked it into his pocket. Breaking from his mumbling, he turned to his audience.

'You bring this? You see my Alva?'

Aralia stepped forward and placed a hand on the bars. 'We saw your daughter and she asked us to give you the letter.'

'Was she happy?' he asked, his eyes wide and sad.

'She looked happy and your brother looks after her well.'

Alva's father bowed his head to hide a tear. 'How can I thank you? I have nothing to give.'

Whilst Aralia and the man spoke, James watched the strange

look on the guard's face. It was puzzled, her eyebrows drawn together in a deep frown. Judging by her expression he guessed she didn't understand a word of English. Nudging Will to the side, James moved to stand beside Aralia.

'There's something you can help us with,' he said quietly. Aralia folded her arms in objection, but he continued anyway. 'We need to go somewhere else in the prison, but we don't want the guard with us.'

'What can I do?' the man asked quietly. 'I have no power here.'

James grimaced and straightened the edges of his cloak. 'You could create a diversion. If you make a scene, we could then slip away. Will you help us?'

A small glint appeared in the man's eyes. 'I not ask why you need help, but I will. Keep speaking and I will help.'

'Thanks,' James muttered in reply.

As the word left his lips, the man suddenly began to shout. He grabbed the bars and shook them before flailing his arms wildly in the air. Brought to attention, the guard rushed to unlock the cell gate and swiftly entered. The man winked at James briefly before continuing his act. With the guard occupied, James swiftly opened the passage doors beside him and slipped through, followed closely by his friends.

They found themselves in a wide circular courtyard, laid out under a huge dome. It was lined with cells five storeys high, the bars all facing outward. The cells were built along strange, curved balconies, starting one level up from the ground. The ring directly surrounding the courtyard was set with several locked metal doors. A huge concrete pillar stood in the middle of the space, its base resting in a large puddle of rainwater which must have leaked through the roof. The whole space was cold and smelt strongly of mould.

'Where now?' Will asked. 'We won't have long before the guard comes after us.'

'We look for a place storing records,' Arthur replied simply and quickly scanned the surrounding area. 'Somewhere behind one of the doors maybe?'

Splitting up, each of them went to one of the doors and stood listening. James pressed his ear hard against the cold metal, trying to detect any sounds. Hearing nothing, he reached out to give the door a push, but it was locked fast. He moved to the next door and listened closely again. Several voices reached his ears and he stepped hurriedly away, shaking his head at Will who had come up behind him. As he was trying the third door, he heard footsteps somewhere behind him and swiftly leapt behind one of the pillars which supported the first row of cells. He saw Will dart behind one too, but Arthur and Aralia were nowhere in sight.

A man in a blue cloak entered the circular space and stopped to draw a large bunch of keys from his pocket. Disentangling a small silver one from the rest, he approached the door set directly between James' and Will's hiding places. Peering out from behind the pillar, James watched as the man inserted the key in its lock and passed through the door. Sliding out from behind his pillar, he crept silently over to the door which stood slightly ajar and peered through. All he could see was a metal staircase spiralling round and out of sight.

Before he could explore any further, he heard footsteps again and hurried back behind the pillar. The blue-cloaked man reappeared holding a file of paper which he tucked under his arm as he fumbled for the key again. The slamming of a door across the courtyard made him stop in this activity and he looked up as another man in grey entered. He wildly gestured for the blue-cloaked man to follow him, calling out in his own tongue. At his words, the man near James hurried after his colleague, a grim expression on his face. James waited until they had gone before he moved from the pillar and went towards the door.

'D'you think they know?' Aralia's voice asked quietly. 'Know that we're here I mean?'

'He left in a hurry and forgot to lock the door.' Will's voice also sounded, hushed with excitement. 'Come on, let's see what's through it.' Without waiting for a vote, he pushed it open and slipped through.

James also passed through the door and stepped straight onto the spiral staircase. As he landed on the first step, the staircase began to move, twisting round of its own accord. Will was already several turns up and he looked down at James' expression of amazement with a grin.

'Never been on one before?' he asked.

'Not like this,' James answered, eyes still wide.

The stairway continued to spiral up until it reached a metal door resting on a small landing. James leapt hurriedly off the top step as it began to fold back into itself and then disappeared completely. He watched it for a moment longer before turning to the door and giving it a push. On finding it locked, he held out his palm, readying himself to break it with magic.

'You can't use magic, it's still forbidden,' Arthur said from behind him. 'We're in a prison where people go for breaking laws like that.'

As if deaf to Arthur's words, Will had pulled up his sleeve and was standing with his wrist exposed to the door. James, Arthur, and Aralia stared at him in confusion, but he didn't turn to look at them.

'What're you doing, Will!' Arthur hissed.

There was silence but as the three of them watched Will in his madness, there was a click and the door suddenly swung open.

'How did you do that?' James gasped, looking at Will in amazement.

'Most doors like this can be opened using identity magic,' Will responded. 'They're enchanted to reject the prisoners, but anyone else can get in. Technically we're using magic, but it's part of the prison system so we can get away with it. You'll all have to show your symbols too.'

Following Will's lead, they each revealed their symbol and moved through the door into the room the other side. It was small and apart from a desk and chair at one end, the space was filled with metal cabinets. A picture hung askew on a bent nail; a painting of a beautiful place with purple hills and blue skies which starkly contrasted the harsh landscape outside the prison walls.

'There might be something in here,' James said hopefully. 'All these cabinets must have papers in. If we all look in different corners of the room, we'll be able to cover more space.'

Every cabinet was alphabetically ordered and heading to the back of the room, James searched for the section under 'A'. On finding it, he pulled open the first drawer and removed the thick stack of papers inside. Running his eyes over the top sheet, he saw rows of notes all handwritten in an unrecognisable language. Unable to understand it, he sighed and shoved the stack back in its place before moving to the next drawer. This one contained similar files and he returned the sheets with a sinking feeling. File after file revealed nothing about Arvad but he continued to rummage, desperately searching for anything that might give them a clue.

'Over here,' Will suddenly called from the other side of the room. 'I think I've found some prison records.'

Slamming his draw shut, James leapt up from the floor and rushed over to Will. The open drawer contained hundreds of folders filled with papers which were stapled together in thick wedges.

'Let me see,' James urged, grabbing the sheet Will held. A list of names was written on it, each followed by a short, tightly scrawled paragraph.

'They're only names, not full records,' Arthur commented, leaning over James' shoulder. 'I think they're all recent crimes too. Look how new the paper is.'

Will nodded with a sigh. 'You're right, they do look like they've just been written. Maybe they don't keep old ones anymore, especially ones written in Arvad's time. That's if Arvad even existed. Celaeno could have lied for all we know.' He took the paper from James and returned it to the drawer.

'There must be something useful in here,' James said despairingly. 'She couldn't have lied, why would she? Maybe we should try another room,' he tried hopefully. 'This can't be the only one here.'

A soft thud at the back of the room made them turn sharply. Aralia stood in front of a tall cabinet, pushing against it with all her might. When she caught sight of the boys watching her, she stopped and folded her arms.

'Maybe one of you could help?' she inquired and gave the cabinet another push.

'What're you doing?' James asked with a slight edge to his voice.

'Trying to move this thing. There's another door behind it, can't you see?'

James followed her pointing finger to where the edges of a door just peered out above the top of the cabinet. He watched as Will and Arthur pushed it slightly to the side, allowing a small gap to squeeze through. Aralia slid up to the door and turned the handle, but it wouldn't move.

Inspired by an idea, James went over to the picture on the wall. Unhooking it from its place, he tore off the piece of wire attached to the back and took it over to Aralia. She stood to the side as he inserted the wire into the keyhole and wriggled it around. There was a click but when he pushed the door it still didn't open. Hiding his hand from the others, he raised it and showed his symbol. The handle glowed for a moment and when he tried it, the door swung open. A large room came into view and James stared at it in awe. It had a smooth polished wooden floor running from end to end and a low, dark-beamed ceiling. Every wall was covered with rows of square shelves, packed tightly with high stacks of files and books. These shelves were attached by wide curves of wood which joined in the middle to create a wide archway down the middle of the room. To James, it looked like a more compact version of the library in Arissel.

'How on earth are we going to find something from hundreds of years ago in here?' Will asked, his voice hushed with admiration.

No one asked James how he'd opened the door and he felt relieved. 'No idea,' he said back to Will and walked up to the first shelf. 'It's all alphabetical again,' he announced after glancing at the files. 'This is Z so A must be the other end.'

He moved down to the other end of the hall with the others following behind. Each picked a corner and began to flick through files one by one. James sat on the floor between two rows and pulled out a yellowing file. Inside was a stack of paper labelled with the name 'Alph' and an indistinct year. The file below it read 'Arrin' and James cast it to the side with a sigh. Each folder was the same apart from the name and year, but there was no sign of Arvad.

Tired of searching, he looked up to refocus his eyes. On the dusty shelf beside him he noticed a mark etched into the wooden surface. Wiping away the thick dust with his already grubby sleeve, he ran his fingers over the grooves. The uneven letters had been scratched by a hurried hand and read 'The Lost Years'. This meant nothing to James but still he pulled out the stack of files above the words. Slowly, he turned his back to the others and held his hand over the papers, watching as a soft light glowed. One by one the papers began to turn themselves over until they stopped on the second to last. The page was blank but when James held a light to it, a symbol of a circle set with a six-pointed star appeared. Beside it was the name 'Arvad'.

Chapter 19

JAMES ran his fingers over the word and smiled to himself. This was it, the document about Arvad the Wanderer and information about his conviction. He waved the papers excitedly at his friends.

'Come quickly, I've found it!'

Will, Arthur, and Aralia set down what they were doing and hurried over, joining him on the floor. Taking a deep breath, he moved his eyes to the words below Arvad's name and began to read.

'Convict for the folowing cryme: attempted slauter of rare creetur with powers, Alati.' He stopped as the writing suddenly changed language. What he had been able to read was written in a similar way to the myth about the crystals.

'Attempted slaughter,' Aralia breathed. 'But—'

James interrupted her and exclaimed, 'Alati!' Seeing the others look at him in confusion he explained. 'Outside the amphitheatre one of the slaves grabbed my arm, d'you remember?' He directed the question at Will and Arthur who nodded. 'After you'd walked away, he grabbed me again and kept saying the same word, "Alati".'

Will's eyes darkened. 'How does that link in? I mean how did he know that we were looking for Arvad? He can't have.'

'Alati isn't from the Garian language.' Aralia spoke abruptly across Will. 'It means winged or lion, but I can't remember which.' She put a nail between her teeth, deep in thought.

'Why would a lion be important in finding the firestone?' Arthur asked. 'What would Arvad have to do with that?'

Will was reading the sheets of paper again, but his head whipped up at Arthur's words. 'Alati must mean lion. The lion is one of the most powerful creatures, king of the animal world. Don't you see?' he questioned, looking at the blank faces around him. 'King, power, fire. The lion is a powerful creature, linked to the sun in symbolism. The sun is power and fire.' He paused and waited for someone to answer.

Aralia smiled and let her hand fall. 'The sun is also an eternal fire,' she added.

James nodded slowly. 'It makes sense,' he murmured. 'The only problem is that Arvad gave the fire a gift to make it eternal. The sun is already eternal, so that doesn't fit. There must be something we're missing.'

The smile fell from Will's face and silence descended. All of them were wondering the same thing, each mentally debating whether the myth was true. The evidence of Arvad's existence through the prison records was only a small comfort. James replaced the papers in their file and slipped them back onto the shelf. As he was doing this, he noticed the engraved words again and pointed them out to the others.

'The Lost Years,' Will read aloud. 'What does that mean?'

Arthur suddenly delved into his pocket and drew a piece of paper from it. He held it out for the others to see.

'I found this in the town, I forgot I still had it. It's just a sheet of paper but it has the same words on it.'

James took the sheet and looked at it closely. 'Do you think it's important?' he asked, directing his question at no one in particular.

The sound of a door thudding somewhere made him jump and his hand knocked against a stack of files which crashed to the ground. The others leapt up in panic and started to frantically gather up the cloud of paper which floated to the floor. Another bang sounded and they all froze, piles of crumpled paper clutched in their hands.

'We have to move quickly,' James said, his voice tense with fear. 'We have to get out before they know we're in here and find us.'

Will uttered a short cough, trying to catch their attention. 'There's something I didn't tell you about the magic we used,' he muttered quietly. 'I think you should probably know.'

'Was it illegal?' Arthur inquired, pursing his lips.

Will shook his head. 'It wasn't illegal but breaking into the prison was. Identity magic fulfils its name by recognising the identity of anyone who reveals their symbol. Anyone who passes through a door enchanted with it is instantly exposed. It was the only way to get into this room, but it was a risk.' He lowered his eyes. 'What I'm trying to say is that the guards will now know exactly who we are, and possibly where we are.'

'Are you serious?' James snapped in disbelief. 'Why didn't you tell us before?' He continued without waiting for an answer. 'Come on, we've got to go!'

'We're fugitives,' Aralia uttered in a hushed voice. 'We're criminals and they know who we are.' Her words were strained as if she was trying to hold back tears.

The office was still empty, and they dashed through and out onto the metal staircase. James was just about to step onto the stairway when voices sounded directly below and he stopped short. Noting the cracks between the steps, he knelt and peered cautiously through. A thick-bodied man stood directly below him, accompanied by a woman dressed in brown. Two guards stood opposite them, arms folded and faces grimly set.

'I'll pay you. Where are they?' It was the man who spoke, his harsh voice cutting through the silence.

The voice sounded familiar and James shuddered. He knew without doubt that the man standing directly below him was Kedran. Feeling a tap on his arm, he looked up to see Aralia looking fearfully at him. She said nothing but he nodded at her and with his finger drew a line down his face, miming Kedran's scar.

'Sir, with all due respect I am under no obligation to share any information with you.' The guard spoke in a clear accent which contrasted the guttural tones of the Garian people. 'All prison matters are in hand and any imposters will be dealt with.'

James pressed his face to the crack again, watching the scene below with a mixture of curiosity and fear. Kedran grabbed the woman beside him by the arm and shook her violently.

'This young woman claimed she saw them, three boys and a girl. You saw them, didn't you?' he snapped, directing the words at his captive.

'Sir,' the guard said again. 'Please take your hands off the prisoner.'

'What if I don't?' He bared his teeth. 'She's only a grubby little inmate anyway.'

'I will have to remove you,' the guard replied. Turning deliberately to the woman, he then addressed her. 'Is it true?'

She looked at him with a languid, pale lipped expression. Raising her head upward to the heavens, her eyes met with

157

James' stare. He went stiff and tried not to blink while her eyes lingered on his for a moment before she dragged them down to meet the guard.

'No,' she said quietly. 'I saw no one.'

'What?' Kedran shouted and raised his arm as if he were about to hit her.

As the guard stepped forward to detain him, two others ran in from a side door. They approached their colleague and muttered something in his ear before exiting hurriedly. The remaining guard stared after them before turning large, bewildered eyes onto Kedran.

'I must escort you from the building and return the prisoner to her cell. A matter of extreme urgency has arisen.' He gave Kedran an urgent shove towards an exit and the prisoner followed dutifully behind.

As soon as they had disappeared, James rose. One by one they hurried down the stairs and out through the metal door. Once in the courtyard again, they kept close to the edges where the pillars kept them in intermittent shadow. The wet floor made it difficult to hurry and they were forced into a steady walk. They crept on around the outer courtyard until they came to the same set of doors the guard had disappeared through. James pushed at them gently but like all the others, they wouldn't open.

'The doors must lock as soon as they're closed,' Will whispered.

His words were drowned by the shrill tones of a bell which suddenly echoed around them. They all froze, looking wildly around for the source.

'They know!' Will shouted over the noise. 'They know we're here.'

His words awoke fresh urgency in all of them and raising their hands, they each cast a bolt of light at the door. It burst open violently in a flash of light and they hurried through into the cell-lined passage which lay the other side. The bell still sounded around them, echoing in the passage behind them as they hurried on. Driven by fear, James began to jog down the passage but was suddenly stopped by a hand which reached from one of the cells and grabbed his arm. Jerked backwards, he collided with Will who was just behind him. Apprehensively, James turned to see who had stopped him. He saw an unhooded woman standing by the bars of her cell, a soft smile on her lips. Her pale red hair was matted down with grease and grime and her face looked somehow familiar. Looking closely, James realised she was the prisoner who had been standing underneath the staircase. He stood still as her hand dropped from his arm, unsure of what to say.

'You're the eyes,' she whispered to him gently. 'I saw you watching. Are these your friends?' She cast a quick glance over the others and James nodded.

'Why did you save us?' he asked, his eyes narrowing.

The woman placed a light hand on the bars of her cell and sighed. 'There's so much suffering,' she said quietly. 'I do not know what four young people such as yourselves would want in a place like this.' She didn't directly ask them, but her head was tilted questioningly.

James avoided her question, eyeing her with suspicion. 'Is there anything we can repay you with?' he asked awkwardly.

She smiled at this suggestion. 'There's only one thing I want and that is my fair freedom. Many innocents wait in here for that, but many remain until they die.' The woman brushed a hand over her tired face and sighed. 'I am bound by magic, by the most unbreakable bonds. They stop me from wandering away.' Her tone was tinged with a deep sadness and she looked away. 'I've been in here a long time; I've forgotten much of the world.'

She fell silent and placed her other hand on the bars before her. As she did so, her sleeve fell back, revealing a dark symbol on her slim wrist. It was unlike the other marks James had seen; a diamond inked onto the skin like a tattoo rather than growing within the flesh itself. Following James' eyes, the woman quickly lowered her arm and covered the symbol again.

'I have no name, not anymore,' she whispered. 'Like all the prisoners here, I carry the Burn of Death. I am bound to die here under this roof as prisoner number 131.'

Absently, James traced the groves of his own symbol. 'Do you come from here, from Garia?' he asked.

'I came from the Hidden City which no one can ever find but has the answers to everything.'

The Hidden City. James remembered those words from before, from the ghost girl in the woods. She had also mentioned the place which hid all secrets and held the answers to everything. An idea came to him and he stood contemplating it for a moment before he spoke.

'Where is the city, the Hidden City?'

The woman uttered a short laugh. 'It is a place that not many can find and when you've been once there's a chance you'll never find it again. It lies within Garia, but I have long forgotten the way back. Those who live or have lived there are bound by magic and can't tell anyone of its secrets.'

She seemed to be growing fidgety and kept glancing nervously down the passage. James wondered whether this city would have the answers to his questions about Arvad and the firestone. If he and his friends could find the way there, perhaps he could finally learn the truth. He would know if Arvad was real, if the firestone existed, and if the dark force known as The Belladonna was really racing against him.

'I can hear footsteps,' the woman suddenly said, her eyes alight with fear. 'They'll be coming back. You must go now, before they find you here. Go! I will protect you for as long as I can if they come asking.'

James was about to ask another question when a voice came from the next cell along. It belonged to a woman and sounded both gleeful and malicious.

'I won't kep a secret. Ya can count on me. They already know, I told them ya was here. Ya'll have trouble finding a way out before they catch ya.'

The occupant uttered a wild cackle and running forward, flung herself against the bars. James saw a gap-toothed, middle-aged hag standing with her face pressed to the bars which made deep grooves in her skin. Mad fire filled her eyes and she spat on the ground with a wild grin. Aralia retreated in disgust and the woman laughed heartily, the sound echoing down the passage.

'They'll come runnin' now,' she howled loudly. 'They'll catch ya quick as anythin'. I knows you goin' to the Hidden City, I'll tell 'em. You won't be runnin' for long before they'll catch ya and put ya in 'ere with us lot.'

Will, Arthur, and Aralia turned swiftly and began to hurry down the passage, followed by the cackles of the prisoner. James lingered for a few moments more, resting his attention on their friend who stood quietly in her cell. Seeing him pause, the others also stopped and restlessly waited.

'What's the factory town for?' he asked quietly. 'What do the slaves do?' He looked at the woman searchingly.

She leaned her head towards him and he pressed his ear to the bars. 'They look for a place where magic is forgotten,' she whispered, 'a place no one can reach. They are cursed to search for it forever until it is found.'

James drew his breath in sharply, the meaning of the words suddenly hitting him. Everything became clear to him in a split second, the slaves, the town, and his role in it all. His own world was a place where magic didn't exist, a place Albert had said no one from this world could reach. The slaves were searching for it, the world which had been spoken about but never found. They were trying to find a way into his world, the place on the other side of an almost unbreakable boundary. It all made sense to him now. Only he had been able to cross between and he was the single link between the worlds. He was racing the darkness for the firestone, but they also wanted to use him to break the boundary.

'Oh my God,' he muttered under his breath. 'They want to crush the light, to start a war. It's worse than I ever thought.' He shook his head in disbelief, but he knew it was all true.

The woman and the others were all staring at him but he looked right through them. He knew now that his task was to not only discover the truth, but to find the firestone and protect his world from exposure. He felt a huge weight fall onto his shoulders and a loud sigh escaped his lips. Mumbling his thanks to the woman, he hurried past the others and headed down the passage towards the door. On reaching it, he glanced back one more time and saw the woman watching him with a puzzled frown. His friends followed him, urgency and confusion written on their faces.

No one said anything and they walked in silence. Turning left, they saw a small barred gate in front of them, fixed onto the wall opposite an open archway. Above the gate was a sign etched with the diamond Burn of Death. Leaving the gate behind them, they headed through the archway and found themselves standing on a small balcony. Thick grey clouds hovered in the sky, looming darkly over the prison. Behind them, the bell still tolled loudly, ringing through the depths of the prison.

'There's no way out this way, we'll have to go back into the passage,' Will said, looking around the small space.

He stepped towards the archway but as he went to pass through it, something knocked him back. With a sharp grunt of pain, he stumbled backwards holding his head.

'It's blocked, they've blocked it,' he uttered wildly.

Frowning in disbelief, Arthur went over and raising his arm, thrust it forward. It struck something solid, an invisible wall which could not be penetrated. Arthur retracted his hand and grimaced. In the ensuing silence, they all became aware of the sound of running footsteps.

'This is it,' Aralia mumbled in a small voice. 'They've found us.'

They stood frozen as the sound grew closer, mingling with the toll of the bell. Suddenly, Arthur uttered a brief exclamation and they turned to see him leaning over the balcony edge.

'We have to jump,' he said. 'It's the only way.'

James went to the edge and, peering over, found himself staring straight down into the water of the black lake. The balcony appeared to be placed at the side of the prison where the walls stretched straight down into the water. The drop wasn't very far but the lake beneath looked less than inviting.

'I'm not jumping down there!' Aralia stepped away from the edge with wide eyes. 'I can't, you know I hate heights.'

'Nor me!' Will exclaimed. 'No way.'

Arthur shrugged and hauled himself up to the ledge. 'I'm going, you can stay if you want to. It's not far, don't be cowards.'

A shout came from behind them and they all turned. Three grey-cloaked figures stood by the arch and bolts of light lit up the passage around them. In sudden panic, Aralia ran over to the wall where Arthur helped her up and took her trembling hand. She cast a frightened look at the guards before nodding to her brother. Another light glowed, this time penetrating the wall of magic and bouncing onto the small balcony. Will and James leapt onto the wall too, following Arthur's lead.

'Now!' Arthur yelled and he jumped, pulling Aralia with him. Her scream echoed back to Will and James who gaped after them.

'Quite high,' Will managed to gasp before he too jumped.

James turned to cast one more look back. The three guards were moving through the archway and all had their hands pointing towards him. Reaching inside his pocket, he felt the gold clock there, cold against his skin. Part of him wanted to take it out and turn the dials in the hope that it would take him back home. The escape would be easy, but he knew he couldn't leave the others. Closing his eyes, he stepped forward on the wall, feeling himself hovering on the edge. Before he could change his mind, he felt something strike his back and he stumbled, cold air rushing up around him.

Chapter 20

JAMES felt the freezing water of the lake hit him, tearing at his skin as if with sharp claws. It surged around him, trying to drag him further down into the black depths. Choking for air, he pushed against the rough force until he felt the pressure around him lessen and a beam of light struck the rippling layers just above his head. With one last push, he broke the surface and felt cold air strike his face. He sucked it into his lungs hungrily, taking great, greedy gulps. Once sated, he turned his eyes upon the rest of the lake, scanning it for any sign of the others. He caught sight of Arthur and Aralia a short distance to his left and Will wasn't far behind them. Raising his hand, he waved vigorously to try and gain their attention.

A flicker of light caught his own attention, shining somewhere within the black, watery depths around him. He held himself as still as possible, trying to reduce the number of ripples dancing away from his body. The light came again, this time a little closer and brighter. From a distance it had looked like a formless splash, but James now saw it was jellyfish. Although small, it moved with quick, short movements across the lake in front of him. Another flash caught his eye and looking around, he realised the lake was filled with hundreds of the fish, darting here and there like fireflies. A voice was calling somewhere and James realised it was Will's. He rotated himself and saw his friends hovering in the water, hardly moving.

'Keep still,' Will called. 'Whatever you do don't move.'

James watched as the jellyfish drew closer and settled around his body. They clung to him, small balls of yellow glowing light. He could feel their long tendrils wrap themselves around his fingers and brush against his skin. Although his body trembled slightly from the strain of keeping himself afloat, he didn't feel afraid. The jellyfish were strangely beautiful and their soft glow was somehow mesmerising. He felt lost in a sea of light, drawn in by the flickering dance. As he waited, the jellyfish slowly began to release their hold and dart away into the depths of the lake. He saw Will start to swim and forced his arms to move too, propelling himself towards the bank.

The four reached the edge of the lake at the same time and dragged themselves from the water. Their sudden movement disturbed the calmness of the water and it burst into frenzied chaos. The jellyfish shot across the water until they became one large, teaming mass. Aralia screamed and Arthur hauled her out of the water. Will and James reached the bank at the same time and dragged themselves out, terror in their faces.

'The Alam Sotsuc, Evil Guardian,' Will panted. 'They respond to movement and can electrocute a live man with their sting. The lake was a trap, made to prevent prisoners from escaping.'

James nodded blankly. He didn't want to think about what could have happened if they hadn't listened to Will. Turning to look at the prison he became aware of the bell still tolling somewhere within its depths. The sound brought him back to life, refreshing his sense of urgency.

'They're still after us, we have to go,' he announced to the others who nodded in agreement.

'Where now?' Will asked through chattering teeth. 'We're fugitives of the law and enemies of the dark. There are people watching us everywhere.'

James bent his head and watched the water trickle from his shoes into the grass. They had risked their lives to find out about Arvad and nowhere was safe.

'The woman in the prison mentioned a place called the Hidden City, a place where all questions can be answered. We still need to read the missing pages of Arvad's story; I think we could find them there.'

Will shook his head. 'It's impossible to get there. The woman said it's difficult to find and the name kind of suggests that too. Where would we begin?'

James shrugged. 'Right now, we need to get away from the prison before we're found.'

He began to walk again and his friends joined him. The air was bitingly cold and they shivered in their wet clothes, stumbling along numbly. A path ran away from the lake to their right, winding lazily up a soft slope. It wasn't steep but their progress was made slower by the rough trees and grass which grew across the way. They walked in silence for a long time, each trying to work out the almost impossible answer of how to find the Hidden City. The landscape gradually changed around them; the soft slopes replaced by jagged grey rocks which ran alongside the path.

Every now and then the rock fell away, revealing a sheer drop. Aralia and Will kept safely to the other side of the path, glancing nervously over at the rock edge. As the day wore on, they began to grow tired and looked out for a place to rest. Nothing suitable revealed itself until Will spotted a small indentation in the rock to their right. Three sides were sheltered by rock and the fourth lay open to the rugged land which ran beside the path. James threw himself on the ground, resting his head on a clump of wiry grass. His friends sat too, and Aralia unwrapped several of the food packages Rolf's wife had given them. James took his out too, starving after long hours without food. It was wet from the lake but the meat inside was still intact and filled his empty stomach.

Once satisfied, they all lay down to rest. James for once felt peaceful. Although the clues they had found were impossible to decode, he still felt they were a little closer to knowing the truth. The ground was hard and cold but he was used to such discomforts and drifted easily to sleep. Beside him, Aralia and Arthur slept too whilst Will sat on watch with his cloak wrapped tightly around him. As they slept a light snow began to fall, covering them and the land around in a thin blanket of white.

Suddenly James jumped awake. The sky was dark apart from the small stars which pricked it with their faint light. He sat up, forgetting where he was for a moment until his eyes adjusted to the rocky wall around him. His body was cold and stiff under his clothes which were damp with snow and rising from the ground, he stretched out his numb limbs. Feeling his way forwards, he stepped to where the rock opened and immediately saw what had woken him. A bright light shone directly in front of him and he darted backwards to avoid being caught by the beam. The light had a strange blue glow to it and James started. It was one he would know anywhere, one which only belonged to a screen.

Will's voice came from behind him, a soft whisper. 'What is it? Why're you standing there?'

Within the glowing circle stood a shadow, a wavering, indistinct figure wrapped in a long cloak. The light cast a long beam outward and the shadow suddenly turned around, swinging the light with it. Its beam lingered for a long moment on the rocks against which James pressed himself, hardly daring to breath. A drop of light caught the edge of his wavering cloak, but he didn't dare reach down to tuck it out of sight.

'What're you staring at?' Will's voice came again, a little louder this time.

James didn't answer. A new realisation was dawning on him, one which made him more afraid than ever. There were no screens in this world, as far as he was aware, and the blue light must therefore belong to his phone. He was suddenly and horribly aware of the dangers his phone could bring. The dark was somehow using it to track him down, to follow him at every stage of his journey. He was exposed and his world was thrown into danger with him. Refocusing his attention on the light, he waited with a sickening feeling as it began to fade and then went out. Peering around the edge of rock, he saw with surprise that the figure too had gone.

'Didn't you see it?' he asked in a quiet voice. 'There was a figure out there holding a light.'

Will shook his head. 'I didn't see anyone, and there definitely wasn't a light.'

'He's right, there was nothing,' Arthur's voice came from the darkness behind them.

James frowned in confusion. 'Someone was standing there, holding a light that I recognised. It came from something only used in my world, the same thing that I lost in the Ona caves. The dark are using it to follow me somehow, using it to find the clues we've already uncovered.' He paused to slow his breath which was coming out in rushed gasps.

'They're using you to find the firestone?' Will questioned, a puzzled note in his voice.

'To find the firestone, and me. There's something else I haven't told you. The woman in the prison told me what the slaves of Garia are digging for.'

'A place where magic was forgotten,' Arthur interrupted. 'We heard.'

'Yes,' James nodded, 'but that place isn't anywhere in this world. They're looking for my world which is divided from this one by an almost unbreakable boundary. The dark wants to find the firestone, but they also want me because I come from the place without magic. I can either let them destroy both worlds or I can keep fighting for the light.'

Silence fell between them as neither Will nor Arthur knew what to say. James felt a drop of water trickle down his cheek, perhaps once a snowflake, and reached out to catch it. His mind turned back to his world where it must now be winter, maybe even Christmas, but he couldn't tell. He could picture himself and his parents having breakfast together, the one day of the year where that happened. The thought created a faint pang of homesickness and he let the picture fade.

'Why do they want to break into your world?' It was Aralia who spoke, her voice piercing through the silence.

'I don't know, I don't understand,' James replied. 'Maybe they want to start a war.'

'A war!' Will said incredulously.

'A war between magic and non-magic. If they break into my world, they can destroy the light everywhere, not just here.'

'Why didn't you tell us before?' Arthur asked quietly. 'We shouldn't be sleeping now; we should be searching for the

Hidden City.'

James shivered and pulled his cloak about him. 'I didn't know until we spoke to the woman in the prison.' He paused. 'Why couldn't you and Will see the light? It was right there.'

'It must have been an illusion, but I don't know why only you saw it,' Will replied. 'If someone had been here they would've found us by now, it can't have been real.'

'It's time to find the missing pages before the darkness does,' Aralia added softly.

Nodding to one another in agreement, they stepped out from their shelter. In the dim light of a moon, the hills around them curved softly with the newly fallen snow. The trees too were hung delicately with white, layering the branches with a crisp frosting. They walked along the outer edge of the rocks, the movement keeping them from freezing. After a while the landscape became steeper and the long grass under their feet grew more straggled, drowning under the snow. The sky remained a heavy grey, matching the weight in their legs as they walked on.

After what felt like hours of stumbling along the path, they came across a wide gap in the rock surface. Unlike the hollow they had rested in, this was more like a cave. The entrance was tall enough for someone to fit through and they stopped to peer into its depths. Gripped by boyish instinct, Will, James, and Arthur stepped into the opening, leaving Aralia lurking behind. Complete darkness swallowed them, and their searching hands met only with air.

'Come on,' Arthur called back to his sister.

'Is it safe?' Aralia asked, taking a few tentative steps forward. 'I can't see anything!'

Alone in the darkness, James found his hands meet a jagged

rock surface which snagged his fingers. A faint whisper had lodged itself in the back of his mind and he closed his eyes, trying to hear it. It sounded both close and far away and was impossible to catch. Stretching out his arms, he ran his hands over the wall. Nothing new revealed itself to him and he began to feel along the wall to try and gage the cave's size. As he moved, his hands suddenly caught on something different. It was a handle of some kind, rough and uneven.

'Here, there's a door I think,' he called to the others.

Without a second thought, he gave the knob a sharp twist. There was a click and he was pushed violently backwards as a heavy door swung open. After regaining his balance, he braced himself and, feeling for the door frame, stepped through and into the unknown space beyond.

Chapter 21

JAMES had the immediate sensation that he was not underground but within the rock itself. The air around him felt spacious and he stopped, staring into nothingness. Light footsteps sounded behind him and he guessed that his friends had found their way through too.

'I wonder how big the cave is?' James asked the darkness. He took a step forward and suddenly tripped, falling on his knees down a small flight of steps.

'James, are you alright?' Aralia's voice called.

James rubbed his knees and stood stiffly. 'I fell down some steps. There are only a few but stay where you are.'

As he stood there came a soft sound, a low murmur which was joined by another and another until the cave was filled with an indistinct whispering. The murmur grew gradually louder until one voice singled itself out from the rest and began to speak.

'Who enters the tomb?' it questioned in a drifting voice which echoed faintly in the surrounding space.

James looked about blindly in the darkness. He paused for a moment before answering, unsure whether speaking out was wise. 'We're looking for the Hidden City,' he said at last. 'Can you help us?'

There was a long pause and then the voice spoke again. 'I am not concerned with the woes of men,' it stated coldly. 'Like all things hidden, I rest in the shadows where the light can't reach. I am the end at the end of all endings. You may only enter when you tell me my name.' The last word faded into an echo and the whispering also died away.

'We don't want to enter the tomb,' James replied calmly. 'We're just looking for the Hidden City. You must know something that can help us?' He didn't know who he was speaking to but the only sound that came back to him was the eerie echo of his own voice.

'Can we leave?' Aralia whispered. 'I don't like the idea that there are tombs all around us.'

There came the sound of someone scrabbling by the back wall and after a moment Arthur's voice sounded.

'We can't leave, even if we wanted to,' he called. 'The door's gone. We're trapped unless we work out the name and go into the tomb.'

James put is face in his hands and thought hard. 'What could the name be?' he whispered aloud.

He heard footsteps treading carefully down the steps and felt someone brush against his sleeve.

'There are hundreds of names, how're we going to find one?' Will's voice was close to his ear.

'It's got to be easier than that,' Aralia said lightly. 'There must be something obvious that we're just not seeing.'

'Voices, whispering voices, death,' James murmured to himself. 'There must be a logical answer. The voices of the dead, voices silent after death, silence.' He nodded to himself. 'Maybe it's silence?' he suggested in louder tones.

174

'It can't be silence, we heard it speaking,' Aralia replied. 'It must be something more closely related to the tomb.'

'Grave, bodies, souls?' Will suggested in quick succession.

'The voice said something about being the end of endings,' James said. 'What's another word for ending? The clue must be to do with word logic. It must be something to do with the word 'end'.'

An idea was forming in his head, but he wasn't sure about it just yet. He was about ask the others when Will called something past him.

'Soul,' he blurted. 'It must be, the place where the soul leaves the body! The soul leaves the body at the end of life. Your name is…'

'Death!' James exclaimed, jumping over Will's words in sudden fear that he would say the wrong thing. 'Your name is Death.'

There was absolute silence and James stood calmly waiting for the reply. When the voice came, it was so close behind him that he felt shivers run down his spine. He could feel a presence behind him but didn't dare turn around.

'Very clever,' came a hiss. 'I take your answer. Indeed, I am Death as you put it. Death ends life, resting at the end of every ending and each man will one day meet me.'

'May we enter the tomb?' James asked tentatively.

There was a pause and he felt the presence disappear. A light began to grow around him, pushing the darkness into the far corners and making the shadows seem more mysterious. The light was not whole but made up of tiny glowing particles which hovered like fireflies in the air. They danced together and then parted, turning the tomb into a whirl of beautiful light.

Looking ahead of him, James saw they were in a vast hall

which resembled a church or cathedral. The floor was paved with large, square flagstones, worn smooth by feet that must have walked over it for centuries. The curved roof, decorated with finely engraved gold leaves, was held up by fifteen large grey pillars. There were six on each side leading up to a large window and the other three stood in front of James, marking where the tomb ground began. Swirls of gold light ran across the window, making it look like moving stained glass. The space between the pillars was filled with rows of tombs, some with stone figures resting on top in stately fashion.

'Some important people must be buried here,' Aralia murmured as the lights began to settle into a still glow.

James took a few steps forward until he was standing in amongst the first set of tombs. 'People must not come here anymore,' he breathed. 'It's so hidden away.'

'And why so close to the prison?' Will asked. 'It can't be for the prisoners.' He went to join James by the stone slabs, running his fingers over their rough surfaces.

'Or the slaves,' Arthur added, remembering the acrid black smoke with a shudder.

James shook his head and reaching out, let one of the small lights hover in his hand. 'It must be here for a reason,' he insisted. 'There's magic in here too, it must have different rules because it's a tomb.'

He began to wander between the tomb stones, his shadow enlarged by the strange light. The tomb was eerily beautiful, and his footsteps seemed to taint the mysterious silence. Each tomb bore a different symbol, carved by some unknown hand. Slipping behind the pillars, James came across another opening to his right. It was an arch, thrust into semi darkness and only just high enough for him to pass under. Before he slipped through, he reached out to draw another light into his palm.

The room he entered contained fewer tombs and the walls were lined with statue-filled alcoves. James felt as if he'd entered an unseen world were the dead had rested undisturbed for many years. As he passed between the graves, he ran his eyes over the symbols etched on each. Each was unique, no circle or line ever the same as the one beside it. He found himself remembering Arvad's symbol, the circle filled with the six-pointed star. The grave in Lover's Wood and the prison records had both born the same symbol. It was a clue, a trail of symbols leading towards their destination. As his mind processed this thought, a new and wild idea came to him. Burning with excitement, he rushed over to the archway and called to his friends who were lost amongst the maze of tombs.

'What is it?' Arthur asked as he entered the smaller tomb. 'Have you found something?' He looked around as if expecting to see something obviously striking.

James shook his head but nodded quickly after. 'I haven't found something exactly, but I've had an idea. 'These symbols on the graves made me think about Arvad's six-pointed star again.' He paused for effect.

'What about it?' Will asked impatiently.

James grinned at him. 'I've been convinced all along that it's the blood ruby we're looking for, but I think that's wrong. Elra showed us another type of ruby in the caves, the star ruby with the asris inside.'

'Asterisk,' Will corrected.

Arthur however nodded to James in understanding. 'You think the star in Arvad's symbol might link to the star in the ruby,' he stated. 'A crystal which represents his own symbol.'

James nodded. 'Exactly! It would make sense, but I could still be wrong. We need to find the Hidden City and then we'll know for sure.'

Arthur and Aralia nodded in agreement and turned to go. Only Will remained still, his face turned to one of the alcoves carved into the cave wall. Reaching into his pocket, he drew out a small coin and placed it on the narrow shelf before turning to follow his friends.

'Respect for the dead,' he whispered to James who was staring at him with a puzzled frown.

James nodded and they passed out into the hall again. A door stood to their right between the pillars, a small wooden rectangle which they hadn't noticed before. Arthur tried it and it opened easily, revealing a wintery scene beyond. Unhesitatingly, they all stepped through and only James paused for a moment to look back. The whispering had started again and as he looked, the lights inside the tomb began to fade. Tearing himself away, he shut the door tightly behind him and watched in awe as it merged into the rock, concealing the secrets of the tomb once more.

James hurried to join his friends who had moved a little distance ahead. The surrounding landscape was bare but strangely beautiful with its clean white decoration. There were no houses in sight and only a few trees were scattered here and there. Bending down, James scooped up a small handful of snow and unable to resist, flung it at Will. It struck his friend directly in the back and he turned around laughing before sending one back at James. In their desire to forget their troubles, all four of them soon became lost in a haze of powdery white. It was soft and wet but they didn't stop until their hands became too numb to scoop up the snow. Laughing and shivering they began to walk again, moving swiftly to keep themselves warm.

'The Hidden City must be somewhere in this region,' James panted.

No one answered him as they were all thinking the same. They found themselves walking alongside the craggy line of rocks again. It grew colder as they went, the warmth from occasional rays of sun fading as the freezing dark clouds set in. Nothing in the landscape changed until, after hours of walking, they spotted a cluster of overhanging branches up ahead. The leafless limbs spread thickly over the layers of rock which towered above them before drooping down over a long ridge. On reaching this scene, James pushed the fronds firmly aside and looked behind them. Hidden on the other side was a small opening, a roughly cut tunnel which was only a few feet long. Driven by curiosity, he dropped to his knees and after beckoning to Will, Arthur, and Aralia, crawled forward.

Chapter 22

ON the other side the landscape changed completely. Emerging from the tunnel, James found himself in an open hollow set between high faces of rock. The snow had not settled here as the space was protected by these mossy ridges. Set right in the centre was an open body of water which stretched out a short distance before disappearing between two vast, naturally formed columns. Anyone standing on the heights above could have looked straight down into the water and the surrounding hollow.

The rich scent of moss hovered in the crisp air and tingled in James' nostrils. Walking over to a smooth rock ledge, he sat and gazed out at the lake in silent wonder. His friends came to sit beside him, staring at the scene with a similar sense of awe. It grew darker around them and a half-moon slipped out, illuminating the water with its soft yellow glow. Its path fell directly between the two columns, disappearing behind them just as the water did. Aralia suddenly went rigid beside James and pointed at the water.

'Did you see that?' she asked in a hushed voice.

'See what?' James frowned and followed Aralia's finger with his eyes. 'I can only see the lake.'

'Between the columns, I saw something. I don't know what

it was.' Aralia stood and went to stand at the water's edge.

'I can't see anything either,' Will said and Arthur nodded in agreement.

'Look again, right between the rocks where the water seems to disappear.'

James focused his eyes on the edge of the water where the light faded. He couldn't see anything and opened his mouth to speak but Aralia held up a hand. She knelt by the water and stared hard at the space between the columns.

'Don't you see,' she said with a smile. 'We're looking at the way to the Hidden City.'

'The Hidden City?' Will moved to kneel beside her. 'That's impossible. We can't have found it that easily.'

Aralia smiled again and pointed to the path of moonlight on the water. 'Like all things hidden, it rests where the light can't reach.'

'What are you talking about?' Her brother, quiet until now, looked at her as if she were mad.

'Death,' she replied. 'The voice in the tomb said the same words. It was a clue, but I didn't realise it until now. It was another riddle, the answer to finding the city. The city is hidden in shadow behind the columns apart from when the moon shines between them. The light reveals the city.'

James gaped at her. 'Genius,' he whispered under his breath.

He focused his eyes on the water again, waiting for the moon to emerge from behind a cloud. As he watched, several shapes appeared between the columns that could easily be mistaken for wavering shadow. If Aralia hadn't seen it first, he would have doubted the vision and the city would have been lost.

'Is it real or just another of those illusions like the Lover's Wood?' he asked quietly.

Aralia gave a small shrug. 'I don't know, it could be.'

Something else was moving on the water but James couldn't tell what it was. He pointed to it and they all watched it grow closer with increasing apprehension. Afraid of being seen, they stepped back into the entrance of the tunnel and watched from the shadows. The shape came closer, making the water ripple gently around it as it glided along. As it came towards the bank, James realised it was an empty wooden boat. He waited for it to come to rest by the bank before stepping out from the tunnel with a laugh.

'It's just an empty boat,' he commented.

Aralia came to stand beside him. 'Is it a trick?' she asked, looking suspiciously at the vessel. 'It's tiny and it hasn't got oars.'

Ignoring his sister's doubts, Arthur stepped down into the boat. He reached out an arm and helped a reluctant Aralia in before Will and James climbed in also. As soon as they had settled themselves, the boat began to move again of its own accord. None of them spoke but they clung onto their seats as the boat glided across the glassy blue water. To their left a waterfall came into sight, cascading down the side of the ridge and spraying into the water. In his seat at the bow of the boat, James felt the spray strike his face. Leaning over the side of the boat, he let his hands trail in the water and watched as the ripples merged with the boat's wake.

Halfway between the vast columns and the shore, the boat began to slow and came to a sudden halt. James, Will, Arthur, and Aralia stared at the expanse of lake that surrounded them before turning to each other in confusion.

'Why's it stopped?' Will asked, voicing everyone's thoughts.

Will silently raised his left palm to the front of the boat. A gentle yellow light glowed for a moment before flickering out.

'The boat won't respond to magic,' Arthur told him calmly. 'It's already enchanted, that's why we can't use magic on it. You were right, Rai, it was a trick after all.' He fell silent and peered dismally into the water.

'We could paddle with our hands?' Will suggested half-heartedly.

James shook his head. 'If the boat won't move, then we'll have to.' He looked over the edge of the boat into the water with a strange expression on his face.

'No way,' Will replied with a horrified expression. 'Anything could be in the water. You can't have forgotten the black lake already!'

Ignoring Will's protests, James slowly removed his shoes and lacing them together, hung them around his neck. His friends watched him as he slowly stood up, causing the boat to lurch beneath him. With unsteady legs he stepped onto one of the wooden benches and after a moment of contemplation, jumped. The water was much colder than he had expected, and he felt it close all around him. Squeezing his eyes shut against the sting he propelled himself upwards until he felt himself break out into the open air.

'I'm fine,' he called over to the boat. 'Are you coming or not?'

There was a sharp splash as Arthur leapt in, followed by Will and a shivering Aralia. James grinned at them all through chattering teeth.

'Let's swim and get out of the lake quickly, its freezing.' He turned in the water and began propelling himself towards the columns.

'Where're you going?' Aralia called. 'The boat was a trick and the Hidden City must be too. Let's turn back.'

'I'm going to find out if it's there,' James snapped. 'I have to.' He turned back towards the pillars and began to swim.

His muscles began to ache after only a short distance. The pillars which had looked close from the boat now seemed far away. The water felt cold around him and it splashed into his nose, making him sneeze. He could hear the others splashing behind him and couldn't help feeling relieved.

'It's so cold!' Aralia's stuttering voice reached him. 'It's got worse, I'm sure.'

'It's fine, just keeping swimming,' Arthur called as he powered ahead of James.

James took a great gulp of air. 'It is freezing I can hardly move my fingers,' he commented to Aralia.

Will swam up beside James, his teeth chattering behind his lips which had turned blue. 'James, listen to me,' he said urgently. 'It's another trick, a game. The water will get colder until we freeze to death.'

James suddenly felt sick. He could feel his arms going numb and the columns were still a good few feet away. When he breathed out a white cloud froze in the air above his face and he shivered uncontrollably.

'Swim for your lives!' He tried to shout but his voice was dying inside him. Will was right, it was all an elaborate trick which he had fallen for.

They all tried to breathe slowly and move their limbs as quickly as possible. Every now and then the thin wisp of moon went behind a cloud, plunging them into complete darkness. The water became even more threatening and James felt his chest constrict as darkness swallowed him. At last the clouds drew away altogether and seeing the columns directly ahead, James gave one final push and crossed between them. Turning to look behind him, he saw Arthur and Will propelling Aralia forward over the last stretch.

As they passed through, the air underwent a sudden change and the lake disappeared behind them. The cold freshness of the air was instantly dominated by the rancid odour of smoke, mingled with the unhealthy stench of mould. Houses and buildings appeared from nowhere, lining the edge of the water which had now narrowed into a small channel. It looked ugly and green in the moonlight and James could feel himself tingling in its grimy warmth. The houses and buildings were made from brick, stained dark by the smoke that hung invisible in the air. Craning his neck, James noticed other lanes of water between the buildings and streets too. It reminded him of Venice which he'd visited once, only this place was much less beautiful.

Here, there was a different kind of history written in the air, one riddled with magic and darkness. The people walked with a purpose, never stopping or bumping into one another. It was as if each person was wrapped in a world of their own. No one noticed the strangers in the water, in fact no one looked up at all.

'The Hidden City,' James breathed to himself, gazing at it in wonder.

The wall running alongside the channel was low and James pulled himself up easily. He looked down at the others and saw Arthur was supporting a white-faced Aralia in the water.

'James, can you pull her up and me and Will can push her?'

James sat on the wall with his feet hanging down and his clothes dripping wet. Holding his hands out, he grabbed Aralia by the arms but as he tried to lift her up, she slipped back down into the water. On the second attempt, he managed to grab her wrists and with a great effort, heaved her onto the street beside him. She fell onto her back, a small moan escaping her lips. He leant over her but was pushed away by Arthur who had clambered hurriedly out of the canal.

'She's cold,' Arthur said, his voice cracking. 'We need to get her into dry things.' He stood up and scanned the street. A woman was walking along on the opposite side, close to the houses, and Arthur hurried over to her.

'Excuse me, can you help?' There was no reply and the woman kept walking, her eyes fixed ahead. 'Can you hear me?' Arthur tried again and when she didn't answer he grabbed her sleeve. She stopped abruptly and turned her cool grey eyes onto him.

'My sister needs help.' He pointed to where she lay.

The woman looked at Aralia and her expression changed. She hurried over and knelt beside her, touching the cold skin with her own warm hand.

'Can you lift her?' she asked the boys and they nodded in reply. 'Then follow me.'

Arthur supported her head and arms while Will and James took her feet. Keeping their heads bent and covered, they hurried after the woman who walked at a swift pace. The shadowed streets and buildings ran alongside the canal channels and everywhere reeked of rancid smoke. Several of the buildings had rundown signs over the doors, announcing their purpose. James glanced at these as they walked, murmuring the names aloud to himself. They passed several apothecaries' and necromancers' lairs and one odd shop with a complex symbol over the door. James glanced inside as he went past, but the interior was dark.

Eventually they came to a small house which was built with

its back to the water. The woman cast a furtive glance inside before holding the door open. The boys carried Aralia through a front room and into another where a rough bed lay strewn with blankets.

'Leave her with me,' the woman commanded softly. 'Go into the front room, no one else is here. If anyone does come in, tell them nothing about why you are here.'

The boys left Aralia with the woman who ushered them out into the adjoining room. Arthur glanced suspiciously behind him but the woman closed the door and his view was cut out. The room they entered was dimly lit by an orb which hung over a cluttered wooden desk in the corner. Shelves lined the walls, crowded with dark bottles, boxes, and unidentifiable things. Beside the desk was another door leading to a third room which lay completely dark. The boys waited in fearful silence, hoping the woman would come back quickly. Will reached out to one of the shelves and took a small stone into his hand. He held it up to the light, observing the strange mark on its surface.

'What is it?' James asked.

'It's a mark of alchemy,' Will replied, running his fingers over the engraving. 'I've read about it before, but I've never seen it done.' He hurriedly placed the stone back on the shelf.

'Is alchemy a form of dark magic?' James asked. 'Do you think the woman is a sorcerer?' He looked from Will over to Arthur who stood toying with a small glass ball.

Will shrugged. 'Alchemy is the art of turning metals into gold. It isn't dangerous like some magic, but this city is a strange place and we've got to be careful. We have to find the missing pages and find out about the eternal fire.'

As he stopped speaking, a new voice sounded. 'What do you want with eternal fire?' it asked.

Chapter 23

THE boys whipped around to see a short man standing in the doorway of the dark room. He was leaning heavily on a walking stick, although his light brown hair suggested he was not yet old. James held his breath, horrified that the man had heard Will's words. He hadn't forgotten the woman's warning that they should not tell anyone why they were here and he swallowed uncomfortably. He watched as the man entered the room and took a seat at the desk.

'You are strangers to the Hidden City, seeking knowledge like many others. What do you wish to know?' His voice was harsh and demanding. The boys looked at him in silence, unsure of what to say. 'Do speak,' he said smoothly. His eyes were dark and expectant, never once blinking.

James lowered his eyes to the ground before he spoke. He knew it was too late to tell lies and the truth about their search for the eternal fire must be spoken.

'Is there a magic that can make fire eternal?' he asked quietly, keeping his eyes fixed on the ground.

The man looked at James sharply, his eyes bright in the light from the orb. He rose from his chair and stared piercingly at each one of them in turn before reaching for a book on his shelf.

'Such magic is almost impossible,' he whispered, 'but for a small payment I will tell you what I know.'

They each began rummaging through their pockets, looking for something to pay the man with. All came out empty handed and they looked back at the man in disappointment. Seeing their faces, he turned to the shelf behind him and removed three small black bottles from their resting place. Placing them on his palm, he held them up for the boys to see.

'In these bottles are three substances necessary to perform the art of alchemy: salt, sulphur, and mercury. Deep in the vaults underneath the city there is a gold coin. These vaults hold some of the most protected secrets on earth, secrets and objects that are rare or have been banned from view. This gold coin bears secrets which alchemists only dream of knowing. I will tell you what I know in return for this coin. You must bring it to me. Are we agreed?'

James looked at Will and Arthur questioningly. He was willing to risk fetching the coin if it meant learning about the eternal fire. They looked at him blankly and turning from them, James locked eyes with the man.

'We'll do it,' he stated, his voice coming out more quietly than expected. 'What can you tell us about the eternal fire?'

The man stroked his chin thoughtfully as he opened the book he had taken from the shelf. Holding his hand over one of the pages, he let a red light glow briefly over the inked paper. As this light faded, he beckoned for the boys to come over and turned the book so that they could see. On the page before them was the image of a fire, burning brightly.

'There is magic which can do everything,' the man began, 'but to make a fire eternal one would need power beyond human forces alone. Such magic requires both natural and human forces combined. Once created, eternal fire can only survive within something else. This might be within an object or perhaps something more complex like a living being.' He paused and pointed to the image of the fire on the page. 'It can only be made eternal by receiving a gift, for no fire is naturally born to live forever.' He stopped and slammed the book shut with a snap.

The boys looked at each other, faint smiles on their lips. The man's words confirmed what they already knew, that eternal fires did exist. They were also right about the gift making the fire eternal. Such a fire must live and breathe within the alati, a lion.

'What kind of gift creates eternal fire?' James asked. He could feel his heart beating wildly with anticipation.

Rising from his seat, the man returned the book to the shelf. 'I know of none myself. Fire is a strange, ephemeral substance which men have tampered with to make eternal. You three would be better off not meddling in these things.' His face had grown hard and he eyed James suspiciously.

A soft click made them all turn to see the woman standing in the doorway of the room Aralia was resting in. She stopped short when she saw the man and her expression grew icy.

'I didn't know you were here, Papa.'

He returned her look with an equally cold stare. 'You should know better than to invite strangers in.' He moved across the room towards the front door where he paused and turned back to the boys. 'Don't forget our deal, I know many who could wipe you out in the blink of an eye. You have a day.' Casting a final glance at the women he left the building, slamming the door behind him.

'She is well, your friend,' the woman said quietly. 'No harm done.'

The door behind her opened and Aralia emerged, dressed in dry clothes. Arthur hurried over to her with a grin and she flung her arms around him.

'Rai, you're alright!' he breathed. 'I thought...,' his words trailed off.

'We can go soon,' she answered softly, leaning against the wall beside her. 'I feel alright now. Dina gave me a drink which helped.' She gestured to the woman who smiled in response.

After a brief silence Dina left the room, only to hurry back with a tray of steaming mugs. Her hood had fallen back and her long hair flowed in coppery waves over her shoulders. Under her delicate brows, her hard eyes flickered around the room, resting on each of their faces. There was something different about her, something strange. Her neck bore a small tattoo of a butterfly and her hands were also decorated with ink, the black lines looking like scales. Setting down the tray she handed round the mugs with an indifferent expression on her face.

'Drink it and you'll feel better,' she commanded. 'It's a special mix.'

James sniffed the liquid with distaste, unsure whether to trust it. It smelt of smoke and salt and he choked as he drank the first sip.

Brushing liquid from his chin, he looked at Dina. 'Is there a library in the city?' he asked quietly. It was the same question he had asked Will back in Arissel, a time which now seemed so long ago.

She looked at him suspiciously, resting her hand on the frame of the open door. 'The underground vaults hide every book ever written, every poison, the rarest jewels. Down there you will find many secrets locked away.' Her voice dropped to a whisper and she looked slightly uncomfortable. 'What deal did my father make with you?'

James looked at his feet. 'It was nothing,' he mumbled, 'he just wanted something.'

Dina sighed and went to sit at the desk, toying with a fountain pen she found resting there. 'My father is not a good man,' she said directly. 'You should never have made a deal with him, but now that you have you must abide by your promise. If you are strong enough to come with me, I can show you the way to the vaults.'

They all nodded and Dina passed across the room to the front door. Arthur gave Aralia his arm and gently helped her out onto the street. Turning left, they passed between buildings until the canal came into sight again. Dina approached the water's edge where a set of metal steps led down to a small boat, much like the one they had travelled in. Seeing their troubled glances, Dina laughed.

'It's alright, this boat won't trick you.' She began to carefully descend the steps and gestured for them to follow.

Arthur, Aralia, and James sat on one bench whilst Will sat beside Dina on the other. She kept her eyes fixed in front of her, staring at the channel ahead with glazed eyes. The boat began to move of its own accord and looking behind, James saw a faint haze over the water. He knew instinctively that is must be the imprint of magic. The streets on either side of the canal were scattered with people. They walked past in their black gowns, the same as anyone else, but in this part of the city they wore no hoods. Most had grey hair and walked quickly, all unconscious of the boat gliding along beside them. There were fewer women than men and no children at all.

'This is where the elders live,' Dina announced. 'Those who

don't live in the temple at least. They guard the greatest secrets of the world and have more knowledge than anyone. They are considered holy and have great powers in necromancy and the other arts, both light and dark.'

James leant his chin on his hand and stared at them. An old woman was walking at the same speed as the boat and he looked carefully at her face. It was extremely old, framed by snow-white hair and so wrinkled that the features were almost entirely lost. Despite her aged appearance she walked with a confident step, never once stumbling. As he watched, James noticed her eyes were blank and hazy. Surprised, he looked at the man walking just behind her and saw that he too walked blindly.

'Is everyone blind?' he asked with slight repulsion.

'The elders are.'

'All of them?' Aralia looked puzzled. Some of the unnatural paleness had left her face but she still looked tired.

'Yes, all of them.'

'Why?' Arthur turned his eyes away.

'They give up their sight in order to access the most inaccessible places of their minds. The most powerful magic can't be seen by the naked eye.'

'How does someone get to be an elder? Are they just old?' James stared again at the people walking past.

Dina laughed. 'Some are too selfish to commit themselves, it's like a religion I suppose. Some are never born with the gift.' Her voice sounded slightly bitter and she stopped talking.

The boat pulled up against a wooden pathway and they climbed out. More buildings rose before them, a vast metropolis of windowless blocks and towers which suffocated under smoke and ivy. This area was riddled with the shadows of night and the air bore the scent of poison. The ancient wisdom of evil things lurked in the gloomy avenues and even the trees stood silent, as ancient and wise as kings. It was a haunted, loveless place, where all the secrets of the world lay buried beneath the ground.

Following Dina, they turned onto a street beside another strip of canal. Ahead there was a group of people, leaning against a wall and laughing loudly. It disturbed the peace of the place, but no one seemed to care. As Dina led them past the group, a young man extracted himself and stood in their path, grinning at them with a drunken smile.

'Visitors,' he said. 'How interesting.' He directed himself at Dina and muttered in a slurred voice, 'Who are they?' He rubbed his gingery beard with a fumbling hand.

'Customers, Marcus,' she replied sharply. 'You know our customers remain anonymous.' Her eyes flashed dangerously.

The young man's eyes paused for a moment on James. 'Children?' he scoffed to himself, 'Just children.'

'Please go,' Dina's voice sounded almost pleading now.

He leaned down close to her ear as if he was going to whisper something and she closed her eyes as if in pain. Then he stood again, no words having come and sauntered back to his friends. Dina continued to walk and the four of them hurried after her.

'Who was that?' Aralia asked quietly.

'Just someone I know,' Dina replied sharply. 'Now come on.'

They turned down another street and stopped abruptly. A circle of houses faced them, four half crescents with pathways in between. These looked unlived in and they surrounded a small, derelict courtyard. The walls of the buildings were damp from the waterways and had turned slightly green with the uncontrolled growth of moss and sludge. In the centre of this courtyard was an old stone block, looking like some sort of hut with two holes for windows. Dina pointed towards it.

'Here I must leave you,' she said quietly. 'There are many rooms down there, it's all very protected. You must understand that only a few of the vaults are publicly accessible. The others you must enter with a pass and some are forbidden. This entrance will take you to a safe place. Be careful.' She said these last two words softly, as if she really cared.

'Why have you helped us?' Will asked. 'We're strangers.'

She smiled. 'My sister was imprisoned because of my father. I don't want the same to happen to you.' She paused before continuing. 'Get a pass if you can, otherwise be careful of the guards.'

James nodded gratefully to her. 'Thanks,' he murmured and waited as his friends echoed him.

Together, they crossed the courtyard towards the stone hut. Just before they slipped through the rough doorway, James glanced back at Dina. She stood silently watching them, a sad expression on her face. She reminded James of someone, but he couldn't quite remember who. Seeing him looking at her, Dina raised a hand in farewell and he waved back before disappearing through the gloomy entrance.

Chapter 24

A set of stairs led directly downwards for a short way. On reaching the bottom, James found himself standing on a small square of floor surrounded by walls. He went to stand with Will, Aralia, and Arthur who were partly hidden in shadow. Suddenly, the floor began to move beneath them, first slowly and then dropping with neck-breaking speed. They all grabbed hold of each other as they continued to drop until the ground went still beneath them, thudding to a sudden halt. Everything became solid again and they were flung out onto an earthy floor where they lay panting.

'Where are we?' James asked, standing and brushing himself off. 'What was that?'

'No idea,' Will replied a little breathlessly. He too stood and rubbed his knees which had broken his fall.

Looking around him, James saw they had been flung out in front of a tall metal gate which reached to the ceiling. On the other side of this was a clean, bright passage which was lit by orbs. It looked out of place in the ancient city, filled with its dark alleys and shadowy secrets. Aralia reached out and gave the gate a small push.

'I don't think this is going to open,' she announced.

Above the central spine of the gate was a small plaque which glinted in the light. Several letters were etched onto it but they were muddled and made no sense.

'Is it in a different language?' James asked, pointing to the words.

Aralia shook her head. 'It doesn't look like it. I think it's an anagram of some kind. The letters must form a word which will open the gate.'

Arthur gazed at the letters, trying to rearrange them. 'Veny, yevn, nyev, eyvn? No I've tried that,' he muttered.

'We should've asked Dina,' Will said glumly and shook the gate. 'She could've told us. Come on, James, you're good with logic.'

'Not with words I'm not,' James replied.

He went to stand beside the gate and put his head in his hands, trying to think. Copying Arthur, he began to sort the letters into different word orders in his head. No logical words came easily to him and he sighed. The voices of all four of them merged together, whispering half formed words repeatedly.

'En, evy, vey,' Aralia murmured to herself. 'Envy!' she suddenly said loudly. 'That's it.'

As she spoke the word, the letters on the small plaque began to move into order and the gate clicked. James leapt up, grinning at Aralia as the gate swung open to let them through.

'Why envy?' Will questioned as they passed through. 'What's that got to do with anything?' No one answered as they all wondered the same thing.

A little way down the next passage another gate blocked their path, looking exactly like the first.

'Riped,' Aralia read out from the plaque in a puzzled voice.

'Redip, drip, pied,' Will murmured to himself and Arthur's

voice joined him.

'It's pride,' James stated abruptly. 'I think it is anyway.' He traced the letters out in the air but a clicking sound confirmed his answer.

'I think I know what the words are here for,' Will said with a grin as the gate swung open. 'Pride and envy are two of the seven deadly sins.'

The others looked at him in amazement and James clapped him on the back as they passed through the gate. After a few metres they reached a third barrier. The answer was 'lust', followed by the fourth, fifth, and sixth which read 'wrath', 'sloth', and 'greed'. At last they reached the seventh and final gate through which they could see a long room. Like the passage, it was painted brilliant white and was set with ten identical painted blue doors. Apart from these, the room was empty. Raising his eyes to the last set of jumbled letters, James read the word 'tnugloyt'.

'Which sin haven't we said yet?' Aralia asked, looking blankly at the letters.

'Envy, pride, lust, sloth, wrath, greed,' Will reeled off. 'I don't know what the last is.'

James had heard of the sins before but had never taken note of them. He stared up at the letters on the plaque, trying in vain to figure them out.

'There's a G, but we've already had greed,' Aralia said.

'I don't know,' Will replied blankly. 'No idea.'

'Gluttony?' Arthur shrugged doubtfully as he said the word. 'Is that even a word?'

'That's it!' Will exclaimed, making them all jump. He looked up at the gate and pointed to the shifting letters. 'Gluttony!'

The gate opened and they slipped through into the room

beyond. The space felt cool and heartless and was completely silent apart from the light tapping of their feet.

'Which door?' Aralia looked from one to the other. 'Do we choose any?'

James went over to one and reached for the brass handle. It felt cold to his touch and he gently twisted it until he heard a click. On the other side a set of stairs slanted downwards. He listened carefully but on hearing voices somewhere below, quickly closed the door. Will too tried a door and shut it, placing a finger on his lips. The first safe door was one along the back wall. No voices or any other sounds came from behind it and they all passed through. They hurried down a short staircase and found themselves in another bright passage. It was lined with doors like the room above, but these were painted black.

The four started down it in single file, an unspoken rule of silence resting between them. Every so often they stopped to wait and listen, but no sound came from behind any of the doors. As they neared the end of the passage Will stopped and tentatively opened a door to his left. Behind it was another identical passage and the others followed him through. Each door they passed through offered the same view and it was soon impossible to tell where they were.

'It must be a maze,' Will said loudly, his voice echoing in the passage. 'Everything's the same. It must have been built to make sure no one finds anything down here.'

'If all these doors have passages behind them, we'll never get anywhere!' Arthur said. 'There must be some logic to it.'

Will groaned and rested his head against the wall. 'Why did we think it'd be easy? Now we have no idea where we started!' He began pacing up and down the passage they were in. 'There must be some logic to it like Arthur said. There're fourteen doors on each side I think.'

James nodded whilst mentally counting the doors again. 'Yeah, fourteen,' he confirmed.

He too began to pace the length of the passage, cutting past Arthur who was standing in one of the doorways. His mind was racing, trying to figure out some sequence in the numbers which might give them a clue. The number fourteen bore no significance to anything as far as he knew.

'Fourteen,' he whispered to himself. 'What goes into fourteen? Seven, seven is fourteen divided by two.' The doors reminded him of several logic and labyrinth games he played on his phone and suddenly a new idea struck him. 'Seven!' he said loudly, his face lighting up in excitement. 'Fourteen divided by two is seven. There were seven gates leading to this place because seven is a magic number.'

'What're you talking about?' Arthur asked. 'We've looked behind so many doors and there's nothing there.'

James grinned. 'We've looked, but not in the right way. If I'm right, every seventh door will have a room behind it, or something other than a passage at least. There are several seventh doors, depending on which side you start counting from.'

Without explaining any further, he hurried down the passage until he stood outside the seventh door. Resting his ear against it, he listened for any sound coming from the other side. Hearing nothing, he smiled to himself and pushed it open. He was immediately faced by a dark brick room but as he entered a light flickered on. Inside were rows of cases filled with tiny insects and birds and James recoiled. Behind him, Will, Arthur, and Aralia entered and stood gaping. James turned to grin at them before exiting the room and walking to the other end of the passage. He counted the doors again and arriving at the seventh, opened it. Behind it was another room, glowing in a soft light.

'How did you work that out?' Arthur asked, following him in.

James bit his tongue to stop himself telling the whole truth. 'Something from my world made me think of it,' he said, avoiding Arthur's gaze. 'Here in the middle are the four possible seventh doors, but they have to be deliberately counted for it to work.'

The four of them entered the second room one by one. Glass cases glinted all around them, their edges bound with gold. They were display cases, filled with bottles, bowls, and boxes holding invisible contents. Some items rested on their own whilst others were crowded together so tightly that each could hardly be distinguished from the next. Under each case was nailed a blank gold plaque. James reached out to touch one and writing suddenly appeared under his fingertips. It said something in a language he couldn't understand but the case above it was filled with tiny bowls of powder. He went to the next plaque and touched that one too, watching in fascination as the words appeared. This case held a large blue bottle which stood beside a small vase and box. The words said, 'Elixir of Life, Necromancer's Vase, Bottled Nightshade'.

'These must all be rare things,' Arthur commented, leaning over James' shoulder. 'Elixir of Life, they must be trying to keep that hidden.'

'Bottled nightshade,' Aralia murmured. 'That's a deadly poison which comes from a plant. Its other name is Belladonna.' She stopped short as if suddenly realising what she'd said.

'Belladonna?' James asked. 'Like The Belladonna?' He could feel the air tingling on his skin, indicating that he was in the presence of strong magic.

'I guess so,' Aralia replied, eyes wide. 'She's as poisonous as her name. The plant is deadly and so is she.'

James turned away from the case. 'It's all poison and medicine in here and no books,' he said, changing the topic. 'Let's go look for another room.'

At every seventh door they stopped to peer inside, awestruck at the genius of the maze. In some of the rooms there were more glass cases with bottles, bits of jewellery and even animal parts like horns or scales. One room held a full display of rare feathers. It was much like the museums James had been to before, only much more complex and riddled with magic. He couldn't believe some of the things he saw existed, such as an iridescent dragon scale and a sea serpent's fang. There were still no books, but they continued searching through the rooms, lost in the magic of what they saw.

It was a long time before they came across a room containing books in great glass cases. Once inside, they split up, each searching a corner in the hope of finding Arvad's tale. The spines of each book were on display but many of the titles were in strange languages. Many looked too fragile to touch and had crumbled away at the corners. Walking between the cases, James found himself wondering if the languages here were the same as those in his world. He'd never been good at languages and therefore couldn't tell. As he looked through various titles, he caught sight of another glass case resting higher up on the wall. He tried to crane his neck and peer inside but couldn't quite reach.

'Will, give me a leg up so I can see inside this one, will you?'

Will came over and put his hands out and James climbed onto them, wobbling unsteadily. He gripped the edge of the case and looked inside, pressing his face to the glass. There was nothing inside and he sighed. Just as he was about to go down again, he thought he saw something red inside. He blinked and looked again but it was still empty. It had evidently been some trick of his imagination. Will lowered him down and he moved to look at another case. As he stood there, footsteps sounded outside the door accompanied by the faint murmur of voices. The four of them moved as one and darted behind the door, straining their ears.

'You understand exactly what I'm talking about,' a male voice said quietly.

'Yes, Zir, I do, but it's not of much value.' A woman's accented voice answered, sounding rigid but faintly nervous.

'Why would you 'ave it locked up then?' the man demanded.

James took a sharp intake of breath as the man's voice sounded again. He recognised it from Arissel; it belonged to one of the men he had heard down the alley in the underground city. He held his breath again and listened.

'Well, it's not a complete set,' the woman continued. 'There's a high price for viewing such an item down here.'

'Well tell me and I'll pay it. That doesn't bovver me at all. I can't take back nuffing to ve boss. Just show me ve coin and I'll go, no complaints, no trouble.'

At the word coin, Arthur, Will, and James all stared at each other. Dina's father had also told them of a coin and they wondered if it was the same one.

Outside the door, the woman cleared her throat. 'You are aware of the legends surrounding the coin, are you not? That's why you ask to see it, I would presume. Such a coin has been in the vaults for centuries, it is said it belonged to—' She stopped abruptly. 'It's in room 205. I will take you there, Zir, after we have filed some papers. Follow me.'

The footsteps and voices slowly faded away but the four remained still until they were certain the pair had gone. Will stuck his head out to check and nodded to confirm it was safe.

'The man,' James breathed. 'I recognised his voice from Arissel. I'd forgotten all about it but back there he was talking to another man who was threatening him. He called the man Scarface.'

Aralia gasped. 'He's working for Kedran?'

James nodded. 'He must be, which means he is also working for the dark. We have to get to room 205.'

'The coin,' Will added quickly. 'It must be the one Dina's father wanted us to find. D'you think he is working for them too?'

James shrugged but said nothing. He didn't know the answer, but he needed to find out. Driven by curiosity and a slight sense of fear, they all ran down the passage past the rows of closed doors. Pausing for a moment, Arthur bent to look at the brass handles on which the room numbers were etched.

'Room three hundred,' he called softly. 'Only a few more to go.'

They ran through numerous doors, pausing to check the numbers as they went. On several occasions they took a wrong turn, ending up in the opposite direction to the one they needed. After passing through the high 200s they began to feel more hopeful and James picked up the pace. The numbers on the doors began to count down and they reached row 220 choking for air. Turning into the next passage, they suddenly caught sight of two figures ahead. One was male, the other female and horrified, they ran back to the previous passage.

'Another door,' Will gasped, 'must lead to the same place.'

Fearfully, they turned from one passage to the next. The numbers rose and fell as they went but number 205 eluded them. At last they stumbled into a dimly lit passage. It wasn't bright and white like the others; the paint having faded to a dingy yellow. The lights too were darker, hardly giving off any glow at all. Squinting at the door handle beside him James read 211 and walked forward until he stood outside room 205. Pressing his ear against the door he listened for voices. All was quiet and he gently opened the door.

The room inside was the largest and most crowded of all the ones they had been in. There were things heaped everywhere, stacked on top of each other in no logical order. A huge pile of boxes rested in one corner, perching between two tall shelves. On the other side of the room were several glass-topped tables and numerous stacks of musty books. James went over to the boxes and lightly kicked one, only to release a stream of tiny beads onto the floor.

'Over here,' Aralia called. 'There are some coins on this table, but how do we know which the man was looking for? We don't even know why he wanted it.'

'We should be looking for the tale, not for some coin,' Arthur responded, looking about the jumbled room in despair.

James ignored them both. A faded red book had caught his eye, resting at the edge of one table. Hauling it from its resting place, he blew the dust from its cover and squinted at the faded writing. Unable to decipher it, he opened the book and began flicking through the pages. Right at the back he stopped, his hand hovering over the second to last page. On it there were six words scrawled in grey-black ink. They said, 'The Tale of Arvad the Wanderer'.

Chapter 25

'IT'S here, Arvad's tale,' James called. 'I've found it.'

The others stopped mid search and hurried over to where he stood. He held the book out and they each glanced over the pages in turn.

'Why's it in this room?' Aralia asked in a puzzled voice. 'Do you think the man we heard was really after the tale and not a coin?'

James shrugged. 'I don't know. Why would it just be thrown into a stack of books? I thought it'd be in a special case at least.'

'Well let's read it before the man gets here.' Arthur's sense of urgency interrupted his usual patience.

James glanced over the tale until his eyes came to rest on the part where his copy had ended. Although the tale was incomplete again, it was longer than the copy he'd found in Arissel. The words were written plainly, unlike those in Kleon's crystal book, and he began to read the tale aloud.

'Arvad had with him four gifts that he believed would suffice as an expression of his gratitude. To the fire he gave a piece of gold which he knew could bring eternal life. He asked the fire to hide the crystal within its eternal depths until someone came who would be able to use it for good. After accepting the gift, the fire did as it was bidden and taking the crystal from Arvad, hid it from mankind.'

He stopped reading and looked at his three friends. 'That's it, that's all it says.' His voice was riddled with disappointment. 'There aren't any details.'

'A lump of gold,' Will repeated.

'That doesn't tell us much,' Aralia said discontentedly.

Taking the book from James, Will traced over the words with his finger. His eyes gleamed with a strange light and he looked pleased with himself.

'Not just any lump of gold,' he said quietly. 'A piece of gold. A coin.' He let this last word linger on his tongue.

James stared at him, hardly trusting himself to speak. 'The coin, the one the man is looking for. It's the gift!'

Will nodded. 'And Dina's father also wants it.'

'Why would he want it?' James took the book from Will and closed it with a soft thud. 'He can't have known about Arvad and if he did, he wouldn't have told us about the eternal fire.'

'He's an alchemist,' Will replied. 'He heard us talking about eternal fires and must have known we'd be looking for the coin. He was lying when he said he didn't know about Arvad's gifts. Alchemists are always after gold and if this coin can make fire eternal then it isn't just ordinary gold. He's used us to get the coin for him.'

James tucked the book between some boxes. 'We have more than one enemy in this city,' he said quietly. 'Let's find the coin quickly and get out of here.'

They all spread out again, starting in the corners and branching out. Aralia moved back to the table of coins and after a while, James joined her. The coins varied in size, shape and colour and glittered beneath the glass tabletop. Some were tucked away in their own individual cases, whilst others rested on rich velvet cushions. A glint of gold caught his eye in the corner of the case and he leant closer. He found himself looking at a simple gold chain and sighed in disappointment.

A soft call from Aralia made him turn. She was standing on her tip toes and trying to see into a glass case on the wall above her.

'Come and look,' she urged.

She drew a glowing orb into a palm and held it up to the glass. James, Will, and Arthur gathered around her, trying to see inside. Resting behind the glass was a thin glass box and inside was a coin.

'This must be it,' she whispered.

'How d'we know it's the right one?' Will asked.

'You're not looking at it properly! It's engraved with a star.'

James also craned his neck and suddenly realised her mistake. 'The star has seven points,' he said quietly. 'Arvad's symbol only had six. It can't be the right coin.'

'It has to be,' Aralia insisted, 'unless Kedran's accomplice has also made a mistake. This is the only coin in here that's engraved with a symbol.'

'Let's take it out of the case,' Arthur suggested. 'We can look at it properly then.'

'There's no way in,' James returned.

Arthur ignored him and reaching out, pressed his palm against the glass. A thin curl of green light trailed from his fingers and ran onto the surface of the case. For a moment nothing happened but then the glass began to waver and ripple like water. James watched on, completely mesmerised by the process. Beside him, Will gave a sudden shout.

'Arthur, it's melting,'

There was a loud sucking sound as Arthur pulled his hand

from the glass. His skin was raw and burnt and he held his hand to his chest. Aralia hurried over and tried to take his hand, but he brushed her away.

'The glass,' he breathed. 'We have to erase my handprint!'

'There's only one way to do that,' Will answered and the two boys exchanged a glance.

'We have to break it together. Rai, James, you have to join in.'

They all formed a line in front of the case and raised their palms to face it. James closed his eyes and cleared his mind, letting the magic fill him. Gradually, a light began to form, and he opened his eyes. Four separate beams swirled towards the glass where they met and swelled. There was a flash as they struck the case and the glass shattered. The coin box fell to the floor and darting over to it, James pulled it from amongst the shards. Slowly, he lifted the lid and stared at the gold coin resting inside. It lay in a soft hollow and another dent beside it suggested that it might have been moved around.

'It has to be the coin of Arvad the Wanderer.' Will's voice was deep with excitement and satisfaction.

Still suspicious, James carefully drew out the coin. It felt cold in his palm and strangely heavy for its small size. Turning it over, he looked for the inscription and let out a small gasp. The back was engraved with two words which said, 'ara Arvad'.

'What does ara mean?' he asked and held the coin out for the others to see.

'For,' Aralia replied promptly. 'It means for Arvad.'

'You were right then,' James breathed. 'This is the coin and Arvad's gift. This is what made the fire eternal and is the key to finding the firestone.'

Will said something but James didn't hear because something

else had caught his eye. A light was coming from the passage and he blinked in confusion. The orbs in the room had dimmed and the four of them stood in a spotlight coming from the doorway. Will fell silent as he too noticed the change and he moved to stand behind James. Arthur and Aralia also huddled closer and the four stood together as a group.

Two figures were standing in the doorway and silence fell for a moment. It was abruptly broken when one of the figures cast a light into the room. James darted behind a shelf, quickly followed by Aralia, Will, and Arthur. There was a clatter as several boxes and bottles fell to the ground around them. Peering between the shelves, James watched as a man and a rough looking woman entered the room. The latter was dressed in a light blue cloak, emblazoned with a crest of what looked like a lynx and a boar. The woman sent another light towards the shelf and James ducked as several more objects fell and shattered.

There was broken glass everywhere, strewing the floor with dangerously sharp shards. The four companions watched in fear, frozen in their position of hiding. The man and woman came closer, advancing through the room and throwing aside everything in their path. Simultaneously, Will and Arthur sent flashes towards them but ducked as they ricocheted off the walls. The man and woman seemed undeterred and continued to forge their way forward. Will was breathing fast and turning to Arthur he flicked his head in the direction of the door. James saw Arthur nod and before he knew what was happening, Will had grabbed Aralia and was heading across the room. Arthur sent a curl of light towards their enemies, distracting them from Will's and Aralia's movements.

Alone with Arthur, James felt his courage seeping out of him.

Mustering his strength, he formed a weak light in his hand and sent it bouncing towards the woman. It faded before it reached her and she let out a short laugh of scorn. Suddenly a strange new light filled the room with a sharp, bluish glow. James felt his head begin to spin and he shuddered violently. Concentrating hard, he moved his legs a few inches until he was standing in view of the door. There was a straight path to it but for some reason he couldn't make himself walk.

The next thing he knew was that the light was in his eyes, so bright that he had to shut them. In the blindness of his own mind he leapt forward, filled with sudden anger. He felt himself collide with someone before he was thrown to the floor with such force that he lay winded and still. Forcing his eyes open, he saw that Arthur had disappeared. The room was deadly still apart from the blinding light which flickered into his eyes again. He squeezed them shut and listened as the sound of heavy breathing filled his ears.

'So it's you,' the man's voice said. 'Bin escaping us the whole way, running for your li'le life. Not so good now, my young friend.' James could smell foetid breath and he gagged in disgust. 'I wouldn't mind taking nuffing back to the old scum bag,' the man continued, 'but to 'er I do. She's terrible but very clever you see.'

James felt the heel of a shoe digging into his ribs and tried to wriggle away. 'Give me my phone,' he managed to choke. 'The light, turn it off and give it to me.'

'What's vat?' The man sounded sarcastic. 'Stupid boy, it's not yours anymore. It belongs to ve dark and I 'ave to deliver it to 'er. I might take you wiv me too, she'd be 'appy wiv me ven.' He pressed the screen to James' face again. 'I would kill you, but I can't do vat. She needs you.'

'What for?' James asked even though he already knew why. The Belladonna wanted to poison him until he became a tool for her to use against his world.

'None of your business,' the man hissed and kicked James again.

Angered by this, James began to move his limbs. As they loosened, he raised his hand and let a flash of light shoot from it. This time it did not miss its target and struck the man straight in the stomach. He staggered against the shelves behind him and the phone fell from his grasp. James darted forward and picked it up before turning to look at the man who'd slipped to the ground amongst the debris of the shelves.

'What're you doing,' Arthur's voice suddenly sounded in the doorway. 'Leave him, James, and run.'

James turned to the door with his phone gripped in his palm. For some reason, he felt the clock in his pocket tick faster against his leg and this made him look back at the man.

'The dark can't chase me forever,' he said boldly.

The man looked up at him and laughed. 'Ve blue light mark you always,' he whispered. 'It's bound to you, bound to your quest.' He stopped and raised a hand as if to strike.

James closed his eyes, feeling strength growing within him. Another light burst from his hand and sparked against a beam cast by the man. He then turned and ran towards Arthur and together they began to hurry down the passage.

'Through here!'

James found himself looking at Aralia's face through a crack in a door to his left. She reached for his arm and pulled him through into another passageway. Will stood at the far end and looked relieved when James and Arthur appeared. He pressed his ear to the door beside him and raised his palm.

'All clear,' Aralia said. 'Come on!'

They hurried down the passage with James at the back, his head still spinning. Will ran in the lead, blindly passing through doorways without knowing where he was going. They moved from passage to passage and became lost again in the maze of vaults which ran beneath the city. They were already exhausted when they became aware of voices shouting and footsteps running behind them. To James, it sounded like there was a whole group of people somewhere in the corridors behind them and he picked up his pace.

'We're in row one hundred and thirty,' Arthur called. 'We need to find door number one.'

The footsteps came closer and somewhere a door slammed. Aralia looked back and tripped, colliding with Arthur who was just in front. As they paused to collect themselves, a flash of light came down the passage behind them and Will flung open the nearest door. A room rather than a passage greeted him and he moaned in disbelief.

'Back the other way, wrong door,' he panted.

Their pursuers were halfway down the passage behind them and they ran to the other end. They passed through the last door on the left and James slammed it shut just as another burst of light smacked against it. They stood with their backs to it, looking at the passage ahead of them which was set with only five doors. Will tried them but they were all locked apart from the last. It was their only form of escape and one by one they slipped through. On the other side was a long passage with a set of stairs at the end. It wasn't a small flight like the ones they had come down, but wide and long and reminded James of the London Underground.

Running to the end of the passage, they all began to ascend

the stairway. The steps began to move with them as they went, carrying them quickly to the top where a metal door greeted them. Will opened it with a harsh shove and they suddenly found themselves looking back into the main hall. As they stood catching their breath, James noticed a figure standing by one of the doors. He put his finger to his lips and began to creep slowly across the wooden floor. The others joined him and they all moved silently back towards the seventh gate. They were halfway across the room when the figure spoke and they froze in their tracks.

'Don't move,' it commanded. 'Stay right where you are.'

'Who are you?' Will asked in his direct manner.

The figure still did not turn. 'I know who you are. You know what the punishment is for breaking into the vaults I'm sure.'

As the words trailed away the figure spun around. The form belonged to a woman whose grey-blue eyes fixed them with a blind stare. She was one of the elders and her soft grey hair fell about an old and wrinkled face. Her jaw however was set in a hard line and her lips followed the same stern pattern. She looked at them coldly, as if she could see them easily.

'I know who you are,' she repeated. 'I have been waiting for you to return the coin to me.'

'Who are you?' Will repeated.

'I am someone you made a promise to and I now expect you to keep it.' The figure began to waver and when it refocused, they gasped. Dina's father stood before them, his eyes wide and laughing.

'You!' James exclaimed. In his pocket his hand pressed against the coin box, his phone, and the gold clock beneath them. Just for a moment, he found himself wondering again what would happen if he turned the tiny gold dials.

'Yes, me, Merik.' The man laughed aloud and slicked his hair into place. 'The art of shape shifting can come in handy at times. Now, for the coin. I assume you have it, as you're trying to leave the vaults. There's no need to lie to me, we made a deal after all.'

'What do you want it for?' Aralia asked and flinched as he cast her a scornful glance.

'The coin which can make fires eternal, formed from the ashes and turned into gold. I want to know how it was done, something I can only do with the coin in my possession. I seek to find the eternal fire which lives because of this coin. Now give it to me.'

Will shook his head and stepped in front of James. 'We made a deal to give you the coin in exchange for all you knew about eternal fires. You didn't uphold your end of the deal and we won't either.'

Merik laughed again, longer and harder than before. 'No matter,' he muttered. 'If you won't hand it over willingly, I will take it myself.'

There was a flash of grey light and James found himself falling to the ground. He heard three thuds beside him as Will, Arthur, and Aralia also fell. Lying on the cold wooden floor he tried to move his limbs but found they were completely frozen. When he tried to use his voice, he found that it too had gone. He watched helplessly as Dina's father knelt over him and reached towards the pocket which held the coin. Desperately, he tried to roll away but the more he wanted it, the more difficult it became. His heart sank and he closed his eyes, trying to block out the image of the man smirking above him. He couldn't help thinking that Albert's doubts had been accurate because he was just ordinary and would fail after all.

Chapter 26

JAMES heard the voice in his head saying 'Run, run,' but whether it was real or a memory he didn't know. It irritated him as it went on and on, telling him to do the impossible. He lay like a lump of wood on the floor, not even able to turn his head to look at his friends. Beside him, he could see and feel Dina's father still fumbling in his cloak pocket, desperately trying to find the coin. As he knelt there searching, the sound of voices came faintly from behind one of the doors. A stricken look came into Merik's eyes and he rose hurriedly, looking wildly between James and the exit. With a snarl, he leant over James' frozen form and sneered into his face.

'This isn't over, not yet. I'll come for you and the coin, you can be sure of that.' Having said this, he moved away, out of James' line of vision.

Somewhere in the room something changed, and James sensed the man had gone. 'Believe,' the voice said in his mind, 'believe.' The words kept going round and round in his head until he thought he would go mad.

'I can't,' he thought back. 'It's impossible to move. Believe in what anyway?' He was puzzled as to why he could hear the voice now, even when his eyes were wide open. He couldn't see the figure in the mist, even when he closed his eyes, and this disconcerted him.

No one answered him and he gritted his teeth. Filled with anger, he tried moving his leg an inch, but nothing happened. Slowly, he tried to relax himself and think logically, letting his limbs sink into the floor beneath him. In his mind he focused on his leg and tried again, willing it to move. His knee clicked a little and to his amazement his leg suddenly broke free from its invisible bonds. Smiling to himself at this success he moved his other leg and before he knew it, was completely unfettered. Hurrying over to his friends, he knelt over them and spoke with urgency.

'Try moving, just imagine your body is able to move.' He lifted Will's arm up to help him, but it fell limply back to the floor.

Beside Will, Aralia had begun to move. James hurried over to her and looked down into her anxious face.

'Don't think about it, just let it happen,' he encouraged. He watched as her face went blank and slowly her arms become free.

Leaving her to herself, James hurried back to Will who still lay stiffly on the floor. Aware of the voices growing louder behind one of the doors, James spoke quickly and directly.

'Come on, Will, you've got to do this. Hurry up!' He cast an anxious glance behind him.

Nothing happened and Will remained frozen in position. With Aralia's encouragement Arthur had broken free and stood stretching his bruised limbs.

'Come on,' James hissed at Will. 'You're the bright one, supposedly.'

This comment seemed to spark some irritation in Will and with great force, he flung his arms out. Having done this, he was soon able to move his whole body and rose to stand with the others. As he came to his feet, a door at the back of the hall burst open and three blue cloaked guards emerged at a run. Leading them was a figure James recognised, the drunken man who had stopped Dina, Marcus. James stared at him for a second before his vision was obscured by flashes of light which bounced off the walls. Budged into action by Will, James ran for the exit. The four friends paused at the first gate and Aralia called out the clue, but the iron frame wouldn't budge.

'Why won't it open?' she asked desperately. 'Gluttony, it was gluttony.'

'Let me try,' Arthur said, pushing her aside. 'Gluttony,' he said loudly and clearly.

'No, look, it's changed.' Will pointed to the small plaque. The letters had rearranged themselves upon it and they weren't the right letters for gluttony.

Light flashed behind them, flickering dangerously closer by the second. They heard voices shouting wildly, calling for reinforcements.

'Close the gates and send word to the city. The city must be locked down and surrounded. There's been a break-in and a theft. Ring the bell and let the city know there are thieves escaping. They've taken the coin in room 205, yes that's room 205.'

Trying to ignore the guards, the four friends strained to work out their plan of escape. Will suddenly slapped himself on his forehead and raised his eyes to the ceiling.

'The clues have rearranged themselves but they're still the sins, just in a different order. This one is pride again.'

At this word the gate began to swing slowly open. Smiling faintly, James slipped through, followed by his friends. At each gate they paused to figure out the sin before hurrying on through, chased by flashes of light and racing against time. Imprisonment and death raced at their heels, threatening to take all they had achieved from them. A strip of light struck Aralia's ankle and she fell with a cry, her face twisted in pain. Arthur quickly hauled her up and dragged her along next to him, despite her sharp groans. There was not time to cast light back and they simply moved forward, desperately hoping they would make it in time. As they approached the last gate, they heard a grinding sound. More metal bars were forming over the original frame and the four stared at them aghast.

'Greed,' Will shouted.

The gate began to stutter and jerk, as if fighting against itself. The friends waited with bated breath, hardly daring to watch. After another lengthy shiver, the gate clicked and swung uncertainly open.

'Quick, we're just in time,' James gasped. 'Run through before it closes for good.'

They flung themselves through just as the gate scratched and shuddered to a halt. Before them was the square of ground they had first been thrust down upon. Standing firmly on it, they found themselves rapidly born upwards to the city. Gasping with relief, they mounted the steps and emerged from the stone hut into the dilapidated courtyard.

Snow had fallen whilst they had been underground and although it was daylight, the sky hung thick and dark. The magic of the snowy scene was however ruined by the sound of a clanging bell which rang through the city, announcing the presence of fugitives. It wouldn't be long before guards patrolled the streets, searching for the four thieves. They were hungry but knew there wasn't time to stop and eat or rest. James himself was horribly aware that his phone still rested in the hands of the dark.

'Which way out of the city?' Will asked, looking blankly at the maze of streets opening around the courtyard.

Instead of answering, James began to walk in the direction he thought they had come. They all thought they recognised the first few streets they passed through, remembering the greenish buildings and strips of canal. It was only when Arthur walked over a discarded knife that they realised they were lost. The alley they were in was unpleasantly dark and there were strange smells in the air, different to those everywhere else. Dark buildings closed in on the street, suffocating them as they hurried on through. A small patch of light shone at the end of the alley and they hurried towards it, sticking close together. The street was empty apart from a few rusty bins scattered here and there. Breaking from the darkness, they found themselves beside a new strip of greenish water. No boats rested on it and the streets around were empty.

Suddenly, James noticed a figure standing at the edge of the canal, its back to another dark alley. It looked poised, as if waiting for something to appear on the water. The figure looked familiar but James nevertheless eyed it with suspicion. As he watched, the figure turned and the face of Dina met him. Her eyes grew wide and James himself turned as if to run.

'Wait!' Her voice halted him, and the other three turned to notice her for the first time.

'Dina?' Will blurted the word before he could stop himself.

She approached the group at a rapid walk, looking suspiciously around her. 'What are you doing here, you'll get caught,' she hissed. 'The bell is ringing for you I would guess. There's no time to hang around. follow me, I can take you somewhere safe.'

Will nodded but James planted his feet firmly in the ground. 'I saw him in the vaults, he works as a guard. You're all in it together, you, your father, him.'

Dina looked at him in confusion. 'Who are you talking about?' she asked gently.

'That man, Marcus.' James spat out the words and turned away.

'My father is not a good man; I have told you that before. Marcus was only doing what his job asks of him, can you blame him for that.'

James shook his head fiercely. 'No, but you know him. How do I know that you won't give us away to him? Why should I trust you?'

Dina bowed her head, hiding her face in shadow. 'I am fond of Marcus, but he will never notice me. You will have to take my word that I won't tell him where you are. As for helping you, I will do what I can to save you. The law sometimes takes innocent people, I hate them for that. I had a sister…' She stopped abruptly and turned away to face the canal. 'Take my offer or leave it, the choice is yours.'

Will nodded vigorously at James who stood pondering for several minutes. Eventually he raised his eyes to Dina's turned figure and spoke.

'We will take it,' he said simply.

Without turning, Dinna gestured for them to follow her and started out down the street. They followed her for a while until they noticed the buildings had thinned out, replaced by tall trees. The canal wound out of sight and the four walked on with lighter hearts, leaving the city behind them. After a short distance, the roof of a building came into sight in amongst the trees. It was flat but ornamented with large carvings which could be seen even from a distance. Although none of them knew what it was, the sight of it offered the prospect of food and safety from the bell still tolling behind them.

'I can take you no further,' Dina said, coming to a halt. 'Follow the trees to that building, you will be safe there for a while. It is where the most revered female elders live and work.' Without another word she left them and walked away, back towards the city.

Breaking through the trees, the four companions found themselves standing in a small clearing directly in front of a large building. It rested at the edge of a wide, clear pond which was tucked between banks of moss. The building itself was beautifully constructed, set with ornately carved pillars that appeared to run the whole way around the structure. It was higher at one end than the other, the low end covered by a flat slat of roof. Just outside, standing distant from the rest of the building, was a stone statue of a young woman. It was completely white and its plainness contrasted with the ornateness of the temple.

'You are strangers here, at the Temple of Electra.'

Everyone whipped around at the sound of the voice coming from behind them. A woman stood in the doorway of the building, clothed fully in white.

'Erm, yes,' Aralia stuttered, unsure if this was a question or not.

The woman's face softened a little. 'Come in and welcome. You look cold and hungry. I'll have some food made for you.'

James turned to his friends with suspicion in his eyes, but they ignored him and followed the woman inside. Lingering behind a little, he tried to dismiss his fears before slowly entering the temple. Once inside, he gazed in awe at the ceiling of the hallway which was decorated with gold leaf and painted pictures. Chairs lined the walls and there were orbs everywhere, lighting the way. The woman led them through a door and into a side room which contained a long table, set with chairs. There were small alcoves all along the walls, each containing a miniature replica of the statue outside, presumably of Electra. Several were made from stone or metal, but many were cut from white crystal. At the other end of the room was another door and beside it an empty fireplace.

The woman gestured to the table and they sat silently. 'I'll bring food,' she said in her gentle voice and left quickly.

James sat with his head resting on the table, trying to stay awake until the woman came back. When she re-entered, she was carrying a tray set with four steaming bowls and some cups of water. After setting these down before each of them, she sat herself in a chair at the end of the table. Raising his head, James looked at her properly for the first time and realised with a start that she too was blind.

He began eating in silence, aware of the woman's milky eyes passing over him. The food was some sort of stew and he gulped it down hungrily, grateful for its warmth and substance even though it tasted plain. When he had finished his last mouthful, he looked up at the woman with a question on his lips.

'Are we still in the Hidden City?' he asked in a thin voice.

The woman smiled. 'In a way you are, but you need not fear. No one can harm you here, you are safe.' She spoke as if she knew they were fugitives and James shivered.

Rising from her chair, the woman proceeded to gather their bowls and without saying a word, left the room. James immediately turned to the others.

'Do we stay or go? They'll find us here, we didn't go far enough.'

'Let's stay,' Will replied with a sigh. His head fell onto his arms and his eyes slowly closed.

'We have the gift,' Aralia agreed. 'We don't even know where to go next. Without the gift, the dark can't reach the firestone. We've paused the race. Arvad's eternal fire is what we need to find next.'

'You speak of Arvad the Wanderer.'

None of them noticed the woman had returned to the room. Aralia felt herself blush deeply and looked down at the table to avoid James' angry stare. Arthur froze, his mug of water resting still against his lips.

'One of the seven brothers. There's no need to be afraid. You are not the first to come looking for the crystals of Arvad's legend and I'm sure you will not be the last.'

'What d'you know about Arvad?' James asked, his mind suddenly coming alive.

'I know many things. Not many people know the whole tale anymore. The full story was forbidden many years ago, the copies burned. People say it no longer exists in its entirety.'

Aralia leaned forward with curiosity. 'Have you read the full tale yourself?'

The woman turned her face towards Aralia and shook her head. 'No, I have not, but I suspect the full tale does exist somewhere. I have learned of Arvad over the years however, Arvad the Wanderer that is. Arvad is a different person entirely.'

'What, what d'you mean?' Will raised his head from the table, instantly engaged. 'There's only one Arvad isn't there?'

'No, there were two, but few people know this. There is a book, The Famort, kept here in this temple which tells of these facts. It is one of the three forbidden books and is seen by very few.' She paused to rearrange the corners of her robe before continuing. 'There were seven brothers you see. The sixth was called Ira and the seventh Arvad. Arvad was good and kind, but Ira was known as a liar and thief. When Arvad died, no one knew what had happened to him, he just disappeared.

'Ira was abroad at the time and seeing an opportunity, came back to his country under the name Arvad. Everyone thought it was the seventh brother. He changed his symbol to look like Arvad's, the seven-pointed star. He got away with this for the rest of his life until after his death they discovered his symbol was still that of the sixth brother. The secret was out. When they found out the true Arvad had died, they decided to name him not just Arvad, but the wanderer.'

As she spoke, James felt himself grow cold and a sickness rested in his stomach. In the space of a few moments everything he had believed and figured out crashed down around him. The clues about Arvad, the symbols, the grave, all lay in shattered fragments.

'Where did Arvad die?' he managed to ask in a strained voice.

The woman smiled gently. 'Arvad died at the place the legends tell of, the place where the crystals were born. They placed a monument to him in a tomb not far from here.'

Will's mouth fell open. 'A tomb?' He turned to the others. 'The tomb we went to, it must be!'

James looked at him in bewilderment. 'How did we miss it? We would have seen it, surely!'

'Then where did Ira die?' Aralia sat perfectly still, her hands folded neatly in her lap. Her question brought complete silence to the room again.

There was a pause before the woman spoke. 'Ira died in prison and was buried in a wood named…'

'Lover's Wood,' Aralia finished for her.

'Yes, the Lover's Wood, I see you have heard of it. Ira was in love with a woman named Celaeno. When he died, he was taken from the prison and buried in the forest with her.'

The woman shifted her head a little every now and then, as if she were watching each of them in turn. No one spoke and a hopeless silence filled the room. As if sensing the disturbed glances passed between her guests, the woman rose and beckoned for them to follow her. She led them through several more rooms until they reached a small bedroom, strewn with brightly coloured cushions which served as beds. A pile of embroidered blankets rested in one corner and the woman gestured to them.

'If you are tired, you may sleep now and rest your minds. If you need help, ask for the Sister Miri, for that is my name. All people are welcome and safe here, even fugitives. Not everything in this world is bad or evil. Light can be found in the darkest of places, remember that.'

She then turned to go but James stopped her, a question on his lips.

'What does Alati mean?'

The woman turned back, her hand already on the door. 'Al means wing, ati means fire. Together they mean winged.' Without another word she left them.

Will ran and jumped onto the first pile of cushions, burying his face in them and the other three went and sat, their faces heavy.

'It's nothing to do with the lion,' Aralia moaned, also burying her face in a soft pink cushion. 'Ira was in prison, not Arvad, which means the alati part is pointless.'

'The ghost must have thought I meant Ira, not the real Arvad,' James said in a strained voice. 'Sister Miri is old; she must have got her facts wrong. If not, I've failed. Everything I thought I could prove has failed. They were right, it shouldn't be me. I'm not the one supposed to find the crystals, I was never meant to be.'

He could feel himself slipping into his old habit of disbelieving everything around him. None of it could be real, it was ridiculous to have ever believed it was. For the hundredth time, he found himself wishing he could go to sleep and wake up back home, away from this torturing nightmare.

'We have the coin at least,' Aralia offered tentatively.

'We're fugitives, we're in a hopeless race against the dark, and they have a way to follow me wherever I go.' James sighed deeply and gritting his teeth, moved away to gaze out of the window. 'They can find me and use me to break into my world, to destroy everything. We don't know anything about the eternal fire, it could be on the other side of the world. The Belladonna will find a way to win, and I won't be able to stop her.'

Chapter 27

JAMES awoke with a start and looked around with bleary eyes. He was wrapped in a red embroidered blanket which had wound itself tightly around him as he slept. As his eyes adjusted to the light peeping in through the windows, he remembered that he had been dreaming about Arvad. He closed his eyes again, wishing he could forget everything. With the six-pointed star a false clue, the alati also became meaningless and there was nothing left to guide him towards the firestone. It was lost for good and would soon undoubtedly be in the hands of the dark. Opening his eyes again, he saw someone standing by the doorway and sitting up, realised it was Aralia. She smiled faintly at him and came to stand by his makeshift bed.

'I've been exploring,' she said in a low voice. 'You three were taking ages to wake up. Arthur's still snoring!' Her voice was strained with a false cheerfulness and even her smile looked forced.

'How long have we been asleep?' James asked.

'I'm not sure,' she replied. 'Most of the women are sitting next door. I saw them all through a crack in the door. Come, I'll show you.'

Shaking off his blanket, James followed her out of the room

and across the hall to where another door stood ajar. Aralia beckoned to him and stood aside, allowing him to peer in. A large group of white-cloaked women were sitting on the ground, holding their left palms out towards a statue of Electra. Feeling as if he shouldn't intrude on this scene, James stepped quickly away, following Aralia who had disappeared into another room. Entering the space, he stared about him in awe. There was gold everywhere, decorating the ceiling and walls and seeping out onto the floor tiles. At the opposite end of the room was an alter covered in a gold cloth and set with three tall vases. On the wall behind this was a painting of seven young women, all dressed in white apart from the central figure who was arrayed in gold.

Aralia approached the alter and touched one of the vases, very gently as if she knew she shouldn't. James came to stand beside her, gazing at the painting of the seven women with interest. The golden figure in the middle stood out from the rest and he guessed it was meant to be Electra. A flash of movement beside him captured his attention and turning, he saw Sister Miri standing in the doorway. Her white gown was slightly loose around the neck, revealing a gold chain resting on her throat. She smiled at James who nudged Aralia, making her turn around too.

'You've found the gold room I see,' she said gently. 'The sacred room.'

'What's it used for?' Aralia asked, her voice respectfully quiet.

The Sister moved into the room and gently took one of the gold statues from the alcove closest to her. 'In this space we welcome those who wish to become elders. Here they swear their oaths to our sacred lady Electra and give up their physical sight to see the wisdom beyond.'

Aralia took the statue which Sister Miri handed to her. 'Is

Electra a goddess or a human?' she questioned, turning the cold metal figure over in her hands.

'You don't know?' Sister Miri sounded surprised at this. 'Electra comes from the sister tale of Arvad the Wanderer, the tale of the seven sisters. In myth and legend the seven sisters were stars, known as the Pleiades. The tale goes that Arvad and his six brothers each loved one of the sisters, but before they could claim them, they had to present their bride with a gift. One such gift was this temple here, dedicated to Electra by her lover. We now use it as a place to worship her goodness. The woman Ira loved, Celaeno, was also one of these sisters.'

A knock sounded on the door outside and the Sister stopped speaking, her ears alerted by the sound. With a faint nod she hurried from the room, closing the door behind her. Curiously, Aralia and James crept after her and opening the door again, peered out into the hallway. A man stood on the steps outside, his black cloak contrasting with the whiteness of Sister Miri's gown. He smiled, and James started sharply, recognising the face of Kedran.

'Who enters the Temple of Electra?' Sister Miri's soft tones asked.

'Forgive me.' There was a malevolence hidden beneath the smoothness of his reply. 'I wondered if you might help me?'

Sister Miri directed her guest through to another room and closed the door behind them. Their voices fell silent and James sighed nervously, wishing he could hear what was being said. He and Aralia remained in their position behind the door, waiting for the figures to reappear. After a few minutes, they were rewarded by the sight of Sister Miri exiting the room and hurrying across the hallway. She disappeared through a narrow wooden door, leaving it ajar behind her. Just as he was about to slip out and follow her, James saw Will and Arthur emerge from the bedroom. He stepped from his hiding place and waved to them before placing a finger on his lips.

The faint hum of voices trickled from behind the door through which Sister Miri had disappeared. James crept closer to it, ignoring his friends' puzzled expressions. Leaning to look through the crack, he saw the coast was clear and slipped through. On the other side was a small, empty room with a singular door at one end. Through this, James could hear the voices of two women in conversation.

'He has come asking for answers I cannot give, for I am bound by the secret.' Sister Miri's voice rose and fell as she spoke. 'I cannot cast him out, for he is a guest at the temple.'

'Sister Miri, you are one of three who know of the secret. You must keep it this way, you cannot tell him anything.' The other voice was louder, more definite.

'He has come asking for what we always feared. Somehow, he knows of the dragon in the mountains, our sacred dragon. The secret has lain hidden for centuries but now it is a secret no more.'

'I will send a message to the third one of us when she returns from the mountain at dusk,' the second woman said, 'but hush now. There are unwelcome ears in this place. We must speak no more.'

The sound of movement caused James to leap backwards across the room and out into the hallway again. His friends stood there watching him but at his swift movement, they followed him out into the hallway. No one spoke until they reached the safety of their room again. Drawing the coin from his pocket, James held it out for everyone to see. His voice was quiet when he spoke.

'Wing and fire. What does that make you think of?' Wings and fire. It's a dragon don't you see? We're looking for a dragon, not a lion, a dragon which lives right here in these mountains. It's the last piece of the puzzle; we haven't lost everything.'

Will still looked a little puzzled. 'How d'you know?'

'Kedran is here in the temple. Aralia and I saw him. Sister Miri said he is looking for a dragon, one which lives in the mountains. He was after the coin, and now the dragon. It all seems to make sense.' He returned the coin gently to his pocket.

'Of course,' Will returned, his eyes suddenly filled with understanding. 'Dragons like money, and that's why Arvad gave the fire a coin to make it eternal.'

James nodded vigorously. 'Once given the coin, the fire revealed the ruby but hid it again within a dragon's breath. It's genius.'

Arthur sat down on one of the cushions and nodded in agreement. 'The puzzle is solved,' he said quietly. 'The gift is yours and we know where the firestone is hidden.'

Standing by the window, James looked calmly out onto the wintry scene. Outside, a wide stretch of land ran all the way to the base of the snow-capped mountains which they had first seen on entering the city. A pale sun was shining, hitting the peaks of the lower mountains with a glinting sharpness. The ground between these and the temple was studded with rocks and the only sign of human habitation was a stone hut jutting out of the landscape. The view was beautiful but arresting, and James looked at it with a strange dissatisfaction.

'We're nearly there,' he breathed.

As he watched, he noticed a white cloaked figure emerging from the little hut. The figure turned towards the temple for a moment and James caught sight of a young woman's face.

Before he could look more closely however, she raised her hood and moved away towards the mountains.

'She must be the third one who knows the secret,' James whispered to himself.

His heart was beating fast with anticipation for the final stretch of this adventure. He felt both alive and tired but knew they must leave soon to make up for the time they had lost.

'We should go,' he said decisively. 'We have enemies in the temple and outside it, looking for the same thing as we are. Come on.'

'Shouldn't we say goodbye?' Aralia asked tentatively.

James shook his head and opened the door to the hallway. 'It's too dangerous,' he replied. 'We can't let them know that we've gone. We need to have a head start before anyone realises.'

One by one they slipped into the hallway and out into the sharp air outside. A light mist had started to gather around the temple, obscuring their view to the mountains. They began to walk around the outer edge of the temple, ducking under each window for fear of being seen. As the wall came to an end they were forced to break away from its shadow, but the mist soon swallowed them into the landscape. They crossed the ground quickly and soon reached the stone hut. One by one they peered curiously inside. It was simply furnished with a low bed and simple table adorned with a pile of books. Aside from these items, it was completely empty.

Beyond the hut lay the path leading to the mountain range, now a faint purplish shadow in the thickening mist. A darker shadow lay to the right of this, its green, wavering body suggesting the presence of a forest. James led the way down the path, the thin layer of snow crunching under his feet. The mist trailing over the cold whiteness was unlike anything he had seen before and was strangely eerie. Trying to ignore the cold pressing in on him, he continued up the path which grew gradually steeper the closer they got to the mountains. The rocks also rose higher and their crumbling forms strewed the ground with loose debris.

After climbing upwards for a while, the path suddenly peaked and levelled out, broadening into a rocky plateau. The scene around was hauntingly beautiful, with swathes of mist drifting over the white sprinkled ground. The terrain was rough and difficult to cross, but James forged on, unwilling to lose time by stopping. It was colder on the higher ground and they all shivered, wishing they were safe within the warmth of the temple again.

'How far do we go?' Will called from where he had paused by a rock. 'We've got no idea which direction to go in.'

James drew in a deep breath before pointing to the ground. A thin line of footprints rested in the snow, belonging to a pair of tiny feet.

'I'm following the footprints,' he called back. 'I saw a girl leave the stone hut from the temple window. She must have been going somewhere.'

Too cold to reply, Will merely nodded and began to walk again. As the four continued across the plateau, the mist began to clear and a faint ray of sun broke through the haze. It shed light over the mountainside, glancing off the undulating, snowy slopes. The footprints stretched across the ground before them, a thin trail which was their only guide. They stretched on over the rocky ground, winding their way around the numerous protrusions. James followed the prints closely, leaving a larger print as he stepped carefully from one to the next. He traced the steps right to the outer edge of the plateau before eventually stopping to wait for the others.

'Look, the prints lead up the mountain again,' he said breathlessly. 'Let's climb to the top of this slope ahead. We'll be able to see better from there.' He paused for a moment longer, leaning over to try and tame the stitch which had already gripped his side.

'It's got to be miles to the top,' Aralia said blankly, shading her eyes from a beam of sunlight.

James ignored her comment and bracing himself, continued to walk. The others followed tiredly behind, moving up the path ahead in single file. The ground was slippery beneath their feet, forcing them to move slowly. As they climbed higher, the view grew wider below them. The roof of the temple could still be seen but the Hidden City had disappeared, wrapped in the shadow of its magic. Still in the lead, James paused again by a large outcrop of rocks to admire the view.

'We've climbed higher than I thought,' he commented as Will came to a halt next to him.

'Don't look up,' Arthur laughed, 'there's still a long way to go.'

Aralia remained silent, her eyes fixed on the slope below. Her face had turned pale and she pointed with a trembling hand to something at the base of the mountain. Several dark blots were moving there, slowly snaking their way up the mountain path towards the plateau.

'They're following us,' she whispered. 'There's more than one of them.'

James watched, feeling the inside of his body grow cold. They were so close to the end, but even now the race was still on as it hadn't yet been won. Someone was calling his name and he turned to his friends, only to find them all standing silent beside him. The voice was coming from his head and he closed his eyes, trying to hear it more clearly.

'James, James,' it whispered. It was the first time he had heard his name spoken. 'Do not stop to rest, the dark has a powerful weapon. This is a race you cannot lose.'

Opening his eyes, James waited for the voice to fade before turning to his friends. 'The voice, the voice in my head is warning me. We have to go; this is a race I can't lose.'

Whether the dragon and the firestone would turn out to be a myth after all, he didn't know. There was still a risk that everything could fail, even after all they had been through, but he wasn't going to give up now. He would make this quest work, he would make it his and defy the disbelief which others, such as Albert, had in him.

Chapter 28

'COME on!' James called to the others. They had dropped behind on the slope, but he walked on through the pain in his legs, driven by determination.

The sun had gone behind a cloud which hung in a purple haze over the slope. Any warmth it had provided was extinguished and the air bit sharply. Aralia stopped to pick some wild berries growing on several low bushes, but James didn't want to eat anything. The mixed feelings of anticipation, fear, and excitement all boiled inside him, leaving little room for an appetite. Occasionally, he scooped a pile of snow into his mouth to quench his thirst, but that was all.

The footsteps they had been following came to a sudden halt, but as they were close to the top of the slope, they continued to climb. They reached the summit just as the late sun peered out from behind the clouds again. Stopping with relief, they turned to check if they were still being followed. There was no sign of the black figures, but they were still aware that time was not on their side. Approaching the edge of the ridge, all four of them stopped abruptly and stood gaping. Below them the mountain dropped away in a sheer rock face, plunging down to the jagged ground below.

'There's some kind of pass down there I think,' Arthur said, stepping closer to the edge. 'Look, that thin strip of rock leads down to it.' He pointed at a narrow bridge of mountain rock which curved around to their left.

'What about the footprints?' Aralia asked, eyeing the narrow ledge anxiously. 'I thought we were following them.'

James shrugged. 'They stopped just before we got to the top, they can't have led anywhere.'

'Someone can't just disappear,' Aralia protested back. 'They must carry on somewhere.' She moved away from the edge and began scouring the ground for any sign of footprints.

'Come on, Rai, let's go down,' Arthur persuaded. 'It'll be more sheltered down there at least.'

Sighing, Aralia joined the others who were already making their way towards the natural bridge. It didn't take them long to reach it and they stopped at the edge, weighing up the best way to cross it. It looked narrower from this angle, stretching perilously down in a thin, snowy line.

'Why don't we go up the mountain instead of down it again?' Will asked, keeping well back from the edge.

His question was ignored by James who had already put one foot onto the ridge. He moved forward slowly, holding his arms out to balance himself as if he were on a gymnast's beam. Aralia stepped on behind, encouraged by a gentle push from her brother. Arthur was about to follow when Will darted in front of him.

'I'm not going at the back,' he said decisively. 'No way.'

The first stretch of the path was uneven, making it difficult to maintain balance. On one side the mountain rose in steep, jagged rock formations and on the other it fell away down towards the pass. Uplifted by the crisp, clean air, James moved across the ridge with assurance, never once stumbling. He walked with his eyes fixed ahead, trying not to look down at the drop to his right. After the first rocky stretch, the path grew smooth with snow but they had to look out for hidden bumps at every step. The ridge started to narrow ahead of them too, the rocky sides closing in and making it almost impossible to pass through. The bridge became a thin line, squeezed between the two rock faces.

'I can't,' Aralia gasped, looking at the narrow piece of rock with horror. 'I'm going back.' She tried to turn back but there was not enough room to do so.

'Come on, just don't look,' Arthur encouraged. 'We're nearly at ground level again anyway.'

He reached past Will to give her another gentle push. She moved reluctantly, trying to keep her eyes fixed on the solid mountain ahead. Will himself remained silent, but every time he looked over the edge he reeled back uneasily. Distracted by a waft of powdery snow which fell into his hair, Will suddenly slipped on an unseen sheet of icy snow. He lost his balance and falling on his back, began to slither down the path. Hearing his shout, Aralia jumped to the side and watched in horror as Will slid past before toppling from the ridge. The fall was not far, but there was a soft thud as he hit the snow below.

'Will?' James shouted, leaning over the edge of the rock. 'Will, can you hear me?' There was no reply.

James reached the bottom first and ran over to Will who lay motionless in the snow. He rolled him over onto his back but still no sound escaped his friend's lips.

'Will, are you alright?' Aralia asked, hurrying to join them. She knelt in the snow and tearing a strip of cloth from her cloak, held it to the small cut on his head.

There was a soft groan and Will twitched in the snow. 'I'm alright,' he managed to gasp.

Relieved, the other three dropped to the ground beside Will who grinned faintly and pulled himself into a sitting position.

'Just winded,' he commented breathlessly. 'No bones broken.' He took the piece of cloth from Aralia, nodding to her in thanks.

Looking around, the four found themselves standing in a flat area which was surrounded by mountains on all sides. There was only one small opening directly ahead of them which revealed the dimming sky and the edge of another slope. A narrow pass wound its way up to their right, running alongside the ridge they had just come down. Although sheltered from the wind, this shallow bowl of the mountain felt cold as the air was pushed through the channel of the pass.

Looking back towards the base of the ridge, James suddenly caught sight of several prints in the snow. Standing, he hurried over and knelt beside them. He noticed with excitement that they had been made by a small, human foot and resembled the prints they had been following before. There weren't many of them however and glancing around, he found they stopped abruptly again. He was about to announce this discovery to the others when a faint movement near the pass caught his eye. Squinting, he tried to detect its source, but all he could see was white. Something moved again and his eyes focused on a wavering shape to his right. He pointed wordlessly at it, but found the others already staring in that direction.

All four of them watched as the white blur slowly emerged and took shape. It was a figure dressed completely in white and as they stared, it bent to the snow and touched it with a delicate hand. A strange light shone there for an instant, a shimmering, wavering glow which rested gently on the surface of the snow. Faint patterns appeared within the light, symbols of circles, half circles, and diamonds. They held their shape briefly before fading into the snow, the light disappearing with them. The figure straightened up and drawing the hood further over its head, slowly turned around.

Frozen in position, James suddenly found himself looking into the face of the girl he'd seen leaving the stone hut by the temple. She had an unusually pale appearance, the white skin of her face blending into the colour of her cloak and the snow around. Her eyes, shaded by almost invisible lashes, were such a pale blue that they too could hardly be seen. Even her hair was white blonde and it fell to her waist in straight sheets. The white ends just touched the edge of a thin gold belt which was held together by a buckle set with a tiny red gem. Looking at her, James felt mildly conscious of his own grubby appearance.

'Who are you?' the girl asked abruptly. Her voice was harsh and demanding, unlike the gentle tones James had expected.

There was an awkward pause in which James felt obliged to incline his head. The girl stared at him fiercely, her expression a mixture of youthful petulancy and adult wisdom. It was impossible to tell her age and James felt disconcerted as he looked back at her.

'We're looking for a creature said to live in these mountains,' he said quietly. He stared at her, his dark eyes lost in her pale ones.

She paused, as if thinking over what he had said. 'There are many creatures living in the mountains,' she then replied. 'What do you look for?'

Another awkward pause followed in which Will stood and stepped forward. He too bowed his head before he spoke.

'A dragon,' he stated, his gaze unflinching.

The girl cast a sharp, curious look at him. 'What makes you think dragons live here? There are rumours of many creatures, not all are true. What gives you such certainty?'

'We're not certain,' James responded. 'We came here hoping to find the answer. We came from the temple where Sister Miri helped us. You come from there, don't you?' He threw the question at her and saw her flinch as it struck her.

Slowly, gently, she inclined her head. 'I was from the temple and lived there once and knew Sister Miri well. I've not seen her for many years.' The girl grew lost in thought, her eyes resting on the patch of sky beyond the mountain pass.

In the ensuing silence, James felt in his pocket and wrapped his hand tightly around the box with the coin tucked inside. The glass top was smooth and cold pierced his fingers, but he felt reassured by its solid form.

'Did she send you, Sister Miri?' the girl asked at last in a faintly puzzled voice. 'Did she tell you of the dragon?'

James only paused momentarily before shaking his head. 'No, we left without her knowing.' Slowly, he pulled the coin box from his pocket and held it out on his palm. 'We came to find the firestone.'

The girl started and stared at the coin box in disbelief. She opened her mouth and tried to say something but closed it when no words came. Taking a small step forward she held out her hand for the coin but checked herself as James drew the box to his chest.

'The second coin of Arvad the Wanderer,' she whispered, 'the one that makes things whole. It's impossible. No one has found the gift for seven hundred years.' With effort she raised her eyes to James again. He met her gaze steadily, still clutching the box to him. 'Who are you?' she asked. 'How did you find your way here to where Arvad's secret has been kept safe for centuries?'

James let a faint smile escape onto his lips. 'We've raced against the dark to get here and we came to find the dragon,' was all he said.

The girl moved forward another step and her eyes bored into James. 'How did you know you could trust me?' she demanded.

'You're one of three who knows the secret; we followed your footprints up the mountain.'

Turning to look between Will, Aralia, and Arthur who all stood huddled together, the girl smiled. 'I suppose I must now tell you all who I am,' she murmured. The confusion had gone from her face and only her hand, which gripped the edge of her cloak, betrayed her. 'My name is Nuria, meaning light or fire and I am the dragon keeper.'

'So it is true,' Aralia uttered in hushed tones. 'The dragon exists.'

Nuria turned to her with a slightly disdainful expression. 'Yes, it is true,' she responded, the strength returning to her voice. 'I am the keeper of the Chinjoka dragon, guardian of the firestone.'

'Chinjoka,' Will repeated, 'I've never heard that name.'

'Its other name is the Azure dragon,' Nuria replied. 'It is the only one of its kind and is one of the four revered mythical creatures on this earth.'

'I thought Azure dragons came from the East,' Will said slowly.

Nuria shook her head. 'Once maybe, but they come from there no longer.' She lowered her head. 'I have been its keeper for only a year, hardly any time at all compared to some. Each time a dragon keeper dies, she is replaced by another who has

243

been trained in the arts. Some wait their whole life to be made keeper, others are chosen young. Only the High Priestess of the temple, the Sister, and the keeper know the secret.'

'Does no one ever see you and ask who you are?' Aralia asked, still with her nails between her teeth.

Nuria bowed her head. 'They believe that the one who lives in the hut is a sacrifice, sent to live meanly in tribute to Electra. For centuries, the dragon keepers have lived apart from the temple, ever since Arvad first asked the elements to hide the crystals. The firestone now rests here, in the eternal fire of the dragon's breath.'

'It's in the dragon?' Arthur stepped forward, his blue eyes wide.

James looked around him, searching of any sign of the dragon. There was no place where such a creature could hide as the ground around was flat and bare. Nuria saw his glance and turned around herself, scanning her eyes across snow.

'You are looking for the dragon, I have called him.'

They all watched in silence until they saw a movement beside the gap of rock which revealed the sky. Something white was shifting there, but it didn't look like a dragon. It moved towards them like a drift of snow blowing across the mountain pass in the wind and they watched in awe. Suddenly, it rose towering into the air, flinging the snow away from its huge body. The four ducked away from the spray, staring as the dragon settled slowly onto the ground before them. Like its keeper, the dragon was white in colour and its pale scales blended in perfectly with the landscape. The only colour visible was the red of its eyes which shone like small red jewels, bright and searching. They reminded James of the red stone on Nuria's belt buckle, the jewel signifying her role as keeper.

The dragon looked at the four companions and slowly bent its head. They bowed back respectfully, their awe for the creature silencing them completely. Once this was done, Nuria went to stand by the dragon and placed her hands on its scales. It lifted its head to her face and let her touch its long snout.

'He asks your purpose with him.'

'You can speak to him?' Arthur stared at Nuria with a mixture of curiosity and amazement.

She smiled at him. 'I am the dragon keeper; through me he has a voice.' She reached her hand up again to pat the white scales.

While she spoke the dragon sat still, watching the scene with its startling red eyes. James stared at it in awe and as if sensing his gaze, the dragon slowly turned to him and bent its head. Suddenly finding the huge creature on the same level as him, James stood as still as he could, hardly daring to breath. Boy and beast gazed at each other suspiciously until James remembered the case in his hands. He held it out to the dragon.

'This is my gift, in return for the firestone,' he said, his voice coming out in a cracked whisper. He waited for the girl to speak, but nothing happened until he heard a deep voice resonating in the depths of his mind.

'You do well to come this far, James Fynch, for I indeed hold the firestone within me. Your gift has long been awaited and I welcome you.'

Chapter 29

JAMES looked around to see if the others had heard, but their faces were blank. As he turned back to the dragon, he caught sight of Nuria standing a short distance away. Her face bore a puzzled expression and her eyes glowed fiercely. Trying to ignore her look, James took a step towards the dragon. Bending down, he placed the coin box gently on the snow between himself and the creature. The dragon's red eyes flicked from James to the box and from its throat came a low, murmuring roar.

At this sound, Nuria hurried forward and placed her hand on the dragon's head. The great body writhed in the snow, wildly thrashing cold flecks of ice into the air. James took a hasty step backwards, moving to stand in amongst Will, Arthur, and Aralia. Under Nuria's calm hand the dragon grew more peaceful and bent its long nose to the box. Suddenly, a thin, curling flame shot from its mouth, flickering across the surface of the case. Flames danced around the wood and the glass glowed hot as it slowly began to melt. The container fell into charred pieces, leaving the coin resting on the snow.

James turned to Nuria. 'What now?' he asked.

'You can speak to him,' she whispered. 'You must ask him for yourself. Your gift brings freedom and if he is willing, the crystal will become yours, for good or evil.'

James nodded and went forward to pick up the coin. He held it up within his palm and waited for the dragon to speak again.

'You must cast the coin between my eyes,' the low, rumbling voice said. 'There it will burn into my flesh, but this is what must happen.'

'Will it hurt you?' James found himself asking inside his head.

The dragon bowed its great head. 'For a moment, but my freedom will be greater than the pain. I have been bound to this task for many years and I am ready. Tell your friends to stand in a semi-circle around you and then do as I have asked.'

James turned to his friends. 'Stand in a semi-circle behind me,' he ordered.

Nuria sank into the background of the snowy rocks without saying a word. James held up the coin and gently placed it between the dragon's eyes. His hand met with the rough white scales but he didn't flinch as he'd expected. Instead, he held the cold coin firmly and began to press it down with his fingertips. Before he could control what was happening, he suddenly felt a warm light flickering around his head. Flames surrounded him, dancing in a ring around his body but never getting close enough to touch him. The coin began to heat up quickly, burning under his fingers until he could hardly bear the pain. He supressed his own cry of agony as he heard the dragon utter a long, deep groan.

As the sound died away, the flames also began to fade. James could feel the presence of his friends close behind him but he didn't dare move until he was bidden. Raising his eyes to the dragon's head, he saw the symbol of Arvad the Wanderer burned onto the white scales. He closed his eyes and tried to hear the voice in his head, but the dragon was silent.

'He can no longer speak to either you or I,' Nuria's voice said gently. She stepped out of the shadows, tears glinting in her eyes. 'He's free,' she whispered and raised a hand to brush away the droplets running down her cheeks.

'Where's the firestone?' Will asked bluntly. The ground between James and the dragon lay empty, save for the ashy remains of the coin box.

Nuria stepped away from her dragon with a sad smile on her lips. 'There were two coins belonging to Arvad, one which could hide the crystal and the other which could set it free. The second coin was lost for many centuries, buried by Arvad before his death. In return for the first coin, the fire took the crystal and hid it within a dragon's egg.' Nuria fell silent, letting her hand drift down over the dragon's back and down its tail.

'Every hundred years,' she continued, 'the chosen male dragon brings the egg here to rest protected until it is born. Once the egg has hatched, the adult dies, leaving a new protector of the crystal. You see, the fire is eternal because each egg keeps it alive.'

As her words trailed away, Nuria stepped away from her charge. Slowly, the dragon bent its head and breathed outwards onto the snow. A long stream of fire flowed out of its mouth, rippling over the white ground in shining red and gold ribbons. It was beautiful and mesmerising to watch and the flames continued to dance higher and brighter. Something then began to form in their depths, an indistinct object which glowed red and hot. It was only as the flames began to sink lower again that the shape became more distinct, appearing as a smooth, oval form.

Adjusting his eyes to the dancing flames, James realised that it was an egg, the dragon's egg. He felt the urge to leap forward and pick it up, but Nuria reached it first. The dragon stepped back and as the flames died away, Nuria lifted the egg. It was beautiful, the shell swirled with red and orange, and as she touched the surface a new glow formed around it. After holding it silently for a moment, she held out her arms and gently offered it to James. He took it without hesitation, feeling his arms drop under its weight.

'Thanks,' he whispered. The egg was warm beneath his fingers and he held it up for his friends to touch.

'You must understand,' Nuria half whispered, looking at each of them from under her white lashes, 'that the egg must break for the firestone to be free.'

Hearing her words, James lifted the smooth oval high above his head in readiness. A short bark from Nuria made him pause, unsteadily holding the heavy oval over the uneven ground.

'Not yet,' Nuria said in a rough voice. 'You must find the place where the crystal may be set free. At the base of this mountain lies a forest which will guide you and the egg towards the final resting place. If all is well, your journey may end there.'

James nodded, running his fingers over with smooth egg shell. 'How will I know when to break it?' he asked quietly.

'You will,' Nuria whispered. 'The egg has within it a dragon, the next keeper of the firestone. When you break the egg, the dragon inside must die to let the firestone live.' Her voice sounded strained and she turned her face away. 'This Chinjoka dragon is the last, and I the last keeper.'

Aralia took a step towards Nuria, her face pained. 'Is there no other way?' Tears pricked in her own eyes and she brushed them hurriedly away.

'None,' came the reply.

James looked down at the egg in his hands, wondering at the cruel magic of it. Nuria began to step away from the group, back into the shadow of the mountainside. The Chinjoka dragon also moved, fading into the snowy scene like its keeper.

'Thank you,' James called after them, but his words echoed meaninglessly around him.

The four friends were left standing alone in the hollow of the mountain. Wordlessly, James tucked the egg under his arm and moved towards the steep ridge again. As he stepped onto the base of the path, a deep, low call sounded behind him. It echoed around the mountain pass, a ringing note of distress which broke the strange peace of the evening. James stopped in dismay, realising that the mournful cry came from the Chinjoka dragon. Behind him, Will, Arthur, and Aralia also paused in their tracks, frozen by the haunting sound.

Arthur was the first to move again, stepping determinedly past James and onto the steep path. The others followed him, covering their ears to keep out the sound. James gripped the egg more tightly against himself, grateful for its warmth. Their ascent up the path was made difficult by patches of ice which had grown with the falling temperature. On many occasions their progress was reversed as they slipped on the ice and slithered back down the path. Small protrusions of rock were the only form of support and they clung to these as the way ahead became steeper. By the time they reached the top, the sky was dim with purple clouds which had crept slowly in. A faint but large moon hung amongst them, casting a thin, watery light over the mountain. Stepping from the ridge, they all sighed with great relief.

'Here, I took this from the temple.' The boys turned to find Aralia holding out an open paper package in which rested several bread rolls and some rough oat biscuits.

'You stole it?' James asked, his voice incredulous. Her act surprised him as he knew her timid nature.

Aralia merely nodded and handed the food to Will and Arthur who took it hungrily. James took his share too, unable to resist the temptation. They shivered whilst they ate, exposed to the cold mountain air which stung their hands and faces. A sense of calm descended, created in part by the reassuring sight of the egg resting gently on the snow. Every now and then James paused in his chewing to look down and gaze at its smooth, marbled shell. Although the dragon's cry still resounded in his ears, he knew that taking the egg was the only way to win the firestone.

They remained at the top of the ridge until all the food had been eaten. Partially satisfied by their meal, they began to walk again, back the way they had come. The ridge slowly faded out of sight, replaced by the rocky ground which led down towards the plateau. James felt his arm begin to ache under the weight of the egg but he was unwilling to let anyone else hold it. He suffered from an irrational fear that if he let it out of his protection, it might never come back. This way, the responsibility was his and his alone.

In the gloom of evening, the base of the mountain was hidden from sight and even the way ahead was obscured by shadows. The four stumbled down the slope until at last they reached the plateau again. Now more familiar with the way, they found the path which led across the flat stretch of land and back down the remaining slope of mountain. As they descended, James became aware of the shadowy forest lurking at the outskirts of his vision. The sight of its dark mass against the white of the mountains made his heart leap with anticipation.

'There, the forest,' he announced in a low voice. 'We've almost done it. The quest is nearly over.'

'Nearly, but not quite.' Arthur spoke quietly and raised his hand to the sky. 'Look, the Shadows have come.'

A new cloud had formed in the sky, a dark mass which hovered against the edges of the moon. The sight of it made James feel sick and he turned away. The elation that he had felt moments before was erased by the fear that he could still fail. In this state of confusion, he felt a hand grab his arm and pull him forward. Refocusing his eyes, he realised Will was beside him, desperately propelling him down the remaining part of the mountain. Shaking the fear from his mind, he tucked the egg more comfortably beneath his arm and quickened his pace.

The presence of the Shadows made them reach the edge of the forest more quickly than anticipated. Breathlessly, they stopped to gaze at the thick, dark trees which rose in a menacing wall ahead of them. The faint moonlight cast great shadows from the branches, making the forest seem impenetrable. After only a short pause, they dived forward together and were lost in the shadows. Pushing aside the bushy branches, they passed through layer after layer of dense, sharp foliage. The needles pricked at their skin but they were all unwilling to let this stop their progress into the forest. They moved through the darkness for a long time until the branches began to thin and they suddenly found themselves standing on the outskirts of a small clearing.

'Is this it? Is this the place?' Aralia asked, looking around doubtfully.

The clearing was circular and was faintly lit by the weak moon which was visible through the wavering treetops. Although the clearing was itself bare, it acted as the centre point for several paths which were placed at equal points around its circumference. Several of them lay bathed in moonlight but the majority remained dark. The mouth of each path was strewn with wild brambles but some invisible force seemed to restrain them from entering the clearing.

'There's nothing here,' Arthur commented, 'just trees.'

James moved out of the shadows and went to stand in the middle of the clearing. Turning slowly around in a circle, he looked for any sign of an obvious place to break the egg. Nothing extraordinary presented itself to him however and his eyes merely roamed over tangled brambles and weeds.

'This isn't the place,' he said in a low voice. 'I don't feel anything here and Nuria said I would know. I think we need to go down the paths and see where they lead.'

'We could take one each,' Will suggested.

They all stood gazing from one path to the next, trying to decide which would be the best to take. Each looked the same, each curving through the wild mass of brambles and disappearing beyond the reach of moonlight. There was nothing to suggest one should be chosen over the others.

'There is something here,' Will said suddenly. He pointed to the paths one by one, a wide grin spreading over his face. 'There are exactly seven paths leading from the clearing,' he murmured. 'I understand it now. If we drew a line between all the paths, we could make a seven-pointed star.'

James stared at the paths in amazement. 'We're standing in the middle of Arvad's symbol,' he said with excitement. 'We're in the centre of the star. One of these paths must lead to the place where the egg can be broken and the firestone set free.'

Chapter 30

THE four companions stood looking uneasily at the paths, not knowing which to choose. James paced around the circumference of the clearing, looking down each dark and unknown track. After three turns he came back to where his friends were standing.

'How about Will and Aralia go together and Arthur comes with me?' he suggested. 'That way none of us are alone but we can still cover more than one path. It doesn't matter which path we each choose; they all look the same.'

'How d'we let you know if we find something?' Will asked. 'You're the one who has the egg after all.'

'We could all return to the middle by the time its light,' Arthur said. 'If one path has nothing then try another but let's meet back here.'

James, Will, and Aralia nodded in agreement and they moved towards a chosen path in their pairs. Taking a deep breath, James stepped forward onto the fifth path without a word or single glance back. He walked with a determined pace and Arthur trailed in the shadows behind him. Everything was so still and silent that it made his skin tingle. Every time he or Arthur stepped on a twig he jumped, expecting to be confronted by some ghostly figure. Peering through the trees on the other side of the path, he tried to see what lay between the shadowy branches. The density of growth obscured his vision however, revealing nothing but darkness.

The path took a sharp turn to the left and James suddenly became aware of whispering voices. He sensed Arthur had stopped behind him and came to an abrupt halt himself. Shifting a little to look through the thick branches, he saw with disbelief that the path had come full circle and they were back beside the clearing. It was no longer empty however and three shadowy figures stood within it. Their voices were faint and he crept closer to try and hear what was being said.

'Where are the Shadows now?' a male voice asked. The rough, low tones were immediately recognisable as Kedran's and James shivered at the sound.

'Back outside the forest waiting for your call,' came a woman's reply. Her speech was thickly accented and James only just managed to catch her words.

'They were seen coming in here. One of the dark-haired boys is the one we want, James Fynch.'

There was a laugh and James clamped his mouth shut to keep from gasping. He felt Arthur grow tense beside him but neither of them dared to speak. The two voices in the clearing were then interrupted by the third figure who stepped forward.

'Vey won't never get away, not vis time. Ve Shadows will swarm ve forest and root 'em out.'

'That's what you promised before,' Kedran's voice snapped. 'You've already failed. You're lucky I haven't killed you yet, you disgusting rat.'

'Use ve crystal, I've told you. It'll find him anywhere, vat's what she told me.'

As James watched, a fourth presence appeared close to where he and Arthur stood hidden. The figure was shadowy and translucent and stood slightly apart from the three already gathered in the clearing. As if sensing this new presence, Kedran and his companions turned slowly around.

'I didn't know you were coming yet,' the woman muttered in low tones.

'I'll go and come again, but I wanted to see you were here.' It was another woman's voice, soft and crooning. 'I needed to make sure you were following them, the boy and the egg. Time grows short and you must act quickly.' She paused for a moment and complete silence descended.

James and Arthur turned to each other but couldn't see the expressions on each other's faces. Knowing their hiding place would not be secure for much longer, they turned back towards the path again. Glancing back, James saw the figures in the clearing slowly advancing towards the trees and his heart was gripped with fear. He gave Arthur a sharp push of warning and the two of them broke into a run. The weight of the egg slowed James' pace and the smooth shell made it difficult to grip. Nevertheless, he jogged onwards, trying to keep track of Arthur who had slipped through a gap in the trees ahead. Hurrying through the opening after Arthur, he suddenly felt himself flung aside as someone knocked straight into him. He regained his balance and was about to continue running when a voice hailed him.

'James?'

'Will!' James instantly recognised the voice and whirled around to see his friend standing a few feet behind him. 'How did you get here?'

'Our path broke off suddenly,' Will responded breathlessly.

'We carried on going through the trees but it never came back again. What were you running from?'

Reminded of his pursuers, James glanced nervously behind him. He could see Arthur close by, standing beside the figure of his sister whose blonde hair was exposed to the night.

'They're here,' James whispered. 'The Shadows are waiting outside the forest. It's only a matter of time before they swarm in to find us. Scarface is here too, in the clearing. We don't have much time to hang around here, let's keep on going.'

Gesturing to Arthur and Aralia, James began to jog again and Will came along beside him. A slither of moon slipped from behind the clouds, but it was still too dark to see clearly. Together, the four plunged forwards into the shadow of the forest which grew gradually thicker around them. They had to fight the branches and brambles aside, ignoring the scratches being torn in their skin. A shadow ran across their path and they all froze before realising it was just a rabbit. Pushing through the next clump of undergrowth, they stopped abruptly as a familiar sight greeted them. The clearing lay ahead, but it stood empty and silent as if no one had ever been there.

'How did we get back here again?' James asked in frustration. 'One of the paths must lead somewhere.'

'Are you sure you saw people here?' Will questioned, looking around the deserted area doubtfully.

'Course I am,' James retorted. 'Me and Arthur both saw and heard them. Either they came after us or they've gone back outside the forest. Either way, we don't want to be here.'

Trying to control his annoyance, James stepped away from the others and looked around. A small sound made him catch his breath and he stood completely still, sheltered by the overhanging branch of an old oak tree. His spine and neck tingled as he held still and tried to hear the sound again. He was about to turn back to the clearing when he felt something move behind him. A warm breath brushed over his neck, making his hair stand on end and his skin shiver.

'Who's there?' he called into the darkness.

'James, are you alright?' Will's voice came back to him from a few feet away.

Slowly, James began to move away from the shadow of the tree. He turned around in circles to view the whole area about him, but the darkness lay still. A sudden growl followed by a scream made him jump violently and he ran out from behind the tree. A huge shape stood directly ahead of him, bathed in moonlight. It rested between him and his friends who had wandered into the centre of the clearing. As he watched in frozen horror, he saw Will raise his hand and a flash of light shot towards the great beast. Arthur and Aralia joined in and James hurried to cast a beam of his own.

Under the shimmering glow of light, he could see the creature more clearly. It rested on four legs and its whole body was covered in a shiny black fur which shimmered strangely. Two sharp yellow eyes burned in its head and in between these were set three hard, silver scales. It had the appearance of a wolf but was much larger and had no tail. The animal stared back at James with its yellow eyes and bared its teeth. He knew it had been standing right behind him in the darkness and wondered why it hadn't attacked him then. It was as if it had wanted to separate him from his friends before pouncing.

'James, listen to me,' Will called. 'The creature is known as a Lowane, beast of the moon. They only live in the Northern forests and are harmless unless their peace is disturbed. They have no claws but their teeth can produce poisoned spasms if they pierce the skin.'

'How does telling me that help at all?' James hissed back. He sent another flash of light towards the beast, but it merely bounced off the smooth black fur.

The Lowane bared its teeth again and they shone unpleasantly in the weak, yellowish light. James stared at them in disgusted horror, unsure of what to do next. He saw Will move a little closer to the creature, but it kept its eyes firmly fixed on James and the egg clutched under his arm.

'It can see the egg,' Will said loudly. 'Lowane's are dangerous and it won't leave you alone until it can't see you or the egg anymore. There's only one choice for us. You have to run and hide, and we'll distract it until you're out of sight. They have no sense of smell and they're deaf too, so it won't be able to follow you. You have to go, before the Shadows see the lights and find us here.'

James stared at Will in disbelief. 'You want me to take the egg and go?' he asked incredulously. 'I can't go by myself and I won't leave you here.'

'It's the only way,' Will responded, his voice slightly tremulous 'We'll follow you but for now you have to go on by yourself. Once the egg is out of sight, the Lowane will lose interest and we'll be able to follow you.'

Before James could answer, there was a blast of light so strong that it blinded his eyes. For a moment, all he could see were bright dots dancing over the ground all around him. As his vision gradually came back to him, he became aware of Will shouting to him. Without any further hesitation, he turned away from the scene and began to run. He felt the rush of magic bursting on the trees behind him and forced his feet to move faster. It was slow going over the brambles and the egg felt heavier than before, but he pushed himself on. He tried to ignore the guilt he felt for leaving his friends behind and used his fear of the Lowane to drive himself on.

A small opening revealed itself in the trees ahead and he hurried through it. He found himself standing on a path which was much narrower than the one he and Arthur had been on before. It curved around to the right in a soft bend and after furtively glancing around him, he began to walk along it. The air had a new freshness about it and he breathed it in, rubbing his eyes to keep the tiredness away. He wondered why the others hadn't followed him yet and he paused more than once to wait for them. The path behind him was always empty and he walked on listlessly.

Eventually, the way ahead began to lighten. Slivers of mountain and sky become visible at the end of it, looming over the edges of the forest. James hurried towards the scene until he reached the end of the path where he stopped to look back again. The darkness seemed to waver before his eyes and he blinked several times before checking again. The trees shifted and shuddered behind him and he suddenly realised that the forest was filled with Shadows.

Chapter 31

THE darkness behind James undulated like a rippling wave in calm winds. The shadowed figures blended into the trees, passing through the forest with ease and grace. James watched them with a mixture of awe and dread and subconsciously tucked the egg beneath his cloak. His path was hidden by several large trees, but he wanted to keep the egg covered just to be sure. He knew he had to move quickly and find the place to break the egg before the Shadows reached it. The final few laps of the race were upon him and it was his task to win it.

Glancing furtively around, James moved off the path and into the unknown wild beyond. He kept to the left of the Shadows, treading stealthily over the dry pine needles. At times he lost sight of the figures, but they soon reappeared in their vast numbers, sliding silently through the forest. He walked for a long time and the darkness pressed around him. The egg, clutched beneath his left arm, was still warm and it kept him from shivering.

Fighting his way through a patch of brambles, he suddenly found himself at a dead end. The way ahead was overgrown with brambles and weeds which twisted together to form a tough barrier. Looking around, he was surprised to see the Shadows had disappeared and he was completely alone. As he turned back towards the brambled wall, he became aware of a strange warmth on his left wrist where his symbol lay. It didn't burn but merely tingled with a gentle heat. To his amazement, the egg began to glow faintly, illuminating the wild undergrowth. Nothing else happened and shrugging to himself, he stepped forward into the brambles.

'You haven't much time,' a voice in his head whispered and he jumped. It was the same voice that always spoke to him but he couldn't see the figure again.

'Am I going the right way?' he found himself asking. His voice was quietly desperate and he closed his eyes, waiting for an answer.

'Hurry,' the invisible guide said, ignoring his question. 'The darkness lurks all around you and is greater than you know. Hurry!'

The voice stopped and James opened his eyes again. Instead of giving him answers, the words filled him with fresh fear and he hurriedly took another step forward. The egg slipped a little but he needed his free hand to push away brambles and keep his balance. The thorns slashed at him but he fought back, pushing them harshly aside. On several occasions the brambles grew so densely that he was forced to climb over them, holding the egg above his head. The undergrowth grew gradually thicker and long grass which reached above his waist began to obscure the way. His cloak was ripped, his hands were scratched, and the soles of his shoes had half peeled away. He could feel the grime on his face and pine needles prickled uncomfortably in his hair and down his back.

He had nearly given up hope and was thinking of turning back when the weeds and brambles came to an abrupt end.

Directly in front of him was a tall archway built from honey coloured stone. The keystone was carved with a strange mark which he didn't recognise, a single triangle pointing upwards. Along the left edge two lines of words were written, one in some strange language, the other in English.

'I seek eternal life against the dark. I am the wanderer.'

As James read the words aloud to himself, his mind was cast back to the house in the abandoned village. The foreign words written here were the same ones which had been etched onto the mantlepiece. The Wanderer, Arvad, must have lived in the village many years ago. Kleon had said the crystal book came from there and James guessed it had been buried by Arvad. This was it, he thought to himself. This was the place where the egg must be broken and the firestone set free.

Peering through the arch, he tried to see what lay the other side. A faint beam of moonlight shone in, casting his shadow before him. It fell across a straight, stone-paved pathway which was lined with more decorative arches. Cautiously, he took another step forward, placing himself at the outer edge of the pathway. Looking around, he noticed that the arches all had a ledge built into them and each bore a small crystal globe. A strange light glowed from these as the moonlight touched them with its rays. Behind these crystal balls were thin panels of glass which had smooth ripples of water running down them. The moonbeams bounced off these, casting undulating ripples of light around the whole space.

Noticing his hazy reflection in one of the panels, James stopped to look at it. He saw a scruffy figure with untidy hair and torn clothes staring back at him. As he looked at this alien reflection, he felt something change in the secluded space between the arches. The crystal orbs began to glow with a faint red light which bounced off the watery glass panels to create a flickering, fiery illusion. Looking carefully at the crystal closest to him, James thought he saw indistinct shapes moving within it. Unable to resist, he leaned forward and gently touched the ball. As soon he touched it, a new light glowed and the shapes inside began to shift. He suddenly saw an image of himself standing in Lover's Wood with Celaeno. Behind her was the shadow of her grave and the wispy forms of other ghosts.

Pulling his eyes away from this image, James ran across the path to another orb. When he laid his fingers on it, he saw his three friends standing in a place he didn't recognise. Curious to see more, he lifted a third orb from its thin stand and held it up to the moonlight. The swirling picture inside changed abruptly and he immediately saw his childish nightmares laughing out at him. He could see himself wide awake in a dark room, trying to find his way to the door. He also saw his mother and father with their backs facing him as he sat alone. All his fears screamed out at him, taunting him and calling his name. Trying to block out the noise, he hung his head and hunched his shoulders. The sounds continued to call at him and he began to shake as they hammered on and on, trying to reach into the depths of his mind.

'Close your eyes,' he told himself. 'Block it out.'

He closed his eyes, but the pictures filled his mind. When he opened them again, he saw the glowing ball in his hand had turned a strange blue colour, bright and different from the rest. It forced the others down into a pale glow, the pictures inside them disappearing. James felt the crystal turn cold under his fingers, gradually losing heat until it burned like ice in his hand. The cold, bluish light grew brighter, reminding him instantly of the screens from his world. Even though he was in pain he held on to the orb, determined to fight the nightmares back.

Suddenly, a red glow burst from his palm and struck the orb directly in the centre. There was the sound of crystal smashing, accompanied by the thud of a heavy object falling to the ground. For a split second, time seemed to stop. James was vaguely aware of the egg slipping from beneath his arm but watched it fall as if he were in a dream. In his mind's eye he saw an image of Nuria falling onto a bed of snow, her face whiter than ever. It bore an expression of great pain and the sharpness of it struck his heart. Somewhere in the depths of his mind he also heard the dragon cry out. This sound woke him from his trance and he looked down in horror.

'No!' he cried loudly. 'Not yet! The egg can't break yet.'

Looking down at the smooth oval, he could already see a wide crack beginning to form across its beautiful red shell. Kneeling, he picked it up and clutched it between his hands, hoping the pressure would hold it together. Another small crack formed directly under his fingers and a small bit of shell fell into his palm. In a desperate attempt to stop the whole outer layer breaking, he replaced the broken piece as if it were the missing part of a puzzle. Although he tried to hold it still, a strange vibration started somewhere inside the egg which made it impossible to contain. It writhed with such vigour that a third crack split the edge and in one final burst, the whole shell fell away. Something was moving beneath the fragments and after a few moments a shape emerged. It was white and wrinkled and its tiny red eyes glared fiercely at James.

'Where's the stone, where's the ruby?' James whispered angrily. 'You were supposed to die and give us the firestone. Nuria played a trick on us, she lied about the egg!'

The tiny creature stared at him with innocent eyes and

sticking out its tongue, began to lick itself clean. Shaking his head at it, he turned his eyes to look up the short path in front of him. At the bottom, he could see a statue which appeared to be the figure of a woman, carved from whitish stone. Leaving the dragon on the path, he stood and advanced towards this statue. As he drew closer, he saw that the woman's eyes were downcast. Her features and frame were delicate and she had a stone cloth wrapped around her body and another over her hair. The only apart of her attire not made from stone was a small gold circlet placed on top of her veil.

A bowl rested in her hands, carved from a hard, pinkish stone. James reached out to touch its smooth surface, feeling the cold sink into his fingers. As he did so, he noticed a ring of words inside it, spiralling down to the centre of the bowl where there was a hole. Reading them, he realised they were the same words which had been etched on the outer arch. With fresh frustration, he understood that this was the place where he should have broken the egg. He knew for certain that this time he had failed at the task he had been so close to finishing. Raising his head to the sky, he shouted in frustration, but the sound was deadened by the vastness of the night.

'I'm sorry,' he called to no one in particular. 'I'm sorry but I've failed. I lost the firestone and the dark will win. None of this can be real. I never believed in magic and even if I did for a second, I don't anymore.' He pressed his fingers over his eyes, trying to forget.

A soft whisper forced him to open them again and he looked round in confusion. The voice hissed all around him but there was no one in sight.

'Don't stop believing,' it murmured. 'Now is the time when you must have faith. Everything happens for a reason, you just have to believe.'

'Who are you?' James asked into the air. He glanced nervously at the shadows, fearful of the darkness.

'Look this way,' the whisper continued. 'Look, and you will find me.'

James looked but still didn't see anything until his eyes rested on the statue again. Just behind it was a faint glimmer of something and he stepped curiously towards it.

'Who are you?' he repeated.

There was a brief silence before the speaker finally stepped forward. It was a boy whose face remained hidden in shadow even though his dark hair shone silvery in the moonlight. He was hardly visible and held a pale flickering flame in the palm of his hand. For some reason he looked familiar, but James didn't know why.

'Who I am is something you must answer for yourself,' the boy said gently. 'I am here to remind you of the power within you, the power that has guided you to this place.'

James looked at his feet. 'I thought I was following the right clues, but I must have been tricked. It's too late now and there's nothing to believe in anymore.' He rubbed his temples tiredly.

'There is one thing left to believe in, but that is something you must discover alone. If you stop believing, you can never succeed.'

'I was never meant for the quest,' James muttered. 'Albert and the others knew that all along, but I wanted to prove that I could do it. Now the dark will win. They have a way to break into my world and will destroy everything.'

The boy smiled faintly. 'You come from another world, you discovered this task and succeeded in reaching this place. Somewhere you must believe that the quest was meant for you.'

James shook his head. 'It was a trick and the dark will come. The Shadows are everywhere and it won't be too long until they find me here.'

'Then stop them.' The boy smiled again and began to grow fainter, blending into the darkness behind him.

'I can't, I'm not…, I can't,' James stuttered.

The boy faded from sight and James was alone once more. He turned his back on the statue and began to walk back down the path to where he had left the dragon. The tiny creature hadn't moved and it watched him approach with its unblinking red eyes. Kneeling, James picked it up gently in his fingers, feeling the warm white skin resting against his own. He stared back at it unflinchingly for a few silent moments before turning back towards the statue. On reaching the carved figure again, he placed the dragon on the outer rim of the stone bowl and looked at it sadly. The tiny animal rubbed itself against him, never once letting its eyes wander from his face.

'You're as real as me,' James whispered. 'I watched the egg break and I saw you born from it. If you're real then magic must be too.' He pondered deeply for a moment before a new expression lit his face. 'I suppose I do believe.'

Pressing his face into his hands, he blotted the dragon from his vision. He wanted to believe in the quest but was afraid of failing and losing himself to the dark. Suddenly, a gentle and soft voice startled him, whether in his head or not he could no longer tell.

'I am the firestone,' it said.

Chapter 32

JAMES gaped at the dragon in disbelief, unsure if he'd heard correctly. It was still looking at him with the same fierce gaze as if nothing had happened at all. Eyes wide, he held out his finger to the tiny creature which licked it before wriggling away into the centre of the stone basin. As he stood with his back to the main archway, he had the sensation that someone was watching him. There was a presence on the path behind him and he felt his skin go suddenly cold. Filled with a mixture of apprehension and curiosity, he slowly turned around. A figure stood on the path, its face shadowed by a wide hood. It looked faint and translucent in the half light, as if it was not really there. James looked at the figure suspiciously and instinctively moved his body to hide the dragon.

'I hoped to find you here,' a female voice said. 'I've been waiting to meet you.'

There was a long pause while James collected his thoughts. 'Who are you?' he eventually asked.

The woman uttered a faint laugh and slowly raised her head. James found himself staring at a face which startled him and sent a chill down his spine. It was extremely beautiful, framed with jet black hair and set with dark green eyes which flashed like fire.

'Don't you know who I am?' the woman asked. Her tone was soft and crooning but it held a dark malevolence beneath it. James shook his head curtly and she laughed again. 'I know exactly who you are. I confess I never expected you to be a boy, nor one from the other world. You could be useful to me in many ways you know.' She smiled a strange, twisted smile and took a step towards him.

'Who are you?' James asked again, this time more loudly. He could feel his heart pounding as dark suspicion began to seep into his thoughts.

'I am another shadow who will come to take away the light,' she whispered. 'I will snuff it out inch by inch until there is no spark left.'

James felt as if the breath had been punched from his body. He gasped inwardly and stared at the woman with wide and frightened eyes. By his sides, his hands began to tremble and he squeezed them into tight fists.

'Yes, I thought you might know,' the woman hissed. 'I am the rumoured Belladonna, the Deadly Nightshade. Don't be afraid of me,' she whispered as James pressed himself against the stone basin. 'I can't hurt you here as I'm just an illusion.'

'Why're you here then?' James asked in an unsteady voice. He already knew the answer, but the question gave him time to think.

The woman lowered her head, sinking it back into the shadow of her hood. 'For the same reason I've always been with you,' she replied. 'You have something I desire and you have led the darkness to it.'

James placed his hands behind his back and shook his head. 'I don't have what you want, it was all a trick. The egg is broken and the firestone isn't here.' As he spoke, the double meaning of her first sentence came to him and he stared at her in disbelief. 'Are you the voice, the one that talks inside my head?'

She cast him a curious glance before shaking her head. 'Guess again,' she hissed.

There was a long silence in which the two watched each other's every move. A new idea then came to James and he struggled with it for a few moments, shaking his head in disbelief. Seeing his discomfort, The Belladonna uttered a sharp, malevolent laugh.

'It was you, in the airport,' James said in amazement. 'The lights, the power cut, it was all you.'

The Belladonna slowly inclined her head. 'You have, it seems, worked out my secret. I have reached into your world twice but have never been able to pass through the barrier between.' She paused to sneer at James. 'I'm not the first to try and break the barrier but I will be the first to succeed. Your own world created the weapon which I will use to destroy it. These technologies of yours have the potential for good and evil, but I will use them to destroy the light. Soon the dark will take both worlds and unite them as one.'

James felt as if he was drowning in a sea of words and meanings. Everything that had happened so far on the quest passed through his mind, suffocating him as he stood there on the path. It was all becoming clear to him, the link between himself, his phone, and the darkness. He gazed at The Belladonna through bleary eyes, hardly seeing her anymore. He finally understood that his phone and the technology of his world could be used to destroy the light. The Belladonna seemed to be growing fainter before his eyes and he realised that she had begun to step away. As he watched, he saw her draw out a black crystal from her cloak. She held it up to the light and it began to glow with the same bluish tinge which had filled the orb.

'Stop!' James called out, his voice loud and clear. She held the crystal still and waited for him to speak again. 'There was a power cut on the day I was born, fourteen years ago.' He left the words hanging in the air, unable to form a question from them.

She laughed at his expression, a terrible and malicious sound which echoed in the space around them. 'Yes, I tried to enter your world then and it coincided with the time of your birth.' She paused and the crystal glowed brighter. 'Your coming into this world and having magic was all an accident. The firestone was never meant for you.'

'I don't believe you, not this time,' James hurled back. 'Maybe the quest was meant for me right from the beginning.' He hardly believed his own words, but something compelled him to say them. 'I'm not afraid of the dark anymore,' he continued. 'My parents always told me to look for the light and then I wouldn't be afraid. I will find the light and destroy the darkness.'

Suddenly, light blazed all around them and in a great wave of heat James was thrust forwards. A bright force of flames leapt from behind him, shooting a wave of light down the path. He watched in amazement as The Belladonna's shadowy form wavered in the brightness of its beam, fighting to remain present on the path. It struggled for a few moments before the light forced it to fade and eventually eclipsed it altogether. James found himself standing alone on the path once more. Whipping around, he saw that the bowl behind him was alight with fire. Within its centre was the tiny dragon, standing within a circle of bright flames.

James himself appeared to be standing within a fire as the golden ripples danced on the path around him. Although his hands had ceased to shake, his heart still thudded heavily. Gazing into the depths of the flames, he watched as the dragon became enveloped in tongues of fire. The creature's skin began to turn a mottled red, matching the colours of its flickering environment. Gradually, these patterns and colours wavered and merged until the dragon faded away completely. Suddenly, several flames leapt forcefully from the bowl and rose into the air. James stared in amazement as they swirled against the night sky and began to form fiery letters.

'Another riddle,' he whispered to himself. 'A final riddle. Of course, it isn't over just yet.'

He cast his eyes over the words which had formed, waiting for them to focus. They burned in the air above him, familiar and yet meaningless. His mind felt fuzzy and concentrated hard, trying to make some sense of them.

'I am the body that holds all life,
I am the essence that bears each soul,
I am the tears that unburden strife,
I am the light that warms the cold.
I am the force that feeds, I am that which quenches,
I am the bed for every seed and the force that avenges.'

James shook his head, trying to unravel the words. 'The body, the essence,' he murmured to himself. 'I don't know what it means.' He sighed and rolled his eyes, the bright light burning into his mind. 'The bed for every seed. What could that be?'

'The earth maybe.'

James whirled around to see Will, Aralia, and Arthur standing breathlessly on the path behind him. He grinned at them briefly as they advanced towards him and came to stand by the statue.

No one spoke and they stood watching the flames in complete silence. The fiery letters still hovered above them, never once wavering.

'Earth,' James repeated at last. 'The earth is a bed for every seed.'

Beside him, Aralia began tracing the airy words with her finger. 'The body is earth too and the essence is air.'

James nodded, following her train of thought. 'Which must mean the tears are water, the light is fire.' He turned to her and grinned. 'The four elements,' he whispered.

Turning back to the bowl, he waited for something to happen. For several minutes, the flames continued to dance and waver with the dragon resting calmly within them.

'What're we waiting for?' Arthur asked quietly.

James shrugged, not knowing the answer himself. 'The answer must be right; it has to be,' he said. 'Something should be happening.'

'I have an idea,' Will said suddenly.

He knelt on the ground before the statue and calmly turned his left palm to face downwards. A small light glowed on the path and its wavering curls began to settle into the shape of a five-pointed star.

'The elemental pentagram,' he murmured. 'I remember seeing it in a book once, a long time ago. My dad showed me.'

'Why five points?' Aralia asked. 'What's the fifth element?'

Will rose from his kneeling position, leaving the star at his feet. 'It represents the spirit,' he replied simply.

James stood watching the stone bowl intently. Something had changed within its depths and the flames rose higher and higher. Just as they were about to burst from the basin, they suddenly lessened and faded into a pale glow. The fiery letters also drifted away into the night as the riddle was solved. Eyes alight with wonder, James stared at the red object which had appeared inside the bowl. He reached a hand through the dying flames, gripped by a desire to touch it. The warmth from the fire bit his hand but he was hardly aware of the pain. His mind was focused on the object and nothing else mattered in that moment. He felt a rough warmth brush against his skin and he breathlessly closed his hand around a crystalline form.

'It's true,' he whispered. 'It's really true.'

'The firestone, you're holding the firestone,' Will breathed behind him.

The crystal wasn't polished like the ones in the Ona caves and its dim red form was rough and raw. It felt heavy in James' hand and he held it up for the others to see. Inside its glassy depths rested the white crystalline star, hardly visible in the early morning light. The points of this star touched seven places inside the crystal form which James held with wonder. The firestone, the first of the four crystals of Arvad the Wanderer, lay in his grasp and the sense of its power overwhelmed him. He, James Fynch, was holding the crystal of legend which hadn't been seen for seven hundred years.

'I can't believe you really have it,' Aralia said quietly. 'I almost didn't believe it was real.'

James nodded slowly. 'I didn't know how to believe until I came here and saw the dragon inside the egg. The dragon was the firestone.' He stopped there, choosing not to tell them about his encounter with The Belladonna.

'The quest is over,' Arthur joined, his voice filled with hope. 'We have what we came for at last. You found the firestone.'

'I couldn't have done it without all of you,' James said and turned away, embarrassed by his own gratitude.

Without warning, a flash of light burst onto the path where they all stood contemplating their success. Aralia screamed and she, Arthur, and Will darted behind the statue. James however remained frozen to the path.

'It's not over yet,' a voice snarled. 'It'll only be over when you hand over the crystal.'

A figure emerged from behind the archway and James shuddered. Kedran stood there, the scar on his face burning whiter than usual. A twisted smile rested on his lips and raising his hand, he hurled another beam of light towards the statue. James watched it coming towards him, but still didn't move. Just before it struck him, something else knocked him to the ground. Shards of stone scattered all around him as the statue's bowl burst into hundreds of tiny pieces. A small shaving hit him across the cheek and he tasted blood as it trickled between his lips. A hand was pulling at him and looking up, he saw Arthur was trying to make him stand. With painful movements he rose and turned back towards the arch.

'James, what are you doing?' Arthur hissed.

'I'm going to finish this, right here,' James said loudly. 'I can't let him get away. They'll destroy my world; they'll take it all. I have to stop them!'

'Are you mad?' Arthur returned forcefully. 'You've got what you came for, now let's go. You were only meant to find the firestone, not fight the dark alone. They'll destroy you.'

Arthur's words seemed to register in James' mind and he paused. Absolute silence reigned as he and Kedran faced each other on the path. Casting one last, lingering glance, James finally broke from his position and was immediately grabbed by Arthur who pulled him into a run. Light blazed all around them, followed by the sound of splintering glass. Many of the orbs fell to the ground, spreading sharp layers of crystal over the path. Arthur dragged James away from this scene, making for the trees behind the statue. As he ran, James noticed other figures moving from the shadows all around him. Dark forms slithered through the trees, gliding along in swift pursuit.

'We need to get out of the forest,' Arthur shouted. 'The Shadows don't have long before it grows light and they can't survive in the daytime without cover.'

'Which way?' James called. He had slowed down to look at the endless sea of trees surrounding them. 'The forest is huge,' he continued. 'We'll never find a way out.'

'We have to,' was Arthur's only reply.

They were running again, dodging Shadows everywhere they went. The dark figures glided through the trees, surrounding them in an almost impenetrable web of darkness. They were everywhere, hovering in the sky above and lurking in all corners of the forest. James lashed out with flashes of light, driven by fear. He gripped the firestone tightly between his fingers, unwilling to ever let go. He had to keep it safe, if it was the last thing he did. He had to prove to Albert that he had succeeded.

Lost in thought, he suddenly found himself face to face with a dark, towering figure. It rose high above him and cast him into deep shadow. He stared up at it fearfully, watching as a bright light grew in the palm of its translucent hand. From the corner of his eye, he then saw a figure fall and realised with horror that it was Will. He was about to dart forward when he became aware of new shapes emerging from the trees. Rows of human figures emerged, dressed in white robes which bore golden crests. White light burst from their hands, mingling with the whirling colours which already filled the air. He watched as bodies fell around him and swallowed to avoid being sick.

At the head of the group, he then caught sight of a familiar figure. Albert stood there, looking as calm and collected as James remembered, his gingery hair glowing under the spinning lights. As he stared, he suddenly found himself blinded by a bright light. The firestone slipped from his grasp and he was aware of it rolling away. He dived after it, but the light struck him mid-motion and his mind went black.

Chapter 33

A figure was standing in the mist. James looked at it tiredly, not knowing what to say. He wanted to go home, back to his dull life in the house on Greenwood Avenue. The figure was beckoning to him but he didn't want to move, preferring to stay in a fixed position. As he stood there, the figure began to glide towards him which was something it had never done before. It drew closer and closer until it stopped just a few feet away.

'You've never done that before.' James was surprised to hear himself speak.

The figure shook its head. 'You've never let me.'

'Let you?' James asked indignantly.

'You didn't believe.'

A brief silence reigned before James spoke again. 'Who are you?' he asked. 'I still don't know.'

Slowly, the figure raised its hands and drew back the hood of its white gown. Beneath the shadows rested the face of a girl. She was about the same age as James but had pale hair and soft green eyes. These stared back at James as if she too was seeing him for the first time. He looked at her in surprise but his mouth remained shut.

'I am this,' the girl said quietly.

'Why have you been helping me?' James asked at last. He took a step forward but stopped himself abruptly.

She smiled at him for the first time, her youthful face brightening. 'It is my task to help you in this quest, to guide you when I can. You see there was a girl written in the stars, and that girl was me. We share a fate you and I. I am a part of your destiny.'

'You are?' James stared at her in amazement, but saw she was beginning to fade.

'James, James, wake up!'

Suddenly, he jolted awake. He was lying on a bed of moss somewhere he didn't know with a cloak wrapped tightly around him. He could hear voices and as he lay there, a figure appeared in his line of vision. It looked like Albert, but it couldn't be, not here. As his surroundings became clearer, vague memories came back to him. He recalled lights, flickering shadows, running, and somewhere falling. Without knowing why, he reached a hand into his pocket. His fingers touched his phone and the gold clock and he suddenly realised what he was looking for.

'Where is it?' He sat up quickly and looked around dizzily. 'What happened?'

The figure that looked like Albert knelt beside him and he felt something pushed into his hands. It was cold and rough and he immediately knew what it was.

'You've done well,' Albert's voice said. 'You received and protected the firestone.'

'My friends,' James began. 'They did it too. Are they here?'

As his eyes came into focus, he saw Arthur and Aralia standing behind Albert. He grinned weakly at them and they smiled back.

'Where's Will?' he questioned.

'Safe but resting,' Albert replied.

James nodded. 'How did you find us? Where are we?'

Albert adjusted his cloak and smiled. 'A message came of disturbances in the Northern forest. We are now in a wood just outside of there.' He paused to clear his throat. 'I must admit, I didn't believe it was possible,' he said slowly. 'A boy from another world completing a task that seven hundred years of men and women have failed at.'

James felt himself blush and looked away into the leafless trees which encircled them.

'Where will the crystal go now?' he asked.

Albert smiled again and moved away to the base of a nearby tree. A long box rested there and picking it up carefully, he brought it over to James. He knelt on the grass between James and Will and beckoned for Arthur and Aralia to join them. The box was made from a dark wood and its surface was engraved with strange symbols. Right in the centre was the impression of the elemental pentagram which Will had drawn before the statue.

'This box has been passed down from messenger to messenger over the centuries,' Albert began.

'Messenger?' Aralia asked with a frown.

'There are twelve messengers assigned to guard the box and await the coming of the crystals,' Albert explained. 'I am the twelfth.' Slowly and carefully he prised open the lid of the box and held it out for them to see.

Inside was a soft white fabric, pressed with four indentations. Reaching out to take the firestone from James, Albert gently placed it in one of these impressions and smiled.

'It will rest protected until its companions are found. The race must go on until all four crystals are reunited, either in the hands of the light or the dark.'

James smiled weakly. 'Can I go home?' he asked.

Albert closed the box and gazed past James into the trees. 'Perhaps for a little while,' he murmured. 'You have succeeded and this adventure is over.'

With the help of Arthur, James stood. Albert walked a short distance away, giving the friends some time to speak alone. Will patted James on the back but avoided looking at his eyes.

'You're really going back to your world?' he asked. 'I still find it hard to understand. How will you get back?'

Reaching into his pocket, James drew out the small gold clock. Somehow, he had always known that at the right time, the clock would be able to take him back again. He held it up for the others to see.

'This got me here,' he said quietly. 'It will take me home again I hope.'

Suddenly, they all drew together in a hug. It lasted for only a moment before they drew away embarrassed.

'What will you all do?' James asked them.

'Albert has Ferastia that will take us back,' Arthur replied. 'We're all going back to Arissel.'

'Ferastia are wild horses which travel quickly,' Will added, seeing James' puzzled look.

'I promise I'll find my way back somehow,' James said to them all. 'I'll be back to find you in Arissel.' He raised the clock before him and after a short pause, turned the hands to rest by ten to twelve.

For a moment, nothing happened and he waited with growing fear. Then, a faint mist began to rise around him, growing thicker and thicker until he could hardly see. Turning back to his friends and Albert, he raised a hand in farewell and stepped forward into the swirling haze. Darkness closed in on him and he gasped for air, waiting to be cast back into the haze of No Man's Land. The darkness didn't lessen however and kept on pressing tighter and tighter until he felt his lungs would burst.

Just as he felt his mind begin to grow numb, orange hit his eyes and a breath of fresh air touched him. As his eyes focused, he realised he was standing on a familiar street. At the end of it, he could see the old clock shop gleaming under a streetlamp. Looking down at the clock still ticking in his hands, he smiled to himself. He couldn't help thinking that perhaps he wasn't just an ordinary boy after all.

* * *

Francesca Tyer can be found on her website:

www.francescatyer.co.uk

and

www.authorsreach.co.uk